D0359803

TRACKED

JENNY MARTIN

DIAL BOOKS

an imprint of Penguin Group (USA) LLC

DIAL BOOKS
Published by the Penguin Group
Penguin Group (USA) LLC
375 Hudson Street
New York, New York 10014

USA/Canada/UK/Ireland/Australia/New Zealand/India/South Africa/China

penguin.com

A Penguin Random House Company

Library of Congress Cataloging-in-Publication Data

Martin, Jenny,
Tracked / Jenny Martin.   pages cm
Summary: Phee Van Zant, an orphaned street-racer on the corrupt planet Castra,
gets swept up in the corporate rally circuit and an even bigger revolution.
ISBN 978-0-8037-4012-9 (hardcover)
[1. Science fiction. 2. Automobile racing—Fiction. 3. Government,
Resistance to—Fiction. 4. Orphans—Fiction.] I. Title.

PZ7.M36318Tr 2015   [Fic]—dc23   2014017479

Printed in the United States of America

1 3 5 7 9 10 8 6 4 2

Designed by Mina Chung · Text set in Perrywood

TO CHRIS AND CONOR,
FOR BELIEVING IN IMPOSSIBLE THINGS.
FOR THAT, AND FOR INFINITELY MORE, I LOVE YOU.

CHAPTER ONE

I PACE THE GARAGE LIKE SOME CRAZY-EYED WIND-UP GIRL.

It's too late to back out of the race, but I can't afford this. The extra fuel. The new wheels. The trouble if we get caught tonight and get picked up by the jackals policing the streets. Or even worse, if Hal and Mary find out we're blazing right through the middle of town . . . I can't believe I let Benny talk me into this.

My crew boss is probably upstairs right now, his belly pressed against the desk while he approves every bet and rakes in all the credits. Sure, he's got his hands full too. I'm not the only one risking my neck tonight. Somebody has to keep the Domestic Patrol quiet and off our backs. Someone has to manage the web of bribes and favors that keeps the garage doors open and all our engines running.

1

For the moment, all that dirty work has paid off. It's packed. Benny's shop has become the biggest hive of lawless gear-heads and gamblers in Capitoline—their flop-sweat stink taints the familiar, welcome tang of leather and fuel and degreaser. Seems everyone's itching to hang around and get a taste of the odds. There are always credits changing hands in the dingy betting stalls, but right now, the garage is so busy, you'd almost think this was an actual interstellar circuit race, with pro drivers and corporate stocks on the line.

It's enough to put me on edge. There's too much money floating around over this race, and like Mary always says, where there's money, there's Sixers. And where there's Sixers, there's trouble. At least for the likes of me. Like most South Siders, I don't care too much for the six corporations who helped colonize this planet for profit. The Sixers might as well rule Castra, and the squeeze they put on the rest of us makes it pretty hard to breathe. Break their laws, complain about working for next to nothing, and you're blotted out like a stray drop of fuel sap. I swear, one false move and . . . *If Benny hasn't paid off their hired goons in the DP . . .*

I can't think about that right now. I have to escape the noise and get on the road. Before I change my mind.

I move back and forth across the length of the place,

past my crew-mates and rivals, between the bay doors and the crowded odds booths and the rickety stairs going up to Fat Benny's office. I don't stop to talk to Eager or Harkness as they slouch against their spit-shined rigs. No high fives or friendly trash talk before we gear up to run against one another. We're past that now—too close to go time. At this point, all I can do is count down the last few minutes in quick steps and shallow breaths. I don't stop moving because I can never shake the bone-deep tremble in my limbs before any race, let alone one this big. If I win tonight, outrunning every decent street rig on this side of the planet, I get double my usual share.

Benny's never split the take fifty-fifty before. I've been racing for him for two years now, since Bear and I turned fifteen and could quit school for good, and he's never offered this kind of cut. And I haven't questioned it, because every driver knows the deal. You pay your dues, running for the best crew boss who'll take you on. You start out sweeping floors and cleaning parts until they let you behind the wheel. If you're lucky, you work your way up and out and maybe someday you save enough to build your own tin-roofed shop. That's the way it works. Benny Eno gave me his best rig and a choice spot in his garage, and in return I'm supposed to keep handing over the biggest cut of the winnings for another two years.

I can live with that if it buys Bear and me a chance for something more, a real shot at making a living on Castra, this dust speck of a planet. And if it puts a little more food on his parents' table and keeps the landlord from rattling their clinic doors, that's more than good enough. That's all I'm asking for. A little less trouble for my foster family.

I walk to the center of the garage, where the floor is permanently sticky, sap-stained by all the fuel that's been loaded into rigs over the years. My sleek black Talon's up on the lift and Bear is standing underneath it, double-checking adjustments on the vehicle and noting everything on the razor-thin flex screen in his hand.

Suspension sensors calibrated. Check.

Fuel cells loaded. Check.

High speed triggers set. Check.

If I squint, his face softens and it's as if we're six years old again, sitting in emptied surgical supply crates, pretending to race circuit rigs and fly fighter vacs. Even then, he was always the navigator, and I was the pilot. That much hasn't changed. I drive. He paces the routes, squawking through the headset and watching out for me at every turn. I guess you could say we're still playing that game.

Bear withdraws, quietly tying himself into the kind of knots only I can untangle. When he turns on me, I catch the twitch rippling through his shoulders. My own satellite, he drifts closer than anyone else is allowed, and I have to look up to meet his ice-blue eyes. But it's not so bad to stand in his shadow. Most days, it's a pretty safe place to hide out.

"Everything looks tight, Phee. You're good to go . . . if you still want to do this." His last few words curl like a question.

I don't answer, for the same reason I'm ignoring the pile-up of Mary's frantic texts on my flex card.

ML: WHERE ARE YOU? WHAT TIME ARE YOU COMING HOME? HAL AND I ARE WORRIED.

I tune it all out because it costs too much to argue. I don't want to hash this out with Bear again or lie to his parents. So I stuff the blinking flex deeper into my pocket and jerk my chin at the lift. "Bring her down. Let's roll out."

Bear nods. He starts to answer, but stops when my flex buzzes once more. I don't need to pull it out to know who's sending the message.

"You have to tell them something," Bear says. "They'll figure out we're here, anyway. You remember the last time you ignored her texts?"

"All right," I say. I don't need a reminder. I remember exactly what happened. Mary wasted forty precious credits on a cab, rode all the way over here, and pounded on the bay doors until her knuckles split and every one of Benny's goons had a good laugh at her expense.

But like it or not, she knows nothing will keep me away from the shop. We need the money. The waiting room's overrun with the throwaway poor, the people who can't afford the fortune it costs to get even the most barebones care at a Sixer hospital. And if you're a protester who needs patching up after the DP knock you senseless? Forget it. Walk into any emergency room and you're as likely to get arrested as get stitches. Better to take your chances at a back-room clinic like the one the Larssens run.

I look at Mary's latest message.

ML: BE CAREFUL. BE SAFE. TELL ME WHEN YOU'RE COMING HOME.

I start to delete the message on the tiny screen, but the blink of the words reaches something in me. Hal and Mary will always worry. And I will always disappoint them. For better or worse, I am still my father's daughter. He may be gone, but I can't resist racing any more than he could. Even so, the least I can do is give the Larssens, my almost parents, one night's peace. I can pretend nothing's at stake and I'm not in any danger.

I swipe my thumb over my flex to reply.

JUST RUNNING SOME TEST LAPS OUT AT THE DUNES. WON'T BE TOO LATE. DON'T WAIT UP.

CHAPTER TWO

OUT ON THE STREET, I AM SMALL.

My legs aren't long enough to win a sprint and I'll never have enough meat on my bones to scrap my way through a fair fight. Good thing Bear stays close. Anywhere this side of the Mains, his six-five frame is enough to scare off trouble. It's enough to make most guys think twice about wolf-whistling or grabbing at me as I move through the crowd. It doesn't really matter that Bear doesn't have a taste for violence. With his broad shoulders and his stoic face of doom, he *looks* like he does, and that is enough.

My crew has done their job. Ahead, my Talon's polished, parked, and ready to go. After pushing through the last of the bystanders, I snap on my gear, slide into the driver's seat, and buckle the six-point. Here I don't need to be tall or strong. My hands are just right to grip the fuel triggers and my reflexes are quick enough to burn off the competition. Behind the wheel, I am fierce at last.

Bear steps back from the car, but his voice fuzzes through my headset. "I still say watch out for Eager, maybe even One-Eye."

Eager may be a worthy crew-mate, but he lost his edge three match-ups ago, and I'm certainly not scared of One-Eye, the stupid alias Matias Kirk has taken to street race. He can try to look tough and wear that patch all he wants, but we all know he's still got two good eyes and half a brain. Lame new nickname, same old pain in the exhaust.

As little kids, Matias and I tangled plenty, but I've never seen him behind the wheel before. Bet he's just a sellout, another wannabe driver angling for a corporate circuit contract. Doesn't matter. Most of the pro-racing hopefuls flame out or disappear soon enough, too scared to run anymore. I give ole One-Eye two weeks. He's no threat. He won't be any different.

Besides, no one on Castra—nobody on this whole planet—has a ride that matches my sweet black Talon. With no restrictor plate and the right burst of fuel, I'll blow past the other cars like my wheels are on fire. I know when to drop the hammer. I'll let Eager lead until the last mile, but once we clear Merchant's Plaza, once we near the docks, I'll whale on him, leaving him far behind.

"I'm on it," I say.

"I'm just saying, I think you should—"

"Got it. It's fine."

"When you're safe, when you cross the finish line in one piece? That's when it's fine, Phee," Bear says. "Eyes open, okay?"

I try not to growl at him, and I'm not very successful. He laughs, but I know he's still on edge. Bear worries more than enough for the both of us. I can practically see him raking his fingers through his blond hair right now. As baby fine as it is, it's a wonder he doesn't yank it all out. "Yeah," I say, pressing the ignition. "Go time in five. Pulling up now."

I weave through a couple of side streets. I pass too many boarded windows and burned-out storefronts. There's been so much unrest on the south side of Capitoline, more than ever before. You can hardly suck in a deep breath without tasting the choke of desperation. The Sixers are safe, tucked away in their penthouses and gated compounds. But here, in my neighborhood, people are on edge, anxious for decent jobs, better options—the promise of anything that might buy them out of hard times.

Things nearly slid into chaos last month. A three-day labor-protest-turned-riot blazed all the way to the edge of the Mains. Shut down Benny's garage for almost two weeks. Canceling races cost him a bundle, but the howl and clash brought too much attention here. Now the streets are hushed. With Domestic Patrol cracking down so hard, there's an uneasy silence, a forced quiet bought with tear gas and closed fists.

The newsfeeds buzz with talk of splinter cells and enemies of the republic—renegades who want to steal our precious fuel. They warn of terrorists, but they never show the ones wearing DP badges.

It's a gamble to run tonight. I tell myself I'm doing it for the money, that I'm driving to pay off my rig and to put more food on the table, but I know Bear's folks won't accept tonight's winnings. It's dangerous taking this kind of race, right through the heart of Capitoline.

For me, I guess that's the whole point.

After making the last turn, I roll into position and wait alongside four other cars. No fanfare. No dropped flags, like in the circuit arena. Out here, at midnight, on the wrong side of the city, racers get a signal flare. I look up and wait for the burst of light, the starry impostor that doesn't belong in the smoggy sky.

On my mark.

Flash.

GO.

I need this moment, the split second in which my body

strains against the harness after I hit the first fuel trigger. I slam against the seat, and I'm rocketing forward even as the signal flare burns spots in my vision. My gauge screens are filled with rapid blinks, rising numbers, and climbing lines. My Talon is a sleek, three-thousand-pound cage and I'm rattling the bars.

"Hope you can make up the distance." Bear has to shout through the headset. The fuel is still screaming. The whistling won't let up until I hit 150 mph. "No one else is taking your route."

I don't answer. Of course they're not. Oh yeah, the race is off to a predictable start, and I'm already grinning. I can almost taste the win. My rivals Eager and Harkness break right immediately. They'll zigzag a few streets, cutting toward the Mains, the long, straight shot through Merchant's Plaza. One-Eye and the last contender, some nobody in a boxy red Corona (who races in that kind of clown car?) are surely going straight ahead, breaking for the industrial park.

And that's not a terrible idea. The industrial route requires maneuvering, but only fools go for the plaza. Even this late, after the last glittering skyscraper goes dark, there are always stragglers working late. Eager and Harkness think building up honest speed early on the straightaway and pacing their fuel bursts will buy them victory, but it won't. Forget all the bribes Benny's handed out tonight. The surveillance cameras, the Domestic Patrol, the stray civilian rigs—the smoothest road just isn't worth the risk.

I take the rough road.

A curve to the left. At 120 mph, I take it, savoring the careening jolt when all four wheels grab the pavement again. Curb check. There's a skid from concrete to gravel, and I'm off road, a hurricane blowing through a bare stretch of under-developed land.

"Get over. You're too far to the left," Bear says.

I know he's gripping the oversized flex screen, tracking my progress and reading the pace notes. He's terrified I'll smash into a bulldozer or worse. I course correct and now I'm roaring down the rutted bottleneck between construction sites. With the dust clouds I'm churning and the lack of traction, I should be terrified too, but instead I'm riding a raging, sweat-slicked adrenaline rush.

Every cell is charged, every part of me is flying high save one—there's a knot the size of a fist in my core, a dull center of gravity. It reminds me of the race's toll, the stupid risks I take just to feel a pulse. I hate that I can't breathe without this. I hate that I have no weight or substance anywhere else. I hate my father for giving me this fuel-driven addiction, for I'm as trapped as any black sap addict who's got to score a fix to live.

Bear's voice sharpens my focus. "Big pothole ahead. Nudge right."

My nudge is not good enough. My teeth clack and the laws of physics punish me with a jarring leap and fall. My now battered, beloved Talon rocks and rebels against my steering. Still giddy, I dig in and dodge another hole, desperate to avert a full spin. I fishtail, but I've gotten through the worst of it. I must be near the end of the gravel by now.

"How much farther?" I yell.

"Mile and a half. Start—"

I read his mind and anticipate the upcoming tilt. I hug the lazy curve to the right on this makeshift road. I'm at the end of the boomerang-shaped route, so I should cross paths with the other racers in a minute or less. It's point to point, get there whichever way you can, and I pray I'm not behind them all. The gravel may have cost me.

"Where—"

This time Bear reads mine. "Clown car is way behind you. You're nose to nose with One-Eye, it's going to be close for second."

"I'm in *second*?"

"Wait, One-Eye just blinked out. I can't see him on the screen."

"What?" I'm furious now. "Did he cross the finish line?"

"No. I . . . He . . . His marker's just *disappeared*. Wait.

It's back. He's way off course, flying off in the wrong direction."

Something is very, very wrong.

"Harkness. Eager," I spit. "Where—"

"Harkness is out." Bear's words are fast and pitched too high. "Patrol bike zapped his machine halfway through the plaza. Eager had to burn all his triggers just to outrun and escape. He's still got first place locked, Phee. I don't like the way things are looking. Pack it up for the alternate rendezvous point. Don't do anything . . . "

I tune Bear out when I catch the scream of another engine. It's Eager; his bright yellow Evenstar is parallel on the good road and he's running hard. A nose ahead of me. As is, the curve will end and I can safely swerve and duck right behind him.

Unsafely, I can pull two triggers at once and rocket the hell past him and the finish line. Sure, I'll probably overshoot and smash into next year, but when I free-float and the six-point harness snaps me back, I'll rock the biggest rush of my life.

Or it will kill me.

I grip the stick and pull both fuel releases in one hardfist clench.

Yesss.

I surge forward. Two seconds of delirium before

g-forces kick in and I'm pinned against my seat. It's the sweetest blowback, but I can't hold on to it. The moment slips through my black-gloved fingertips. I'm the cartridge in the gun, the scorching round left in the chamber after the trigger fires.

No.

I'm not the hollow shell. I'm the bullet now.

Peak acceleration. I gasp as the fuel stops screaming, kindling the silent burn of maximum velocity. The world outside the windshield loses color, everything blurs into black and white. I'm tearing through, the wet streaks and bright splatters of light blind me. The night is bleeding.

"Phee! Phee! No!" Bear screams. His voice snatches me back, and I'm just a girl again. "You've overshot. I've got a visual of the pier. You're headed straight for them!"

Reflex. I strangle the throttle, but it's too late. I brake, but I've gone too far. I know I won't be able to slow down in time. I've lost any chance to turn away from the docks.

"DP are everywhere." Bear chokes. "Bikes. Two armored cars. Blitz Birds are on me. Rust it, Phee. They knew. It's a trap. They've got m—"

Thump. Static. He's gone. Bear—my safety, my reason— is gone. He's been shot, stunned, or snagged into the air by one of these jet-packed, badge-wearing vultures. The DP must have him now, and they're waiting to arrest us all.

And Bear was right about the pier. I see the ambush, the nest of cops, their silver speeders parked in a row. It's a flimsy barricade, but they have me. *Why* . . . why are so many of them here, already waiting in the perfect place? Who tipped them off? Rearview mirror. The flash of yellow paint. Eager's trying to spin around, but there's no escape for him either. DP swarm to box him in. I'm next.

My Talon wails; it doesn't like my foot on the brakes. Rust it. I don't like it either. I shift, my foot slams back on the accelerator. No surrender. I'm dead, but at least they won't bag me for jail.

Smash.

The whiplash stings, but the twist and snap of metal satisfy me. I cut through, mowing down the patrol bikes like they're tin can ten-speeds. I roar past all their sirens and shouts and flashing lights. The end of the pier. Foot to the floor. I'm flying.

I lie and say the soaring will last. The landing won't hurt, the water won't kill me. I will swim away. I will win.

Flip.

Tumble.

Crack.

I am wrong.

The dash screens blink out and I'm flailing for the harness

buckle and the door handle. Nothing will open for me. The windshield's already cracked. Water pours in and I don't know which way is up. There's not much light—my helmet comes off, but I can't get loose. For once, I can't run or race my way out.

I'm trapped. Gulp the last of the air. My heart and lungs and brain are on fire. Completely under the water now. I feel the buckle snap open, but it's too late. Can't breathe. My arms free float and I feel a hand grab me. But the hand can't put out the fire. I close my eyes. I drift and scatter like ash.

CHAPTER THREE

CLEAN. THE BLANKETS. THE BED. EVERYTHING FEELS CLEAN.

But it smells like the Larssens' clinic. Bleached sheets scorched too many times in an industrial dryer. I lift my head a little, but it's a mistake. The movement, the stink, the sting at the nape of my neck—it all makes me want to throw up. I open my eyes.

There are no windows, and everything from the walls to the floor to the plastic pitcher of water on my bedside table is white. There's only one door and it looks locked and the red eye of a surveillance camera blinks from the far corner of the ceiling. Rust this. I'm out of here.

My bruised body aches and my neck is sore. There's a numb spot back there, below my hairline, but a rim of pain, a shifting tidal wave of hurt surrounds it. Even so, the discomfort does nothing to slow me down. I move, ready to jump out of bed and get out of this hospital or detention center or whatever it is. But I can't. I can only pull against the restraints on my ankles and wrists.

"Let me out!" I half scream, half growl at the sight of the IV needle taped against my left arm.

All my noise, all my rattling of the bed rails only accomplishes one thing. I shake the bed hard enough to topple the pitcher off the nightstand, but I don't stop until a bolt snaps and my door is open.

Once I see the horde of pastel-scrubs-wearing medical types, I think this might actually be a regular hospital. They don't look like mad scientists or Domestic Patrol officers. I have to get them to take these straps off.

I start to bug out again. One of the doctors tries to fake me out with an everything-is-going-to-be-all-right smile. Then I see the syringe in his hand.

"Don't you stick me with that rusting needle!" I fight the restraints so hard, I feel a trickle of blood drip down the inside of my wrist. I'm not afraid to die, but I don't want to be put down like a rabid dog. Something breaks inside of me, and I hate myself for letting the words pass my lips so easily. "Please. Please don't stick me."

Two orderlies pounce and hold me still. I'd bite someone if I could, if they'd lean in close enough. But they know what they're doing. They have me all locked down, ready for the good doctor to do his thing. I still struggle, but I turn away.

"Phoebe," he says. "This is a sedative. I don't want to use this. But I will if I have to."

They have to believe I'm cool and calm. I cannot slip this snare any other way. "Let me go," I plead.

"That's not for me to decide, Phoebe," he says. "I'm Dr. Poole and you're at Capitoline General North. I'm here to patch you up, but if you keep going, you'll tear your stitches."

Stitches. Explains the scorch and numbness at the back of my neck. And I'm at CG North? I'm so far from my side of the city, it's not even funny. I don't understand why an ambulance would bring me all the way up here, where the rich people hole up. I'm not some Sixer's daughter. I'm not here for a nose job or a fat transfer or a rib removal. I don't belong in this hospital.

"My friend Barrett Larssen, is he here?"

He points to a sore spot on my waist and lifts up the arm of my hospital gown. I flinch at first, but then I realize what he's trying to show me. I twist and see the bruise on my shoulder. The handprint is huge. I don't know how he pulled me out, but I know who left the mark. The cool hand in the water. My savior in the dark deeps. I should've known.

My throat closes up. Bear hesitates. He worries. He talks me out of stupid ideas. He doesn't pull suicidal stunts. The marks on my shoulder and my waist grow warm. Maybe it's the drugs, but I can almost feel him reach for me. Somehow Bear—my would-be bodyguard and best friend—saved my life.

"Where is he?"

Dr. Poole ignores my question. A DP officer steps just inside the doorway. His coal-black uniform makes him an inkblot, a stain in this spotless room. "Phoebe Van Zant, you're under arrest."

I frog the second orderly, knuckle punching him near the groin. For a second, I think my thrashing will break the cords at my wrists. "I want a lawyer! Cut me loose. I want out of this place!"

I hear Dr. Poole sigh. The needle sinks into my hip. I drown again.

With a chin-snapping nod, I wake up in the back of a moving transport. I'm groggy, but upright, locked into a seat between two DP officers. When I blink and swallow and try to shift my feet, I realize . . . they put me in sync boots. Rigid, heavy, evil red-toe-light blinking sync boots.

"You can't just haul me off like this," I plead. "I'm a minor, and you haven't even notified my guardians."

"Oh that's right," the officer mocks. "How did we forget about that? Just say the word, and we'll be happy to bring in your whole family for questioning."

He smiles, and I catch the glint of perfect teeth. He knows the threat's enough to gut me. Across town, a world away, Mary's probably out of her mind, bent over a sterilizer panel, cleaning instruments and pretending to keep it together while Hal paces the floor and texts me a thousand times.

No, bringing up my ties to the Larssens would be asking for trouble. Their medical supply business is a good front for the clinic—it lets them operate on the edges of the system, without interference from the Sixers. Any of the Six would probably love to swallow another black-market clinic like so much krill. Especially one that patches up the protesters who shout down their names on the streets.

Transcorp. Agri-tech. Benroyal Corp. Yamada-Maddox. AltaGen. Locus Informatics. I know they helped build Castra from nothing, but it's like they think they own the whole rusting planet. If I coughed up the Larssens to the DP, they'd be shut down inside of eight hours. I can't let that happen.

We slow down. Through the windows, fire-bright colors catch my eye. So many knots of orange and red and yellow leaves. Castra's a desert world, one made for scrubroot and hackweed, but there's a whole grove's worth of Earth-imported oaks lining the gated courthouse drive. What a waste of water. So much effort to keep withered roots alive.

The officers tense as we come to an abrupt, curb-skimming stop. We've arrived. The bone-pale courthouse looms and I've never felt smaller.

Inside the courthouse, I'm herded through a gray-walled warren of holding cells and intake stations. I've never been booked or processed before. Two years of racing under the radar and they've never been able to catch me, so I'm not exactly sure what to expect.

My escort pulls out a flex card remote and fumbles with it. Arrows appear on the floor, illuminating the black-and-white tiles. My soles start to slide across the floor and I flail to keep my balance, but as soon as I surrender, moving toward the arrowed path, the pull relents and I'm free to walk normally. Or at least as normally as I can in these rusting things.

I'm pushed through the booking stations without stopping. I don't get scanned or strip-searched or zipped into a baggy lock-up jumpsuit. The DPs don't even interrogate me. I was so sure that as soon as I got here, they'd toss me in a holding cell and start grilling me about Benny Eno's garage/black-market betting operation, but they don't. They only ask who I belong to. I don't answer.

I'm not selling out the Larssens. Not when they're all I've got.

My real mother split when I was little more than a baby. I barely remember her face, a perfect oval so much paler than my own. And even that image is counterfeit. My father used to store a picture of her on his flex, but now I've only got the memory. My case manager says she got into black sap, and I can only guess my dad didn't want me to know that my own mom became a sunken-eyed junkie. So I carry an image less painful, frozen in time, of someone whole and young and pretty.

And my father? The great Tommy Van Zant, the six-time Corporate Cup champion, the circuit rally racer who couldn't lose? When I was five, one day he up and disappeared. Crossed a finish line and drove away, leaving me and his latest trophy behind. Maybe he couldn't deal with the pressure. Maybe he was burned out. Maybe he was just plain bored.

The only thing he left me is his itch for adrenaline and this hell-on-wheels need to race. Come to think of it, I guess he's the reason I'm standing here in the first place. I should text him a message and thank him.

But of course, I won't. I can't.

Maybe I had real parents once. I've forgotten what that means.

I'm hustled around a corner, down the last stretch of tile. We pass more holding cells; I catch my reflection in their safety-glass windows. My hair looks darker in here. Almost black. And unlike the other prisoners, I'm wearing oversized hospital scrubs that have been bleached so many times, it's hard to tell if they were once purple or actually blue. Swallowed up in this threadbare getup, I look like a walking bruise.

The cells are full of rough-faced prisoners, but there are no clean-cut Sixers here. They never seem to get arrested. Plenty of Cyanese rebels and Biseran drug dealers, though, and plenty of South Siders like me. I can guess what's in store for them. The worst of the lot will be shuttled to prison and exile on Earth, while the petty offenders will get deported or sentenced to a lifetime of hard labor on Cyan-Bisera.

I glance at one of the Cyanese detainees, the man closest to the glass. He's gotta be nearly seven feet tall. Bet he thinks he's really cute with the Cyanese Army flag plastered across his T-shirt. Rebel stars, pale silver, on a field of blue. I imagine the DP got one look at that and tossed him and his friends in here just for looking like fuel-stealing terrorists.

Public menace. For the first time today, I smile. At least I'm really guilty.

"Keep it moving," my guard snarls.

We make it down to the end of the hallway. My ears catch the splashdown roar of water in the lobby fountain as the double doors swing open. A flex screen message scrolls above: Enjoy improved, hassle-free judicial proceedings. These new, expedited services are brought to you by Locus Informatics. We're innovating justice for you!

I'm pretty sure this means my fate has just been outsourced.

CHAPTER FOUR

"PHOEBE VAN ZANT?" THE JUDGE LOOKS UP AT ME.

I'd expected him to look scary. All imposing and serious. Instead, he just looks tired. He's not even perched behind the grand bench at the back of the courtroom. Here we are in this fancy, marble-pillared hall and he just sits there behind an ordinary wooden desk on the periphery of the room. He wears a fine black robe, but it looks too big for him.

My public counsel stands beside me, as silent as the statues lining the walls. I don't recognize the empty, ivory-eyed figures, but I'm sure they're more dead guys— twenty-third-century colonials from Earth.

"Answer yes or no, and say Your Honor," the guard orders.

I clear my throat. "Yes . . . Your Honor, I want to—"

"You are charged with six counts," the old judge interrupts. "Reckless driving. Illegal vehicle. Illegal racing. Resisting arrest. Destruction of public property. Mayhem."

I stand very still and try not to laugh out loud. Mayhem. What the rust is Mayhem? The judge says something else about the damage I caused, but he's mumbly. I'm insulted he doesn't even try to sound intimidating or even make me feel guilty about what I've done.

This place is a joke. All of us, the judge, his bailiff, even my sad little entourage—we're packed in a small corner of this vast, opulent room. Everything is so . . . unused. I look up. There's a faded mural on the dome above. Before a majestic sun, a white-robed angel holds a scale. I recognize the three planets—a much larger Earth hangs in the balance against arid Castra and lush Cyan-Bisera. If the angel could whisper, I bet she'd tell me she's been watching this room shrink for a long, long time.

"How do you plead?" the judge asks.

"Not guilty."

I'm silenced by the dull thud of the judge's gavel. "You have been found guilty. The sentence of this court is that you will remain in juvenile custody at the House of Social Rehabilitation, until you reach the age of eighteen . . ."

One year in juvie. This is happening so fast. I don't

know what I expected. The judge takes a breath and I realize he's not done.

"Upon turning eighteen, you shall be remanded to the Labor Corps on Cyan-Bisera until you earn out. Or for the remainder of your life, whichever comes first."

I gasp. One year and I'm done for, exiled to an uncivilized planet crawling with sap miners, terrorists, and drug lords. Hard to imagine anything worse. If I were a murderer or political prisoner, the judge would put my name on the next deportation list, sentencing me to some hellhole penal colony on Earth, but still. I'll never earn out of the Labor Corps. No one ever earns out the cost of "rehabilitation," the steep room and board fees charged to every inmate. My leg starts twitching and I need to run. I need to run away and find a rig and just start driving.

The guard grabs me and spins me around before I can think twice about it.

"You are dismissed." The judge waves me away.

My counsel never says a single word.

In a daze, I stumble out of the courtroom. It takes all of six seconds for sharp-clawed panic to sink its hooks deep enough to wake me up. I am going to juvie. Then hard labor in the fuel mines on Cyan-Bisera. I can't move. I can't think.

I'm free-falling. Away from midnight races at the dunes. Away from lazy Sundays at the garage. Away from my life with Bear.

I start scanning the room, desperate for an exit. I taste the curse words before they fly off my lips, ringing in this echo chamber of a lobby.

"This is bull-sap, you mother-rusting sons of—"

A hundred heads snap my way. From the corner of my eye, I see the elevator doors open. The prisoner inside. He's so far away. The elevator is packed with guards. His back is turned and the crowd between us is so thick.

There's this foolish hope—I carry this fragile ember inside me—that it's him. I'm so, so stupid to think it could be, that I'll ever see my best friend again. The surge of adrenaline thrums like a distress signal. Please. I need to know it's him and that he's all right and that I'm not alone in this terrible place.

In these boots, I can't stand on my toes, but I will every muscle and tendon to stretch. The effort buys me an inch or so, and I squint to get a better look. He turns, and it's no mistake. Bear is here. The ember stirs and I'm on fire. Before the guard can react, I rabbit-punch him with both fists, then snatch the boot remote from his hand.

Stunned, his partner reaches for me, but I duck. Twice. I flick my thumb over the flex card to turn the boots off. In a blink, I'm running as fast as my boots will let me, launching away from the fountain's edge, zigzagging and cutting through breaks in the crowd.

I've probably got a handful of seconds at best. Already, half a dozen DP are onto me, pushing their way through the long lines of detainees.

"Bear!" I scream.

He looks my way. When he sees me, his slumped shoulders lift. "Phee?!"

Bear's escorts had been leading him slowly toward the courtroom, but the moment he hears me, he wrenches free. The force is strong enough to knock two of his captors on their exhausts. They scramble back up, and the other two try to catch Bear, but it's too late. A beast off the chain, he's halfway across the room, running like I've never seen him.

Someone must have another sync remote. My boots force me to halt. I'm ten yards short, but nothing stops Bear. He practically tackles me, folding me into his arms. I can barely breathe. Not because he's crushing me (he is), but because I can't believe my best friend on the planet is alive and well.

I look up, craning to look into his face. Not quite. I reach up and run my thumb over his right cheekbone. For a moment, he takes my hand and holds it there, over a faded bruise. The protective fury—I can feel it roll off him in waves.

"I pulled you out," he rasps. "Jumped in the second they dropped me at the docks. But they took you away. I thought you were dead. They told me you . . ." he says. "I wanted to die."

I think of a million things, but my mouth can't form a single word. I just stand here, wide-eyed, holding on for as long as I can. His grip on me is fierce, but there's a special tenderness in our meeting too. The kind that comes from years of scouting each other's routes before turning any corner. Bear has run alongside me all my life.

Circling, the guards have come to separate us. I hear the thump of their footsteps. I feel the pull of my boots. I'm being dragged away, by unfeeling hands and ruthless physics. I see the pain flash in Bear's eyes, but all I feel is rage.

The DPs take him by the arms.

"Leave him alone!" I say as they drag me away.

No matter how hard they strain, Bear won't turn his back. One of the guards pulls his stun stick, swipes it to half power and jabs him in the ribs. Bear's face twists in pain and fury, but the warning jolt isn't enough. Again, he breaks completely loose.

The unrest is contagious. In the lines, prisoners murmur, a breath away from insurrection. More guards flood the room, pulling their weapons and barking orders. Lock-down sirens blare and blast-proof doors slam into place, blocking the main exits. Our little rebellion has sparked something far more dangerous.

Quickly, four DPs drag me out of the lobby and into a hallway. A glass door slides open and then shuts behind us. I twist toward it. Through the chaos, I can still see him.

I lunge and strain, knocking my forehead against the glass. "Bear!" I scream.

He is coming for me.

I reach for the door, but the guards swarm. One of them bats my hand away. "Back down," she warns. "Or else."

I ignore her, fighting hard. There are three DPs on me, and from behind, I hear more running to assist. Bear slams into the door, his palms out, fingers splayed against the shatter-proof surface.

I mimic his stance. All four of his guards pounce on him. When they stun him again, I scream and choke and pound on the doors. Two more jolts, but Bear holds his ground. The tendons in his neck tighten and rise. His jaw is locked and his teeth grind with every puff of strained breath.

"Behave." The guard tries again. "Stop or we'll do it."

"Do what?" I snap, breaking eye contact with Bear.

She taps the glass and nods at a DP on the other side of the door. He acknowledges, reaching into his pocket. My joints loosen and melt. I know what's in the guard's fist before he pulls it out.

"Get him to back down," the woman says. "Or it's the needle. We'll pack him off to juvie unconscious."

I lean as close to the door as I can. These tears are only for him. "You have to stop, Bear. Please."

He still won't back off. I have to lie. I have to get angry. "Stop it. Right now. If you don't go with them now, they'll hurt me, Bear!" The pain and surprise shows on his face. When the muscles in his arms go slack, when his head drops and he stares at the black and white, I let my palms slide away from his. Limp, I let them drag me away.

CHAPTER FIVE

THE ROOM THEY SHOVE ME INTO DOESN'T LOOK LIKE ANY
holding cell I've ever seen. I'd thought it'd be some kind of
steel box with a table and chair, maybe a sad, lone lightbulb
hanging over our heads. I did not expect a polished glass
table with built-in flex screen interfacing. The DPs nudge
me into a chair and I sink into the plush velvet. There's a
wet bar at the other end of the room, for crying out loud.

This whole room screams corporate. The crystal vases,
filled with bloodred Biseran poppies. The chroma-climate
paintings that change color with each variation in air tem-
perature. The thick carpet on the floor, sculpted into squares
of ebony and cream. It's a Sixer's boardroom, not an interrogation cell. I glance back at the door, ready to run at the
first sight of a stun stick.

Two men walk in. Both are middle-aged, but one of them

is dressed to kill. Black jacket. Kid gloves. Silver tie. Sparkling ruby cufflinks. Never mind the traces of gray at his temples, he is fit and well-fed—a smooth-skinned, golden-haired suit who is so handsome for his age, it's unsettling. Like he's not himself at all, but a digitally perfected version.

The other guy is probably almost the same age as his boss, Mr. Sixer, but this one is completely different. At first, I think he's nothing special. He's not very tall and his brown hair is common as the coffee grounds on the bar.

It's the man's glasses—his specs—that throw me.

Corporates don't wear them, unless they're for show. Who needs lenses or shades when your eyes are surgically perfected, enhanced for Castra's unforgiving sun? Sure, I've seen Sixers and celebrities wear them for looks, but these black frames are severe and thick; they do nothing for his who-knows-what-color eyes. I can't understand why he'd hide behind them.

And if he's security, I'm the Biseran queen.

They carry no weapons, but I'm no more relaxed. The older Sixer has gloves on and for all I know, his lackey's briefcase is filled with instruments of torture. Maybe an IV line, ready to pump some especially toxic brand of black sap into my veins. I'd trip out on happy hallucinations until my heart pumped hard enough to actually burst. On the streets, I've heard rumors about that kind of thing. What a great way to die. Dosed on the narcotic runoff of the same sticky stuff that fuels my rig.

I don't say a word. I stand up and move to slip past them, but Mr. Specs shuts the conference room door. I hear the lock click. My fate is sealed.

After slumping back in the seat, I cross my arms. Bring it.

Without a word, they both study me. While Mr. Sixer sits and begins to pull his gloves off, Specs sets the briefcase on the table and opens it. His boss smiles placidly.

No stun sticks. No syringes or interrogation tools.

Specs pulls out a single sheet of paper.

Paper. Not a flex screen, which is strange. Hardly anyone actually uses paper anymore. People only buy it for off-the-wire business. Or because they're nostalgic. And I don't think Mr. Sixer is the nostalgic type.

Specs lays the paper on the table and slides it across to me.

I'm cautious, but I don't lie to myself. I want to know what it says. Without touching so much as the edge of the table, I lean over to look.

REGISTER OF CAPITOLINE, SOVEREIGNTY OF CASTRA

CERTIFICATE OF LIVE BIRTH

CERTIFICATE NUMBER: *401-57-410180*

NAME: **PHOENIX VANGUARD**

DATE: APRIL 11, 2375

PRECINCT: 3

PLACE: CAPITOLINE

SEX: FEMALE

MOTHER'S NAME: JOANNA VANGUARD

FATHER'S NAME: THOMAS VANGUARD

There are other things listed, but I don't read past the names, I can't see straight anymore. Although the certificate isn't mine, the details are close enough to spook me. I was born in Capitoline on April 11, and my dad's first name was Thomas, but Phee is for Phoebe, certainly not something as rusting ridiculous as Phoenix. I'm a Van Zant, not a Vanguard, and I'm not . . .

"Eighteen," Specs says. He nods at the paper.

It takes me a second, but I catch on. True enough; the printed birth date is one year off, at least from mine. I can't help but make the mental leap. They are changing my identity. They are here to erase me somehow. My eyes find the door again.

"Some improvisation was necessary." Mr. Sixer's voice is every bit as smooth and artificial as his looks. "For our purposes, you can't be a minor."

Our purposes. The phrase makes my brain itch. I've seen this guy—both of them, actually—somewhere. On a screen, on a feedcast, sometime or another, I'm certain.

I can't take it anymore. "If you're here to kill me, just do it already. If not, you can spare me this whole intimidation routine. Why am I here? Who are you?"

"I see," Mr. Sixer says. "You have a tight schedule? Better things to do?"

An angry heat starts to scorch my cheeks, but I don't take the bait. I don't answer at all.

With a healthy dose of respect, Specs introduces his boss. "I am here on Mr. Benroyal's behalf."

No wonder they look so familiar. Charles "King Charlie" Benroyal is only the most powerful Sixer on Castra. Forget that Benroyal Corp refines more fuel sap than anyone on three planets. His company hires every last DP cop and interstellar soldier; this guy has his manicured hands in just about everything. Defense. Aerospace. Munitions tech. Shaving cream. You name it, they overcharge for it.

Benroyal is the biggest corporate name on Castra. So of course, it's the one I most despise. This man and his bespectacled henchman. They must be expecting me to quake in awe; instead, I tap my fingers on the glass for a second and then stand up as if to leave. As if I really could.

"Pity," Benroyal says, playing along. "I've heard you're the best street driver in Capitoline. I had high hopes for you on the circuit."

The circuit.

Two words that stop me cold. I sink into the chair for a second time.

The circuit is everything right, a sport fueled by the ideals Castrans prize the most. It's burning out your last transmission just to make the next checkpoint. It's leaving your competition choking on your trigger exhaust. It's trembling in the wake of a champion, but holding steady when you beat him on the next turn.

It's also everything wrong, a game infected by the sins I hate. It's taking a corporate mark on your shoulder. Getting your skin inked and your soul scorched with a Sixer brand. Staying on script for live feeds and posing for commercials and showing up for sponsored events. It's about selling out with a smile.

Just like my father.

The thought makes my empty stomach flip and roil. Excitement. Hunger. Disgust. I taste them all at once. "Who do you think I am?" I croak out.

"We know who you are, Miss Van Zant," Mr. Specs says. "The question is, who do you want to be?"

I flinch at his question.

"Are you Phoebe Van Zant, the orphaned daughter of a legendary rally champion?" Benroyal's voice thickens with grand schemes. "Or are you Phoenix Vanguard, the rebellious upstart, the circuit star, the girl destined to outdrive them all?"

Specs, no longer at his master's heels, pulls a flex screen from the briefcase and lays it on the table. No paper this time. No, this is for real. Two taps and a turn of his finger and the document on the flex is projected across the glass tabletop. The name they want to give me is bolded in every blank. It's larger than life. My eyes scan the print. I touch the glass and scroll through screen after screen of clauses. A contract awaits my signature.

I shrug.

"You can stay here, take your chances in juvie," Benroyal says. "You can work in the mines and rot in the Biseran Gap. Or, you can sign with me and leave here today."

It feels much hotter in here. The therma-climate landscapes tell me it's not just my imagination. The plum-colored summits on the canvas start to bleed. The fiery veins of orange and red hurt my eyes. I look back at the contract.

My dad once signed one of these. He raced with the best, driving for the tech giant, Locus Informatics. Played this game and look what it did to us. I stood behind the wall, clutching my little emerald pennant, cheering him on while every victory pushed him farther away, turning him into a tense, distracted stranger who spent most of his time on the practice track and at corporate events.

By the time he finally disappeared, he was little more than a shadow on my bedroom wall, a quick whisper before I fell asleep. Somehow, the pressure to keep winning and packing arenas erased him altogether. How can I expect to fare any better? But what other choice do I have? On this planet, you can turn corporate, you can lay low, or you can die.

Laying low is not an option anymore.

"What will it be, Phee?" Specs pulls off his glasses. "We're offering you a way out. Freedom. The chance to write your own legend."

He says it like he knows me. And in a way, the look on his face says he does. It's as if he reads my past—my hesitations, at least. I know now why he wears the lenses. He hides his intent, probably most of the time. Bet he doesn't like anyone to see the sharpness of his blue-gray eyes. He's allowing me the privilege, but I do not know if I can trust their smoke-signal gleam.

I don't even know if I can trust myself to make the right decision. I can turn corporate, or I can rot. And that would be all right, but it's not just my future, my life on the line. I stop thinking, and just blurt it out. "I'll sign, but only if Bear is part of the deal too. It's both of us, or nothing."

Benroyal nods at his counsel.

"We anticipated that as a possible contingency," Specs says. "Barrett Larssen can accompany your team, perhaps he—"

Benroyal interrupts. "He can be her boyfriend, her bodyguard, whatever. I don't care. Just wipe his charges and put him on the payroll."

A deep breath. I trace a finger over the glass, leaving my mark on the contract. It's done.

Benroyal turns his gimlet eyes on me. His lips curl in a blistering smile; it's a victory pennant he's likely flashed a thousand times before. "It's just as well, Miss Vanguard. The boy can be our best insurance policy. His pardon will remind you who you work for. After today, I don't want you to ever forget. You race for me now. I own you."

Someday, I will claw that smile off his face. I will slash it to ribbons.

CHAPTER SIX

NOW THAT OUR BUSINESS IN ROOM NUMBER ONE IS DONE, Benroyal can't bail fast enough. He abandons us in the adjacent hallway, leaving me standing beside his counsel and the DP who dragged me here earlier. Specs puts his glasses back on—he's quick about it too. I'm certain he feels somehow exposed without them.

And I sense another shift. There was an almost mechanical stiffness in his movements back in the luxe boardroom, but now his shoulders are loosened up, and he doesn't sound so much like a laser-eyed corporate robot anymore.

After the DPs deactivate my boots, I pull them off and hurl them down the corridor as hard as I can. Specs nods at the DPs, dismissing them. At first, they're reluctant to leave, but they finally trot away when he waves them off with a less than polite "Thank you, your services are no longer needed."

As soon as they are out of sight, he puts his briefcase down and pulls a flex card from his jacket pocket. "We'll drive you to your new home. Benroyal has an apartment arranged. For now, your friend can stay with you."

I open my mouth to tell him I already have a place to live, but he cuts me off, handing me the flex. "When you settle in, take a good look at this. Your schedule. Rules. There's a lot of protocol you'll have to digest."

I pocket the card. Even though the thin screen fits in the palm of my hand, I'm not fooled. I'm sure it syncs up with the mother of all hubs. By now, Benroyal has probably set up a digital locker to store data on everything but my bowel movements. On second thought, he'll probably want to track those too.

The man hands me a pair of black leather boots. I put them on. A little too big, but they'll do.

"What's your name?" I ask.

"Let's go," he replies.

I stare him down, unmoved.

He picks up his briefcase again and heads for the nearest exit door. "You can call me James."

"Mr. James?" It's like I'm talking to the pinstripes on the

back of his suit. My feet are still pinched and numb, but I manage to stand again.

"No, Phee. Just James," he says.

He walks out the exit doors and I follow, even though there are no more arrows on the tiles.

There's a boxy rig, almost the size of a tank, waiting at the back service entrance to the courthouse. A sweet, spit-shined Onyx, probably custom made for the likes of Benroyal. Bet the whole frame is armored. Bulletproof windows for sure. James reaches to open the back passenger door, but I flit past him.

He backs off and lets me grapple with it. It's heavy, and I have to climb just to get on the step bar. From there, I haul myself into the backseat. The thick scent of new leather and old wine—luxury—assaults me the moment I'm inside.

James climbs in beside me. We're not alone. A funny-looking man faces us. He's wiry all over, from his coarse black curls to his skinny, too-long arms. He sits there, holding a crystal-stemmed glass filled with who-knows-what-vintage. Something burgundy, fragrant and rich.

And that ridiculous blue jacket with gold embroidered trim—I can't believe I've cast my lot with these corporate goons. Give this one a cap, and I'd swear he's a yacht captain dropping in straight from the Cyanese Sea.

"Phoenix Vanguard," James introduces us. "This is Auguste de Chevalier."

Of course it is. I nod, coughing to cover snorty laughter. I run through my options. What do I call him? Mr. Chevalier? Mr. de Chevalier? Or just Chevy?

The man must have read my mind. "But of course," he says, dangerously waving his glass. "You must call me Auguste."

The accent is so thick, his name comes out as Ah-goooost. My mind can't quite place the muddled roll of his vowels. I'm guessing he's not native Castran, or his parents are Earth-born at the very least. Not surprising. With anyone older than thirty-five or forty, there's always the chance they immigrated here. The Sixers didn't start turning them away until a nuclear strike toasted Earth once and for all. Happened just before I was born, and now we have so many refugees from Earth's scattered, broken tribes, I can't keep track of all the distinctions. Doesn't matter. Native or not, I decide I'll just call him Goose.

"Auguste is your team manager," James says. "He oversees Mr. Benroyal's circuit team, and he's matched you with the right crew chief, pacer, and—"

"I know how it works," I say. "And I already have a pacer."

My new corporate overlords glance at each other. The

uncomfortable looks highlight how little I really know about this whole break-out-of-jail arrangement.

Auguste clears his throat. "Yes, yes," he says. "There's a problem with that."

I reach for the door. If Charles Benroyal thinks he can just ignore my only demand, the most important condition, he can forget putting me on the circuit. Without Bear, I will rot in the mines of the Biseran Gap, thank you very much.

James touches my wrist. "Phee. Wait."

My first instinct is to shake him off, but I don't.

"What's the problem?" he asks Auguste.

"Yeah," I chime in. "Why isn't Bear here already? I thought you could handle the sap-holes in the DP."

"*Ma lune et les étoiles!* I like her, James. You've named her well, she has spark." Auguste gulps a huge swallow of burgundy. "It's not the 'sap-holes,' as you say, Miss Van-guard. It's the boy's parents. We've only just contacted them. The father has agreed to sign a contract, but the mother is *un problème*. It's quite stupid, really. But there it is."

Oh yeah. When it comes to Sixers, Mary is definitely a headache, quietly fighting the corporate machine every chance she gets. I can only imagine how it went over when Benroyal's people offered Bear the circuit deal. But surely there's no way she'd let him face the alternative.

James pulls his briefcase onto his lap. With a click, it's open, and two seconds later, his fingers are working over a flex screen. Good. He's working on it, I'm sure—making our *problème* disappear.

"You busted me out, and I'm a minor. Can't you fix his records the way you fixed mine?"

"It's not that easy," James says. "The DP, the courts, the entire public sector is no problem for Mr. Benroyal. And in your case, you are technically a ward of the state with no one to contest anything. It's easy to tweak your age. But Barrett's real parents are around. Ultimately, they can deny consent on any corporate contract. As long as he's under eighteen, they have a say."

I gasp. I can't believe Hal and Mary would let him go to juvie. "They'd let him rot?"

He reads something on his flex. "Apparently, they would. My sources report Bear's parents have already filed a petition with the court. They think they can seek legal recourse to get him out."

"Can they?"

"Not likely. No."

I turn to James. "Isn't there something?"

Auguste puts down his wine and leans forward. "Listen, I have wasted half a day already on this spitfire little girl. Give them an incentive, James. Apply pressure?"

I sense an ally.

James wipes the flex clear and brings up a new screen. "I suppose I could . . ." The glasses come off again and he stares at me. "Do whatever it takes?"

I see the storm front gather in his gray eyes. This is someone to be reckoned with. He can negotiate anything, I know it. And I cannot abandon Bear. "Yes," I say. "Incentives. Get them to agree. Whatever it takes."

Auguste and I crowd around James. His fingers fly over the screens, the words are a blur, but I start to put the pieces together. By the time I finally read his intent, it's too late, and I realize I've made a horrifying, irreversible mistake.

With a sweep of his hand, James is finished. "The DP should arrive at the Larssen clinic within the hour. I imagine three counts are sufficient. The drug charges—black sap possession with intent to distribute—will be enough of a threat. They'll sign. Let's get something to eat."

"Yes, yes," Auguste says. "Sounds good."

I can't swallow down the acid this time. What have I done? I'm a rusting reckless fool.

I startle at Auguste's voice. I must have fallen asleep, but I don't think I've been out that long. We're still in the Onyx, although we're not moving as fast. I look out the window. Ahead, a thousand high-rises pierce the hazy sky.

James touches his earpiece and I realize he's already on a call. His face colors a shade between annoyed and angry. "Yes, I understand. I realize that . . . but I told you to be there when we arrived . . . No. Not tomorrow. This is important."

"Who is he talking to?" I ask Goose.

"You will meet him soon enough, Miss Vanguard. Moon and stars, that one is insolent. But he is the best. There is no better for you." Auguste waves at James to get his attention. "Where is he? Can we retrieve him on the way?"

James nods and reaches for the bridge of his nose. Just when I think he's going to take his mask off again, his hand drops. "Fine. We're picking you up," he says over the line. When the call ends, he still looks pretty scorched.

"Where is he?" Auguste says.

"Where do you think?" James answers.

"Ah." Goose nods. "Another *problème*."

"Who are we picking up?" I ask.

"Your new pacer." James grits his teeth. "He's south of the Mains."

"At the sap house?" Goose asks.

James answers with a scolding look.

"So," I say. "Your plan is to put me behind the wheel, racing between two and three hundred miles per hour, with nothing more than a tripped-out black sap addict to guide me?"

"When you say it like that . . ." Auguste sighs. "It sounds very bad. But he—"

"Look. I already have a pacer and I certainly don't need anyone on my team who is—"

James shuts me down. "Benroyal agreed Bear could be a part of your team. He never promised he'd be your pacer. We're picking him up. And you're going to give him a chance. And that's the way it is."

I know he means business, but I push back anyway. "Or what? You'll drop me off at juvie?"

James lowers his voice. He speaks softly, knowing I'll still read him loud and clear. "Or the DPs don't just threaten the Larssens, they make them disappear."

CHAPTER SEVEN

IN CAPITOLINE, IF YOU VEER OFF THE GOOD ROAD AND EXIT onto the Mains, you can cut straight through the jeweled heart of the city, casting your reflection on a million panes of mirrored glass. You can race between the Sixers' industrial palaces. After you marvel at their sterile beauty, you can curse the corporate hands that built them.

If you stay off the good road altogether, and you keep south of the Mains, you can hide in the shadows the skyscrapers cast. You can see the other side of Castra's grandest city, the darker half that's thick with violent ache.

We don't have a lot of daylight left, and now we're on a street so far from the gleam, even Bear and I would watch our backs and avoid the alleyways. Of course, Auguste opts to wait in the car (I can't blame him), but James climbs out after commanding me to wait in the rig.

I'm tired of sitting in here and tired of taking orders, so of course I ignore him. I get one of James's patented dirty looks, but he doesn't force me back inside. I sense I've caught him in a weary moment. For now, this isn't a battle worth fighting.

"Follow me," he says. "Stay close and do what I tell you to do. And don't talk."

I don't argue. Getting out of the rig is victory enough.

When I hit the sidewalk, James steers me away from the pawn shop directly in front of us. I sense he's been here before, maybe many times, by the way he makes his way through the bustling swarm. We walk into the Biseran chophouse next door.

The restaurant is a dim, narrow hole in the wall. I can barely breathe for all the smoke from cigarettes and burning fat. Under the stench, the sweet scent of roasted meat tempts me. Even in a place like this, I'm sure I could dine on the tenderest cuts on Castra.

And when I finished my meal, I bet I could slip into some back room beyond the kitchen and find any number of criminals dealing their own wares.

I'm right, of course. James is already pushing his way past the sweat-soaked waiters and smudged-apron cooks, past the chatter and clang of dirty dishes. I follow until he stops at a heavy, worse-for-wear door. No secret knock. No shout through the steel. James just turns the handle and barges in.

The view is pretty much what I expected. We're in a hallway with rooms on either side. On the right, booths full of black sap dealers, measuring doses by the murky vial. The irony never fails to sicken me. The runoff dregs—the by-product of the refined sap that fuels our entire civilization—is also the source of such nightmarish ruin. I've seen it a hundred times, in the eyes of the junkies Mary tries to treat in the clinic. Just one taste and you're hooked. You'll do anything for another brain-burning fix. Doesn't matter if you take it by mouth or shoot it up, the end result is the same. Keep dosing long enough and your memories, your sanity—it's all gone.

The feeds buzz endlessly over the "war on black sap," but I sure don't see the DP doing much to stop it on the streets. No wonder the protesters rage and babble about conspiracies. Even Mary swears they're onto something—that the government's only cracking down on small-time dealers. For whatever reason, they're all but turning a blind eye. She'd kill me for even walking into this place.

One of the dealers offers a few small vials. I catch the hungry glint in his customers' eyes. One of the sticky-lipped addicts flashes a grin at me, and I spy the telltale rot of his gums—no diluting it, or shooting it into his veins. He's hooked enough to toss it back raw. He looks Castran, but there are plenty of Biseran here, even a few Cyanese too. Strangely enough, outside the dealer's booth, no one is squabbling or mouthing the usual slurs; it's a regular interstellar friendship alliance in here.

We pass the dealers by and duck into a room on the left. I can't believe James would bring us into this place. He points at the farthest corner, at a table on the other side of the room. Although the lights are low, I can make out the ring of faces crowded there. No junkies among them, as far as I can tell. For a moment, all are quiet, intensely focused. Then the silence breaks, and I hear the roar, a mixture of shouts and groans.

Gamblers. Pocket flex cards studded with ever-changing numbers and suits. In a place like this, I should have known.

A Cyanese man and woman—both predictably tall and golden haired—look up and abandon the game. After they clear out, I can have a better view of the table. I see a new face, one that's bronzed and crowned with blackest hair. This player is much younger than the others. Unlike the junkies in the booths, he is clean and clear-eyed. He looks Biseran, maybe half-caste, but somehow he doesn't belong in this dim, suffocating room.

James touches my arm. "Stay here," he says. "I'll get him."

I'm not surprised when he leans over the younger gambler, the grinning boy who can't possibly be much older than me. His smile fades when James orders him to leave the table. There's a heated exchange, threats, and sour looks, but I can't hear much over all the noise. The stranger pulls his flex from his pocket, collects his last hand, and taps the stack against his card to settle his account with the house. When he glances at his balance, I see he's furious James picked this moment to pull his leash and drag him away.

Their approach stirs the stale air. I catch the scent of balm leaf. The sweet, light spice tells me he must be Biseran. Which surprises me. Most of the ones who migrate to Castra are hard-luck beggars or toothless addicts. My would-be pacer is neither. He is well dressed and I've already seen his mouthful of pearly whites.

It's only when he moves closer, when he's less than an arm's length away, that I finally recognize him.

"Phoenix Vanguard," James says. "I'd like you to meet—

"Wait—" I spit out.

"I'd like you to meet His Royal Highness," James says. "Prince Cashoman Vidri Pelar Dradha, Duke of Manjor, Knight Companion of the Most Noble Order of the Evening Star, of the Royal House of Bisera, Second Son to Her Majesty, Queen Napoor."

Slack-jawed, I blink, expecting one of them to tell me it's all a joke. Instead, he nods. My pacer.

The Biseran prince.

I can feel my gums start to flap, even before my brain has a chance to process the ridiculousness of this moment. I mumble something, dumbstruck, curse words under my breath. No, not even curse words. It's really just a jumble of nonsense, stuttered consonants and strung-out vowels.

His Royal Highness stares back, amused. When his lazy smile grows wider, the heat works its way up my throat. I can't rusting believe they'd put this preening jackass on my crew. Anyone who watches the circuit feeds knows all about Cashoman Dradha, the runaway-prince-turned-apprentice-pacer. The boy who fled his planet after his father was assassinated, turning his back on duty and country. He is nothing more than a bored, spoiled aristocrat who's here to gamble and play the circuit.

The shock wears off. Mouth closed, arms crossed, I straighten. Now it's his turn. I can see him sizing me up, making his own assumptions. I have no idea what he must think of me in the starved, threadbare state I'm in, and honestly, I really don't care. James clears his throat, and I feel pressured to speak. So I don't.

"Cash will do." The prince holds out his hand. His grip is too warm and sure. "What's your real name?"

"It's Phe—"

James cuts me off. "Phee will do."

Cash will not stop looking me over. Scratching his chin, he keeps studying me, like I'm just another hand to be read, then played. "You as good as they say you are?" he asks at last.

I force a shrug, willing myself to stare back and look bored at the same time.

"Okay, then." Cash's broad smile doesn't match his dark, resentment-colored eyes. He turns on James. "If you and Phee are going to yank me from a twelve-hand winning streak, let's get on with it. To the Spire?"

"To the Spire," James agrees.

CHAPTER EIGHT

WE'RE HEADED TO THE BENROYAL BUILDING, THE TALLEST
tower on the Mains. Maybe other Sixer giants claim command of Castra's lesser cities, but King Charlie might as
well rule Capitoline. They call his place the Spire for obvious reasons—its glass-and-Pallurium frame twists two
hundred and thirteen stories high. Its penthouse pierces the
blood-orange dusk like the fire-tipped end of a spear.

James taps at his flex, occupied with who-knows-what
business while Cash and Goose chat away. They discuss
pit adjustments, paint schemes, and track schedules. All the
latest circuit rumors and all the new tweaks they'd like to
test before this year's Corporate Cup series. Cash thinks
he can work me into shape and Auguste enthusiastically
agrees. In fact, he has high hopes for a season full of pole
position starts.

My manager. This mouthy pacer. We are supposed to be a team, but it's like I'm not even here. I tune them out and watch the sun die a slow death.

The Onyx turns one last corner and rolls into the parking garage under the Spire. It's a long march with a side of small talk before we make it into the elevator. James unlocks it with his flex, and a breath later, we step off onto the 210th floor.

Cool marble tile and silk-draped walls. The foyer's monochromatic—everything is drenched in cream, accented with shades of pewter and gold. It's bright and airy and pretentious as hell. Not me at all.

There are two sets of double doors—one to my right, and one to my left. James points to the ones on the left. "Use your flex," he says.

I wave it in front of the blinking light above the handles. Sure enough, three bolts snap—one after the other—and the door is unlocked. We walk in, and they all trail me as I scope out my new apartment.

It's not so different from the lobby. Lots of oversized, off-white furniture. The flex glass walls gleam iridescent like mother-of-pearl. At will, I can bring up any feed or application. It's all programmed to respond to a few command words or the swipe of my hand.

Admittedly, most of it's wasted on me. I don't really

watch anything aside from racing feeds, but there's plenty of space here, and the kitchen is stocked.

It sure beats the rust out of jail. All I need is . . .

"When is Bear coming?" I ask James.

"Who's Bear?" Cash interrupts.

"Bear is Phee's . . . bodyguard, and he will arrive soon."

"Well, aren't you something?" Cash looks at me and then turns on our keeper. "James, when are you going to hire me my own special goon?"

So. Cash is spoiling for a fight or trying to get under my skin or I don't know what. But I'm too focused on getting answers to take the bait. "How soon?" I say. "Tonight?"

On the glass behind the living room sofa, James swipes his flex against the wall and calls up a map. A red bull's-eye crawls along the good road just south of here.

"Definitely tonight." James's earpiece buzzes. He taps it and clears the wall. I wish he hadn't. I want to keep my eyes on that bull's-eye. He walks out of the apartment, leaving us to take his call.

Cash is watching me again. "Don't worry, Vanguard. You're safe in your ivory tower. Nobody's going to get us up here."

"Look. I'm not worried about my personal safety," I tell him. "I just want to make sure my friend's okay, if that's all right with you."

"Finally," he said. "I've been waiting for some sign of life. The fully poseable girl is actually capable of spontaneous reaction."

I've got a pose for him—I'll put him on the floor. I lunge, but Goose steps between us. He lays a hand on my shoulder and stabs a forefinger at Cash. "You and you, *avez courtoisie!* Grace is a virtue."

"So is minding your own business." I hold my ground and flash the same grin Cash wore for me on the way out of the chophouse.

James stalks back into the room. It's like his presence changes the air pressure. The tension between Cash and me instantly de-escalates—we don't need Benroyal's right-hand man crawling up our exhausts over a little trash talk.

"I have to leave. Something's come up," James says. "Auguste, can you stay until Phee is settled?"

Goose shakes his head. "*Impossible.* I realize you all may find this hard to believe, but I have much work to do. The series qualifiers are in a matter of days. If we are to start tomorrow, I must prepare *immédiatement.*"

"Cash," James says. "Go over the basics with her. Look at this week's schedule. Talk things over, agreed?"

"It's fine," I protest. "I can—"

"Anything you say, James." Cash speaks over me. "We got it."

James takes him at his word, and he's out the door with Goose. I'm alone in my new apartment with Cash. I flop into the nearest chair, sinking so low, the snowdrift of cushions nearly buries me. My would-be pacer is smiling again, but this time he doesn't look one bit scorched. "Well?" I say.

He waits for the sound of closing elevator doors.

"I'm just going to be honest here. I feel for you," he says. "It's your first night in the Spire and I'm sure it's all a little overwhelming. But I've been up for twenty hours straight and I need to zone out for a while. So now that James has vacated the premises, let's just call it quits until later."

I really would like to get a handle on things before I crash for the night. It's my future we're talking about. But no way am I getting all angst-y eyed in front of Cash. "Suits me," I say.

"Good. Get some rest. I'll be across the hall, at my place, but I'll check in later, all right?"

I close my eyes. He can think I'm too tired to answer.

I hear the door close. On my own at last.

As much as I'd like to scope out every inch of this apartment, I'm too numb-toed and tired for anything but a hot shower. I drag myself through the master bedroom and into the biggest bathroom I've ever seen.

I jump in the flex-walled shower, and select the hottest gush I can get, then plant my feet and stand up to the blistering fire hose blast. The purge is enough to break me down. After all I've been through, it's the drench that finally puts a lump in my throat.

I don't know who to trust. I don't know how to reach my only friend. I don't know if James lied to get me here. I've managed to wreck my whole life—my rig, my home, my adopted family are all out of reach now. Tomorrow, I'll become Benroyal's property, taking a driver's mark on my shoulder. Twelve hours from now, the needle and ink will erase Phoebe Van Zant for good.

How could I sign that contract?

Quickly, I reach for my towel before another thought has the chance to plague me. Hanging on the door, there's a downy white bathrobe. There are clothes waiting in drawers and closets. I find a pair of gray cotton pants that fit all right in the waist, but are of course too long in the leg. Although the matching sports tank is also a little big, it will have to do. Either I shrunk in custody, or the Sixers think I'm bigger than I am.

I'm still wet and only half-dressed when I hear the knock on the apartment door. I hustle through the living room to get to the foyer. It better not be Cash. Now that I'm ready for bed, I'm so not up for training schedules and pit rosters. When I answer and open up, it's like someone drop-kicks me, punching out my center of gravity. Relief chases the shock.

There are two DP officers flanking Bear.

"Good evening, ma'am," one of them says. "Mr. Benroyal asked us to escort him here. Is James An—"

Before he can finish, I yank Bear's arm and pull him inside. "Your services are no longer needed," I snap. And then, smiling wide, I slam the door in their faces. Surprisingly, they don't beat the door down. Even more surprisingly, I hear the retreat of their footsteps.

"That felt good," I say.

And now it's Bear's turn to pull on my arm. One whiplash spin and his arms are around me, just as they were on the courthouse tiles. But this time, when I look up, he slides his hands from my waist. His palms cradle my neck, the planes of my cheeks. I'm so raw from the shower; the warmth of his fingers on my jaw is an invasion.

Still rattled, I hesitate. We're so close, the heat in his exhale . . . it prickles my cheek, the edge of my lips. Inside, a part of me quiets and panics all at once. I might as well be drowning again. When our eyes lock, I freeze.

He must sense my confusion. I feel the tremble of uncertainty build in his fingertips. His hands drop and he pulls away.

"Bear." I don't know what to say. "You're . . . Did they . . . Are you all right?"

He doesn't answer. I want him to look at me. I want to read something on his face, but suddenly his eyes won't meet mine. He stares at the creamy marble floor. "I'm sorry," he says. "I was worried. I just . . ."

His face is on fire now. He's embarrassed and beside himself and I'm just letting him twist in the wind. "It's okay, Bear," I say. "I'm glad you made it. I've missed you like crazy. You mean more to me than anyone on three planets."

I mean every word, but somehow it's my own mind that needs reassurance. It's not a question of how deep my feelings run for Bear. Blood could not knit a stronger bond between us. It is no lie that I love him, yet when I ask myself exactly how I love him, when I question the shape of the space he fills in my heart, I stumble. A handful of days ago, Bear was my best friend and almost brother. But now?

The flutter in my chest—I don't know if it's the first wave of alarm or longing. I thought I knew where we stood. We had plans. A partnership. We'd keep racing and get our own shop and someday, just fall . . . together. But now I see the headlong curve in the arc, the shape of our landing, and don't know if I'm ready to tumble into this so fast. I'd never imagined exactly the moment we'd trade fist bumps for fever sighs, and now I realize Bear definitely has. Maybe he always has.

Suddenly, he takes a step back, and I feel the distance.

I look at Bear again and then remember what I asked James to do to get him here. "Are you all right?" I blurt. "Are your parents—"

"Dad says DPs shook the clinic down, tried to pin some charges on my mother, but after they both signed some papers—actual rusting papers, Phee—they backed down and left. Things are a mess, some equipment was broken, but—"

He doesn't know what I've done. The thought buys me a moment's peace, but we've never been anything but honest with each other. I shouldn't keep this from him. "It was my fault. I—"

"It's not your fault Benroyal wanted us."

Us.

I could tell Bear that it really is my fault, and that the Sixers couldn't care less about what happens to him, and that they only wanted me to sign their stupid contract, but I won't wound him twice today. "Are you hungry?" I touch his arm. "Do you need to rest? Do you need anything?"

"I'm fine. Maybe I should . . ." He mumbles and tugs

at the sweat-stained hem of his T-shirt. "Is there a place I can . . . ?"

I point to the hallway. "Take a right, then two doors and take a left. They've got a room for you too. It's right next to mine. You've got your own shower and . . . even fresh clothes, I think."

Without another word, he trudges off to get cleaned up. The slump in his shoulders tells me he's lost. Why didn't I reach for him the way he did for me? I don't deserve his goodness. I pushed him away, and I hate myself for it.

CHAPTER NINE

IF I WAS TIRED BEFORE, I'M DROP-DEAD EXHAUSTED NOW.
But it doesn't feel right to turn out the lights and crawl into
bed yet. I need to say good night to Bear and make things
okay. For everything to be resolved. So I slump back into
the overstuffed chair and wait, palming my flex.

James told me to study these files, but I can barely get
through the mind-numbing rules. After glossing over the
media guidelines, I go straight to my schedule, which
reminds me my days will be jam-packed for the next six
months. There are press conferences and practices and parties and the annual gala, not to mention the actual races.

I'm amused they think they need to list them, as if I
haven't watched the series every year, for as long as I can
remember. The Castran Classic kicks off every season with

an exhibition at Benroyal's own track. It'll be my first chance to drive, but the classic's just for show, to give the Sixers and their bookmakers a taste of the season to come. While the exhibition will give them the chance to decide how many shares to dump into the betting pool, it'll give me the chance to show rivals I'm a real driver, and not just a wannabe from the streets.

After the classic, the real races start. Sand Ridge is the first one that really counts—I've got a handful of days to prepare for 400 laps around Castra's most unforgiving track. The 400 is make it or break it. If I place, it's an automatic bid to the rest of the Corporate Cup series. If I put enough rigs in my exhaust, I might even get to cruise off-planet. The biggest interstellar circuit rally is always the mountain rally on Cyan-Bisera.

A lot of credits will change hands over that one. I mean, I know corporates aren't stupid—most of the time, they don't wager stocks they can't afford to lose, but there have been real upsets. Bank on a driver who can't lose and you can cut down your rivals, a few thousand shares at a time. I think of my own father. His winning record made Locus Informatics, putting them in the game and giving them the clout and prestige to rise to Benroyal's level. Forget politics. You want real power? Own a circuit team.

I've become a part of that now, and win or lose, despite

every thrill, this game was my father's trap. Twelve years ago, he raced the same series, and I lost him for good. Dead and gone, my parents are the old scar my mind still traces in the dark.

The bolts on my apartment door snap. Either James is back or the DPs have forgotten something. If the guards are here to harass me, I'm not going to make it easy on them.

The doors swing open and it's Cash.

Rust.

"Why does your flex open my door?" I say. "Haven't you ever heard of knocking?"

Of course, His Highness isn't really listening to me at all. He just waltzes in with that broad, brazen grin of his. You'd think he owns the Spire, all two hundred stories of it. I stand up and plow toward him, and when I'm just about close enough to give him a good get-the-rust-out-of-here shove, he reaches first and pulls us both onto the couch.

Cash is weirdly crazy-eyed, and I can't tell if something's wrong or if he's playing the worst kind of joke. He drapes his arm around my shoulder. "We should get to know each other. Do you like music?" He skims his flex against the wall. The sluggish rhythm of a slow techno-rock track drifts from speakers in the ceiling. Cash turns the volume all the way up to blaring.

He must be drunk or high or I don't know what. "Have you lost your rusting mind?!" I shove him, my hands pressing into his way-too-ripped chest. "Take your music and get the—"

Instead of backing off, he answers by nimbly lacing us together, his hand on the small of my back. My first instinct is to knee him where it hurts, but he sways me with a panicked whisper. "I'm sorry." His lips brush against the soft, vulnerable spot between my ear and my jaw. The contact nearly drains the fight from my limbs. "Really. I'm sorry. I just needed to talk to you."

I give him the side-eye.

"Privately," he adds, letting go. "It's important, I swear. Wow, can I just say? You smell a lot better than you did two hours ago."

"You've got about three seconds to start talking," I say. "Or I start—"

"Be careful," he whispers. "In the Spire, watch what you say. What you do. Security reports everything and Hank's the only guard you can trust. Outside your apartment, there arc cameras everywhere and—"

"Which one's Hank? How do you kn—"

"I just know."

I press my cheek against his and lean in as close as I can. I'm practically eating his not quite wavy, balm-leaf-scented hair, but I want to get harsh, right up in his ear. "Why should I trust you? You're a prince, for sun's sake. Benroyal's special guest—"

"If by guest, you mean someone who can never, ever leave, then yes, I am very special. I'm here because Benroyal wants me here. Wake up, Vanguard. You and I are in the same prison now. King Charlie owns us both."

"Nobody owns me." I say it like it's not a lie. "And I barely even know you. For all I know, you're just telling me this to—"

"Hey, I just thought you should know. We're a team."

"We are not a team."

"Not yet." He stands, then pulls me to my feet. "But we will be soon enough. Besides, if we don't perform well together, they'll be all up in my exhaust about why, so do me a favor and let me help you stay out of trouble. Agreed?"

I grimace. It almost hurts to nod.

He smiles and the sight of it flips a switch inside me. When he leans in, my gray cotton tank pressed against his white, I don't want to cuss or back away or shove him out of my apartment. Inexplicably, I'm rooted in place. Rust. I am so not this girl, the kind that melts for any scheming boy, handsome or not.

"Just be careful," he pleads again. This time, the warning sends a shiver through me. I believe him—of course

Benroyal's not to be trusted—but surveillance is not the only thing making my mind scream caution. The blood pounding at my temple sings vigilance. It tells me to be wary of this boy whose eyes shine so darkly. My hand on his shoulder . . . his skin is more than bronzed, dune-colored like the Castran desert at midnight. I need to close my eyes and turn away; I don't know who I am with him.

I feel the muscles in Cash's stomach tense against mine. He pulls away. I look up and before I can react, I turn and see Bear looming close.

He swings past me and punches Cash in the face.

Oh sap.

Cash stumbles back but quickly recovers, and I can't believe Bear's fist didn't put him on the floor. Bear is already on the offensive again. He lunges forward again, bent on landing another punch.

"Bear!" I scream. "Don't! It's not what you think."

Bear flinches. There's a second of hesitation, like I might have gotten through to him.

"Calm down, man," Cash says. "I didn't . . . I promised her I'd come back over tonight and—"

No. No. No. No. He did not just say that. Cash might as well have flaunted a red flag in front of a Biseran Boar. Bear tackles him and they both tumble to the floor, crashing into a low, flex glass table on the way down.

Face-up, Bear swings for Cash's nose. Cash ducks, bracing his forearm under Bear's chin. "I didn't do anything," he says to Bear. "So there's no call to get all scorched off and—"

Cash has him in a chokehold, but it's not enough. Bear's right hook searches for his face and I've just about had enough of this testosterone circus.

"Hey!" I yell.

They both pause mid-swing, frozen like two lock-jawed, half-cocked fuel triggers.

Since they're actually listening now, I decide to take myself out of this equation. I let them both have it. "Hey," I say again—this time withering them with my stare. "I am not the prize in your box of flakes. If you two sap-holes don't knock it off, I will drop-kick you both into next week and never speak to either of you again. Ever."

I'm pretty sure I made myself clear, so I stalk into my room, slam the door, and fall into bed. If they don't kill each other first, these two are going to drive me into the wall as sure as a bad rig coming around the third turn.

CHAPTER TEN

I DIDN'T SLEEP WELL, AND I'M LESS THAN HAPPY TO BE AT Benroyal's clinic in the Spire. The technician keeps telling me that the burn only lasts for thirty seconds, and that the whole procedure is so quick, I'll hardly get comfortable in the tube before they roll me out again.

See, she keeps saying that, but as I look at the machine through the glass, I don't think I'll ever get comfortable inside that thing. It's a tiny space, maybe three feet in diameter all around, inside the white Pallurium cylinder. Not a lot of wiggle room.

This is going to suck exhaust in the biggest way. As scorched as I am with Bear and Cash, now I actually wish they'd let someone come in here with me. I don't want to get inked, and I certainly don't want to lie down on that table and slide into the mouth of that metal monster all by myself.

"I could give you a sedative, if you'd like," the technician offers.

"No." I hope she can't hear my teeth chatter. "No needles."

But of course, needles are exactly what I'm going to get once I'm in there. A hundred of them, red hot and tipped in permanent ink, will bear down on my shoulder and brand me with Benroyal's corporate mark. It's a rite of passage for every circuit driver—one I'd prefer to skip.

"Alrighty then." The technician shrugs. "Let's get started."

She makes me take off my robe. Underneath, I'm wearing one of those horrible gowns with the slit up the back.

"Lie facedown on the table, please," she says.

When I comply, she drapes a heavy, protective coverlet over me. There's a cutaway square, baring my shoulder. "When you are relaxed, turn your head to the right."

Relaxed? That's not going to happen.

My jaw clamps shut and I try to score more than a shallow breath. "Get on with it," I say, teeth gritted.

Almost immediately, I regret begging her to push me

in the tube. An electric hum slowly builds until the whole tube vibrates with deafening sound.

For a moment, a slight warmth tickles my shoulder. I gasp, and the warmth turns into a screaming burn. A million pinpricks of pain stab deep into my skin. A sharp throb burrows its way past tissue and muscle and then deeper still. Suddenly, I'm sure they're tattooing the marrow of my bones and not just the tender skin on my back. Just when the wail begins to crawl out of my throat and into my mouth, it all stops. An icy cold envelops the burn and instantly quenches it. No pain. Two blinks later, my whole shoulder is numb.

I slide backward as they roll me out and my stomach drops into my feet. They're lucky I don't vomit on their shoes. My torturer shuts everything off, lifting the blanket away. With the weight gone, I fear I'll float off the table.

"You may resume normal activities after an hour. Some dry mouth is normal," the technician says. "Would you like to see?"

She mistakes my trembling for a nod, and two assistants move in with mirrors. They angle one above my shoulder and one below the table so I can look. I glance down and see the mark etched into my skin.

Benroyal's golden lion rears up and paws the sunlit sky. I

recognize the crest, but it has been altered. Phoenix wings, dappled with the colors of flames, arc and spread out from both sides of the shield. It is beautiful. Majestic. A work of art.

Even as I marvel at the emblem embroidered on my skin, I despise the sight of it. The vibrant golds and reds and blacks remind me I'm marked for life, just a pawn in a rich man's game.

After grabbing my clothes, I barely make it to the clinic bathroom before hurling my five-star, protein-packed, room service breakfast. Somehow, I know it's not the procedure that turned my stomach. It's my fatal allergy to all things corporate. I've been branded, and my DNA is furious. My digestive tract has staged a revolt.

Two fried pies later, I'm full of castraberries and caloric fuel. The Onyx pulls away from the bakery and Auguste instructs the driver to take us out to Benroyal's circuit headquarters, his practice track west of town. I'm not sure why I thought we'd be heading for Sand Ridge Speedway, but I'm disappointed all the same. At least Bear will be waiting for me. Not to mention I'll get to meet my entire team.

Traffic is thick downtown. I press my forehead to the glass when we reach the south side of Capitoline. I know these streets all too well—every alleyway and sand-whipped facade is etched into me, mapped as surely as the brand on my back.

We pass Mercer Street. Eleven blocks from home, but still. I look out the window at the protesters, the weary handful of people still foolish enough to march the streets in broad daylight. They pair up, flex banners stretched between them. VOTE FOR ABASI. More slogans blink over images. Prisoners mining in the Gap. Starving children and withered black sap addicts.

No More Contracts. No More Lies.

Who Pays for Your Prosperity?

There is more truth in these pictures than anything you'd ever see on the newsfeeds, but I don't know why they even bother. It's a joke, really. Everybody knows Toby Abasi's the only politician in Capitoline the Sixers haven't managed to buy off, and you can bet even his days are numbered.

It's just the way it is. We live and die hungry, and the Sixers write the rules. They push through every bill and control every resource, while these people have no voice, no money, no real shot at changing anything. These banners? They'll soon fall to the ground. The DP will see to that, sweeping up another inconvenience for the corporates who pay them well enough. I think of the officer who dragged me into court. The thought almost makes me dry heave.

"Are you all right, *ma chère*?" Goose asks.

I nod. He understands. He knows I'm lying, and that my nausea has nothing to do with breakfast and everything to with what's outside our bulletproof windows. And we both know our place, that we're powerless to do anything about it.

"Perhaps you should rest," he says. "I will wake you when we arrive."

I sit back to appease him, but I don't close my eyes.

It's a twenty-minute ride through the rough edge of the city and then we finally make it to Capitoline's outer rim. Benroyal Racing HQ may not look like much from the outside of the gates, but it is sprawling and I'm sure the plain brick facade of the track conceals plenty of jaw-dropping surprises.

As the Onyx approaches the cameras, the lion-crested gates swing inward to welcome us. I'm on the inside now, and I'm both wary and traitorously thrilled about the high-tech, steel-boned snares that await me.

The driver drops us off at the far end of the track. My new flex gets us inside and I follow Goose down the main corridor. We turn a corner and there it is. Benroyal's main garage.

"Behold." In a grand gesture, Auguste sweeps his hand through the air. "Our fair kingdom."

Go ahead and call me a sellout, because I am more than giddy. I am rusting awestruck.

Even though the cement walls and floors are painted the standard blue-gray, the bay is so beyond ordinary. The open space seems to stretch forever and there are people everywhere. Apparently, it takes more Benroyal jumpsuits to fill out a crew than I'd ever imagined. I'm definitely not in Benny's tin-roofed shop anymore.

In the farthest corner, sparks fly as fabricators smooth out sheet metal and mold it to a frame. Opposite them, two engineers are testing three identical rigs on separate decks. I've seen this kind of setup on behind-the-scenes circuit feeds, but I'm still amazed how they can test horsepower and suspension and chassis by mounting the vehicles in place and spinning the wheels. There's even a synthetic track control that simulates the turns. I watch the engineers. Flex screens in hand, they make notes on the data.

In the middle of the bay, there's another rig, but since it's almost completely draped by a blue-gray slipcover, it practically melts into the background. I almost missed it. A cluster of jumpsuits mills around its frame.

"Shall we?" Goose starts walking their way.

I'm only too happy to follow. When we get closer, I recognize a friendly face. Bear is hanging back, standing behind the crowd, but he's head and shoulders above the rest, so I don't know why I didn't notice him before. Benroyal's tri-colors—the deep red with gold piping and the black vertical stripe—look good on him. The uniform's a little tight in the shoulders, but I'm thrilled to see him blend in with the team.

"Hey there," a voice calls out.

I turn, and Cash is beside me. To say the jumpsuit looks great on him would be an understatement. The high-collared zip-front fits him like a perfectly tailored second skin. And I can't imagine his hair and eyes—all the darkness in him—looking better against any other shade.

Cash owns this look.

I should be civil and say hello, but suddenly my throat wants to close up and I have to squeak out the words. They come out louder than I'd like. "Hi. What's up?"

"Miss Vanguard," Goose announces. "This is your circuit team." He smiles at Cash and passes him a flex screen. "Cash, would you do the honors and introduce each devoted member of the crew?"

Cash is obviously caught off guard, because while I'm sure he's acquainted with everyone, he looks none too thrilled once he takes a look at the roster. "Um, sure. I guess you already know me, so let's start with your over-the-wall guys . . . This is Billy and Arad, they are your tire changers.

Corky and Joshua are tire carriers, and Dev here is your jackman . . ."

In turn, Cash introduces them all, and I know it's going to take a while to keep everyone straight. Dev is huge, the strongman of the group. I'll have to think of other ways to help me remember the others, who are all short, agile-looking grunts.

"Ben is your trigger man, the guy who'll always load your fuel for you—"

"You can call me Banjo," Ben pipes in. "Everybody does."

"Banjo it is, then." I nod.

Banjo's a hayseed blond with a toothy grin. Bet he was born and bred far from Capitoline and only wandered here when he ran out of tractors and dry season tillers in need of repair.

"And these guys . . ." Cash turns toward the remaining stragglers. "They keep things running smoothly in the pit stall and in the garage. Mr. Gil Gates is your crew chief and he's also your chief mechanic. Navin oversees all body-work and he's our detail man. No one makes it shine like he does."

I nearly fall over when Gil offers his congratulations. I've seen the feeds. A million times, I've watched the high-light recaps. He's old-school, a rally legend. There's isn't a driver alive who wouldn't kiss Gil Gates's feet and beg him to join their team. I'm humbled that Gil and everyone else smile at me, a nothing street rat racer. I hadn't expected them all to treat me with such uncommon respect. I shake hands with every person in the room, even the guys Cash doesn't introduce, the nameless grease monkeys who walk over to greet Benroyal's latest driver.

I'm lit like a live wire, practically twitching with excitement, but through it all, Bear is stone faced and quiet. For him, there's no introduction, no explanation of duties. He is lost here, and I don't know what to say to reassure him.

Auguste is distracted, talking shop with Gil, when I notice Cash taking one last look at the roster. His expression clouds, so I look over his shoulder. My eyes sweep to the bottom of the list and find Bear's name there.

Barrett Larssen—floor sweeper

"I had nothing to do with this," he says. "I swear."

"This isn't going to fly with me, Cash," I say. "No way. Not okay."

Bear moves to my side. "What's not okay?"

Before Bear can get so much as a split-second glimpse, Cash wipes the screen. "Nothing," he says. "We were just discussing paint schemes."

For a moment, Cash and I stare at each other. I hope he can read the silent thank-you on my face. They can arrest me, terminate my contract, do what they will, but I'd sooner be cut loose and tossed in juvie than allow Bear to see himself as anything less than a full-fledged crew member. Cash can call himself my pacer to appease Benroyal and the powers that be, but Bear will always be the voice on the other end of my headset.

"Yeah," I say to Bear. "I was just saying that I wanted to see the scheme they've got on my rig."

We've captured Auguste's attention again. He perks up when I mention the vehicle. "Well then," he says, motioning at it. "Take a peek for yourself."

Cash and Gil pull the cover forward. It slips off and pools on the floor like a castoff silken gown. It's the big reveal, the moment I've been waiting for, maybe for longer than I'd ever thought. Can a dream sleep for a lifetime, only to surface and breathe the second it comes true?

My own circuit rig.

It's beautiful. Almost my snub-nosed Talon, only the body curves more subtly, and every plane is smooth as glass. All the seams and rough edges are gone, made invisible with body filler and gloss. And unlike the rig I sunk by the docks, this one is drenched in crimson, a red richer than garnet, deeper than blood. The paint detail is gorgeous. Sharp black pin-striping on each side. The air dam—the low, ground-skimming dip of the front bumper—is painted gold. The glimmer gradually fades up into the ruby blush on the hood. The crest over the engine is identical to the marks on my shoulder, but I sense the car and I are well-matched in ways beyond this.

This is how they get you. With metal and gears, the Sixers dangle the hook you can't refuse. They bait the trap with everything you want to taste. And just like that, they have me. I move closer to the driver's side.

"You like?" Auguste asks me.

I've been staring so intently, I'd almost forgotten where I was, and that there was anyone else here. I've been alone with the most perfect rig in the world—one that was made for me.

Bear moves behind me and puts his hands on my shoulders. It's a gentle reminder to speak, but I'm at a loss for words. A feeble "Uh-huh" is all I can manage.

"I think she likes it," Cash says.

CHAPTER ELEVEN

I'M DYING TO LOOK UNDER THE HOOD, BUT I WANT TO LET
the engine speak for itself. I want to see how this thing
handles first. Gil says they still have a few tweaks to finish,
but they'll need my input before making any more adjustments to my rig, so I beg for a test drive.

Since I've yet to get fitted for racing gear, it's not easy to
get them to roll it out of the garage onto the oval practice
course. Even so, I can tell I'm not the only one who wants
a test drive, because everyone else on the crew follows us
out to the sun-bleached track.

Clear skies. Cool breezes. Perfect day for a ride.

"Listen now," Gil warns me. He's all squinty eyes and
wide nose and gap teeth. "You just take it easy. If something
happens and Benroyal finds out I let you open her up without fireproofing you first, we're all out on our exhausts."

"Just a couple of laps," I say. "I'll be careful on the turns, I promise."

He and Cash step back while I slide through the driver's-side window. I'm not used to a rig with no doors, and I'm a little embarrassed when Bear has to give me a hand. Next time no one's around, I'm going to practice until I can jump in like a rally pro.

I pull, and the steering wheel locks into place. Gil hands me a helmet. After I strap it on, I buckle the six-point. I give it a couple of tugs—it's not as tight as it should be. The crew is going to have to make some belt adjustments to accommodate my runty frame. It'll do for now, but when it's race time, when I rocket through the backstretch at well over two hundred miles per hour, I'll need the harness as tight as it can be to keep me firmly in the driver's seat.

I spy an ignition switch on the dash, but that's about it. I flip it on and the engine hums to life. I don't think I've ever heard sweeter music than its low purr. Even so, I've got a big problem on my hands. Besides the wheel, all I see are dead dash screens. And when I reach for the throttle and trigger stick, they're not there.

No stick? How am I supposed to drive without any control, any get up and go? "Um . . . I'm not really sure . . . ?"

Cash leans through the driver's-side window. "What's the trouble, Vanguard? Never worked a hyper-screen setup?"

"No," I croak.

He smiles; it's an exultant gleam. We're on the same team, but I swear, every time his grin widens, it costs me something. I'm ashamed to admit he's racking up victory points right and left.

"That's all right," he says. "I can give you the lowdown." He pulls down my visor and flips a switch below the ignition. Suddenly the dash screens blink to life and jump right out at me. Literally. I flinch back against the seat as if the floating panels are going to bite. I can still see the windshield, but the tachometer and the rest of the gauges and controls hover near the bottom of my field of vision.

In fact, when I turn my head, they move with me. "VR controls?"

He nods.

"What about the throttle?" I ask. "How am I supposed to—"

He gestures toward the console beside my right arm. There's a flat-deck touch screen panel.

"The center toggle is the throttle," he says. "Swipe it up to open. All the way down to choke. Blinking circle at the top is your trigger. You have three bursts loaded. Just press and go."

Even after I've processed his explanation, my right fist wants to close around a mechanical throttle that isn't there. "This is sooo weird," I say.

Gil shouts from the pit wall. "You gonna sit there all day, or you gonna give it a go?"

"You'll be all right, Vanguard." Cash slaps me on the shoulder. "Just go for it."

When he steps back into the safety zone, that's exactly what I do.

I roar out of the pit lane and into the front stretch. I'm not used to the fancy virtual controls, but my feet still know how to work an accelerator just fine. At first, it's not that hard to obey Gil's warning—I haven't quite adjusted to the setup, so I'm content to keep the RPMs in a reasonable range. Reasonable for me, anyway. Anything less than three thousand feels like a crawl.

I'm not exactly crawling right now.

I'm careful around the first two turns. On most real circuit tracks, there are magnetized panels on at least one of the turns. Get too close to the wall, and you end up skidding helplessly against it. The only way to bust free is to burn a fuel trigger. The feature is designed to shake things up on the track, but the mag walls are every speed demon's nightmare. Waste more than one trigger prying yourself free and you're rusting done, at least as far as the standings go. Nobody's ever won without saving those precious fuel bursts for gaining straightaway speed.

I have no idea if these walls are juiced, so I'm not taking

any chances. Gil would probably string me up and eat my liver if I wrecked his rig during a test run.

I'm just rolling along when I see the exit tunnel built into the back stretch. Looks like Benroyal's arranged it so drivers can make the third turn and keep driving around the oval or they can exit onto a longer, point-to-point rally course. Every Corporate Cup series has as least two regular lap track runs, but I hate them. What's the point in going around and around in circles?

For me, the real heart of rally racing is the cross-country course, the traditional, multi-point routes that hearken back to the circuit's earliest days, when the first colonists sprinted hundreds of grueling miles to stake a claim on their own patch of dirt and sand. Like them, I'm aching to run off this smooth track and onto a rough road with plenty of rolling hills and hairpin turns. Right now, it's all I can do not to break for the tunnel. And oh, how I would love to make off with this rig.

But I wouldn't get very far. And I know what they'd do to Bear if I even tried. So I'm forced to honor my word and I make a nice, clean third turn. As I'm speeding through the back stretch, my eyes finally get comfortable with the virtual hyper-screens. I've figured out the throttle, and it's been too long since I've had my foot on the floor.

I need this.

My mind slips into a zone—I wonder if my father felt this same rush, driving the circuit. Even as I roar down this empty track, I can almost visualize the blur of a hundred thousand rally fans, screaming from the stands. I hear the snarl of engines on all sides. I feel the sweatbox heat of the three hundredth lap.

One last turn. Straight shot. I go for one more lap. Then two. Three. Faster. This time, I'll make this rig scream. My hand slams against the throttle deck and I find the triggers.

Ready.

Push.

GO.

Whoa. The bursts are like nothing I've ever felt. The car runs pretty tight, but only a death grip on the wheel keeps me from spinning out of control. I'm banking dangerously close to the wall and it's time to start praying.

Please. Please. Hold on. Yes.

My tires squeal but valiantly grip the track. I've managed to keep it together and make the next straightaway. My heart pounds and this glorious feeling builds and expands, radiating from the fist-sized knot in my core, until I'm as weightless as laughter. I smile, because this is what I was made for. This moment. Right or wrong, this is my inheritance.

Two last white-knuckle turns and I brake hard near the

front stretch, engineering a series of hard jolt pirouettes across the blacktop. I spin and spin, but I'm anything but out of control. This is my victory dance.

At the finish line, I skid to a rubber-melting stop. The crew runs out onto the track.

Gil says nothing—I know he's sizing me up and weighing the cost of my reckless speed. Bear and Goose look completely horrified, but I can tell Cash is on my side.

"Vanguard?" Cash says. "That was hot."

"Seem to know your way around a track," Gil adds.

Once the engine dies, I punch the six-point release, peel myself off the seat, and slide out of the rig. "Runs great. Spring rate is a little off. I'm tough on tires, so adjust the camber. That's about it."

I walk off the track. I don't have to look—I can hear the sound of their jaws dropping.

After we drive back to Benroyal's high-rise, I expect Auguste to drop us off, but he takes the elevator up with us. "You tucking us in tonight?" I tease him.

"No, no," he says. "The fitting. I take no chances. I must make sure the *couturières* are precise."

I'm not sure about courti-whatsits, but *fitting* is definitely an ominous word. I don't like the sound of this at all. Maybe they're just measuring me for my crew gear? That's what I tell myself, until I catch Bear's uncomfortable foot-to-foot shuffle. Something is up, and he knows it.

"I'm sure Phee is going to love this," Cash says. "All the dresses and stylists. The shoes. And the hair extensions. Just think of all the super-fun possibilities."

I am no one's dress-up doll. I turn on Auguste, my manager/white-trouser-wearing yacht captain. "What?!"

Goose rolls his eyes and waves Cash off. "Pay no attention to him, he is joking."

"Good. He better be," I say. I'm so worn out from our whirlwind day at Racing HQ, I don't appreciate the heart attack.

"Don't be absurd," Auguste chides. "You won't meet the hair stylists until tomorrow."

In my apartment, someone has tidied up. All traces of last night's brawl are gone. The broken table has been replaced and the breakfast dishes I left out have been washed and put away. It seems my corporate prison term includes maid service.

Honestly, at this point, I don't really care who was here, messing with my stuff. I'm more concerned with who is here, messing with me now. I'm ready to tell everyone good night and good riddance. Of course, Auguste will have none of it. Every time I protest, he threatens to schedule additional fittings, and just this one is horrifying enough.

Maybe it wouldn't be so bad if there weren't so many people eyeballing me. Including Cash—I cannot get him to leave. When he and Bear aren't exchanging threatening looks, he's gushing with running commentary on each and every outfit the stylists throw at me. At least, I think these two vultures are stylists. For all I know, Phillip, the man in the purple suit, is really the devil and Bijan, the fabric-swatch-bearing bimbo at his side, is his favorite harpy.

I stand here, and I can't help staring at the creamy throw rug covered with a lifetime's worth of too-tight shirts and skirts and hapless halter tops. It's like the Castran Fashion Feed vomited all over the living room.

"I think the poppy red is a much better color for you than the desert mauve. And that jacket has to go," Cash mocks. "Don't you think?"

Phillip, the eggplant-wearing hell spawn that he is, agrees. He taps his chin. "Hmm," he says.

He says hmm a lot.

"Hold still, Fiona," Bijan says. "And stand up straight."

"It's Phee," I growl. "My name is Phee."

"Uh-huh," she says.

I can tell she's sick of my backtalk. She's getting huffy; her fat-transferred behind jiggles every time she has to push my shoulders back to adjust my posture. She's not the only one who's about had it, though. I'm this close to chasing everyone out, canceling all fittings until further notice.

Bijan has already scanned me with her handheld laser four times. How many measurements of my nearly nonexistent chest does anyone really need? I let Phillip hold things up under my chin. I even let them both drape two dozen cocktail dresses in my face without throwing up all over the silk bodices and strappy shoes.

But I am not trying anything on. No way.

"I don't need these," I say.

"You need them," Goose argues. "Press conferences. Circuit events. Parties. On the circuit and off, you represent the wealth and prestige of Benroyal Industries. Racing is more than the national obsession—no other sport on three planets commands such attention, and you are about to become a part of the spectacle."

If he wanted to win me over, that was not the way to do it. "This is not me," I say. "At all."

Auguste frowns at me. "Yes, yes, Miss Vanguard. That's the point. We don't want you to look like you. We want you to look extraordinary."

There's a blur of words as both Bear and Cash talk over each other. ". . . already are extraordinary," Cash says. ". . . fine as she is," Bear agrees.

I'm a little stunned. It almost feels like I'm not alone,

like we're all in this together. Unfortunately, their mutual faith in my worth as a human being does nothing to neutralize the bad blood between them.

Cash stands up. "I'm out." He looks at Bear and extends a fragile olive branch. "Wanna catch a feed at my place? Ditch the fashion show?"

Bear shakes his head and summons his worst stoic face of doom. "How about you just leave?"

Everyone stops what they're doing to stare at the baldfaced rudeness of the exchange, and even I'm not sure what's gotten into Bear. The boy I know is careful with words, but always, always kind. He still opens doors and carries groceries for every old lady on Mercer Street, for sun's sake.

I could say something to Bear, but I know it would just push him over the edge. And I don't need Cash making a scene either.

"You know what?" I say, pushing the latest chiffon monstrosity out of my face. "I'm done for the night. Everybody out. Right now."

Cash is the first one out the door, and I'm not sure that's a relief. After Bear stalks to his room and everyone else clears the apartment, I'm alone with nothing but brooding thoughts.

〜〜〜

I walk into my room just as the Castran sun dies. I know this because the milky iridescence of the outside flex wall has somehow morphed into transparent glass. Whoever made my bed must have also swiped the wall sparkling clean. I didn't know they made flex walls like this, but as I face the horizon, this window on the world is a gift.

We are above the worst of the smog, the choke and residue of a thousand gritty streets. I can see past the city into the shadow-veined foothills of the Sand Ridge Mountains. The sight of it all is so seamless and clear, I'd swear there was no wall at all. I move closer and the illusion is broken. I see the ghost of my reflection on the shatter-proof surface and it reminds me of all the inescapable boundaries that keep me here. The contracts. The cameras. The threats against those I care for most.

I can race, but I cannot run. I can live, but I cannot breathe.

Something does not add up. Racing is everything here, but I'm an unknown with no real rally experience, just a couple years' worth of small-time match-ups under my belt. Forty-eight hours ago, I was pacing Benny's garage and now I'm living in the Spire.

Why?

CHAPTER TWELVE

I'M SOMEWHERE BETWEEN THE PARALYSIS OF SLEEP AND blinking awareness, in the hazy, just-under-the-surface zone. My side-to-stomach-and-back-again turns have twisted the sheets; I'm tangled up in soft cotton knots. Eyelids and limbs are too heavy to move.

"Pretty girl," a woman whispers, touching my arm. "Such a pretty girl . . ."

My eyelids snap open so fast, it hurts, and blood is pumping and the flow of fear and instinct and adrenaline is pushing, pushing, pushing through veins that are too small to accommodate the flood.

There is someone in my room; I can just make out her bone-sliver shape in the dark, and I'm already moving. I'm off the bed, feet on the floor, back against the wall, in the space of one breath.

Don't panic. Watch. Listen. Sweep the room and look for an out or a defensive position. My eyes flick toward the door, but she is in the way. I can't see her face. She is tall, but her long, long dark hair seems to weigh her down. She is so thin and eggshell frail.

And it seems my jump to the wall has frightened her almost as badly as she has startled me. She starts to cry, the sobs bleed into her voice. "You can't stay here . . . they give you things to make you forget . . . they cook it themselves." She speaks gibberish, talking so fast I can barely keep up. "They cook it . . . don't you understand?!"

She tries to press something into my hand—a flex card— but instinctively, I flinch away, letting it fall to the floor.

"Take it." She scrambles to pick it back up, mumbling the whole time. "Sweetwater. Remember. It's Sweetwater. You have to remember. You have to take it."

This lady is completely unhinged. I could backtrack my way into the bathroom, lock myself in, and summon a flex wall panic button. Or I could tackle this crazy and shove her in instead. Rust. She moves closer. I can sense the impulse; she's going to pounce if I don't move. Still pinned against the wall, I edge right.

"You have to get out!" She lashes, clawing for my hands or arms, anything to hold on to. "Get out or they will give you things to make you forget."

I pivot, grabbing her by the shoulders. Before she can react, I force her into the bathroom and slam the door to keep her inside. I nearly plowed through her—she is no more solid than melting snow. Through the door, the woman keeps calling out to me. *Get out . . . Get out . . . Get out before it's too late.*

No sooner do I reach for my flex to call for help than I hear the boot stomps. Voices. A trio of security guards burst into the room and push me aside. Black shapes moving past me in the dark. The muffled cries of a madwoman being dragged away.

Another slamming door. Footsteps in the hallway. It's Bear. He stumbles into my bedroom. When he sees the guards in my room, he charges forward, but then freezes almost as quickly, scanning the room.

"Bear!" I call out.

He sees me, finally realizing the guards don't have me. He barrels past them and over the bed until he's at my side. He reaches for me, but I stand and push him back.

Bear's eyes are wide, lit with alarm. "Are you okay? Did she hurt you?"

My protector, he tries again, pulling me closer. I know he just wants to shield me, to guard me from the lunatic mess who's invaded my room, but my pulse is still racing. Bear overshadows me, and suddenly I don't want his arms around me. I hear the woman's birdlike shrieks as the guards haul her completely away and it makes this tiny room feel all the more like a cage.

"What happened, Phee?"

"I don't know. Just a crazy woman . . . I don't know how she got in. I'm sorry, Bear, I'm sorry," I say, pushing past him. "I need to breathe."

Still in my pajamas, I run after the guards. Once I make it to the living room, I realize I'm too late—only one member of the uniformed security detail is left. My front doors are still open, but they've already taken her out of the apartment.

In the lobby, I see the other guards hustle her into the elevator. Her back is turned to me, but I recognize the man waiting for her. Even as she collapses against him, there is almost no reaction on his face, just a trace of possessive concern. Mechanically, he smooths her hair and whispers in her ear, as if he's done this a thousand times before. There's something in the tenderness that makes him all the more terrifying. It's the flicker of restraint. He's an animal, the predator too strong to hold this china doll. After he folds her into his arms, Charles Benroyal looks up, straight at me.

The torment in his eyes instantly vanishes. Cruelly, he smiles. The sight chills me to the bone far more than her trembling voice and frozen touch. Benroyal holds a half-empty glass—his cheeks are bright with wine. And he is so sharply dressed; no doubt he's just been torn from a penthouse gala to deal with this woman. She's a beloved inconvenience, someone I was never meant to meet.

But he is not so alarmed. The look on his face assures me that everything is firmly under control and that I need not concern myself with these matters.

The elevator doors close. She's gone. "Who was that?" I ask the remaining guard.

He was heading for the entryway and my near shout brings him to a sharp halt. He pulls an about-face and looks at me. I see that he's not that much older than I am. Bet there'll be hell to pay when he's forced to account for this lapse in security. "I'm sorry, Miss Vanguard. She used an all-access flex, but it won't happen again. Sorry to disturb you."

Maybe he thinks that official-sounding nonsense is a good enough answer to dodge my question, but it isn't. I decide to get up in his exhaust. I'm pitifully short, but when I lean up to get in his face, there's no way he can avoid me. "Who was that?" I repeat. "Who was in my rusting room?"

"Mrs. . . ." He stutters. "Mrs. Benroyal."

"What? Are you kidding me? That's his wife?"

"Yes, ma'am," he answers.

"Which one are you?" I ask. "What's your name?"

"Kinsey, ma'am. Hank Kinsey."

Hank. The only guard Cash trusts.

I lean closer and spy the edge of the flex card he must have taken from her and stuffed into his right hip pocket. Turns out Mrs. Benroyal is not the only one with a talent for nicking things. I'm no thief, but I've seen enough of them at work around Benny's place to spot their little tricks. I'm streetwise enough to distract the guard with a little shove. "Is she—"

"Good night, ma'am. Take care." He backs away, out the door before I can get two more words out of him, but I've already palmed the stolen flex, tucking it out of sight.

Bear and I collapse on a sofa in the whitewashed living room. I'm creeped out enough that I don't want to go back and lie down in my bed. Bear insists on staying up with me, but I don't want that either. Why should we both spend the night sleepless and miserable? There's no chasing him out of here, so we stretch out on the couch.

I sink into one corner and he rests his head on my lap. I feel the tension in his shoulders, so I run my fingers through his hair until he finally relaxes. This is something I've done a hundred times, on nights when Bear cannot sleep. I've known him since we were small, and he's always closed his fists around our worries and kept them close.

But it's me who's anxious now. This place is changing him. Us. Before the arrest, we were inseparable. He's the same loyal, blue-eyed boy I've always clung to, but now I keep pushing Bear away. I care for him. I'd bleed for him. Yet since arriving at the Spire, I can barely look him in the eye.

My hand slides from his blond hair to the cushion. His eyelids are already growing heavy. He doesn't notice I've pulled away. Good. After tucking a blanket around his broad shoulders, I decide I'll lull Bear to sleep with the most boring feed ever. Corporate News.

I gently fish my own flex out of my pocket and after selecting the feed, I turn off all the lights. I keep the volume low and let the talking heads yap softly. It's the tail end of a financials recap. Sixer stock prices flash off and on below the larger-than-life camera shots.

". . . After violent swings throughout the day, stocks ended this afternoon at their lowest point in this year. The Corporate Exchange experienced massive trading as investors scrambled to deal with the fallout of a terrorist attack just east of the Biseran Gap . . ."

The feed cuts to an aerial shot of the canyon, the red rock gash that runs so deep, it seems to slice Cyan-Bisera apart. In the distance, smoke rises from the torched shell of a building. Soldiers herd sap miners into evacuation rigs. Another refinery bombing.

I think of my hearing and the judge's sentence—I

could've easily ended up in that mob of prisoners. Day after day, they'd lock me into a miner's harness, forcing me to rappel all the way down into a dark, sticky hole, where I'd hose up raw fuel sap until the fumes finally wore out my lungs and choked me to death.

Either that, or I'd end up blown to bits in an attack like this, murdered by drug traffickers or Cyanese Nationalists or whoever they're blaming this time. No wonder Cash left home. His planet's a war zone.

The feedcaster continues his canned, teleprompter freak-out.

". . . Deep concerns about the interstellar economy have prompted official statements from several corporations . . ."

The feed cuts to a press conference clip, and I nearly jump out of my seat when I see the next talking head.

James Anderssen, CEO, Locus Informatics, according to the screen.

What? If James runs Locus, the company behind every flex network in the universe, he has a lot bigger concerns than jail-breaking circuit crew for King Charlie. I scowl at the feed. My father drove for Locus. I got a life sentence thanks to their rusting "hassle-free" court proceedings. This whole time, I've been so suspicious of Benroyal, but now I'm beginning to wonder if James is even worse.

On the screen, his frames obscure his eyes, but James's voice carries loud and clear.

". . . I spoke with the prime minister today, and I'm told that Benroyal Corp is prepared to deploy an additional twenty-five thousand Interstellar Patrol officers to secure the Gap. We will not back down. There will not be another conflict on Cyan-Bisera."

The glasses, the pitch of his voice. It's all empty talk, and James knows it. I keep waiting for him to ditch the frames and let the audience at home see the truth in his eyes. Nothing is going to get better. Get used to it. Instead, the feedcaster interrupts with another clip.

". . . Most officials have released similar statements, but once again, Chamber minority leader Toby Abasi opposes the current administration . . ."

Onscreen, Abasi is lean but haggard, and I swear his sun-spotted face is as creased and dark as the cloth we use to spit-shine a rig. He looks nothing like the smooth-talking corporate clones who normally dominate the feeds.

". . . We should not authorize the deployment of any more troops, least of all Benroyal's mercenaries. It is one thing to defend our interests, but it's completely another to hijack control of Bisera, another allied nation. What hard evidence do we have that the Cyanese are actually behind these 'terrorist' attacks? Why aren't we policing the problems on our—"

A flex message flashes over the walls, swallowing Abasi's final words. It's Cash.

CD: ARE YOU HURT? HANK TOLD ME WHAT HAPPENED.

I grab my card and delete the message off the walls, keeping our conversation contained on the tiny screen in my hands. Before I can reply, he texts again.

CD: YOU OKAY?

PV: FINE.

CD: ARE YOU SURE?

PV: CAN'T SLEEP. NO FRESH AIR.

CD: I HAVE FRESH AIR.

PV: ???

CD: BALCONY. TELESCOPE TOO.

PV: HOW COME YOU GET A BALCONY AND I DON'T??!!

CD: COME OVER.

I don't answer for a long time. I could use a breather, but dealing with Cash again . . . I don't know. I look down at Bear. He's fast asleep, relaxed and dreaming at last. I could slip out and get back before he woke—he wouldn't even miss me.

CD: ???

PV: YES.

CHAPTER THIRTEEN

FEELING MORE THAN A LITTLE GUILTY, I SLINK OUT AND PAD barefoot across the lobby. Cash opens his door before I have the chance to knock. Benroyal's interior decorators aren't very subtle. While my apartment is awash in white, Cash's place is a dozen shades of black and gray.

His bed-head and insomniac stare tell me I'm not the only one who's been tossing and turning. Tonight, I don't see a prince or an arrogant rogue. Just a sleepy-eyed boy.

"Heya," he says, lowering his voice and leaning in.

I start to ask him why he's whispering, but then I remember the possibility of surveillance. The thought of cameras makes my skin crawl. I stay close enough to keep our conversation quiet. "Benroyal's wife. What do you know about her?"

He shuts the door. "Well . . . I know she's messed up in the head. And that she's James's sister."

That first detail is obvious. The second is a jaw-dropper. "Really?"

"She's James's twin." He shrugs. "She and Benroyal? Childhood sweethearts."

I raise an eyebrow. "There's nothing 'sweet' about Benroyal. You're telling me he actually—"

"Oh, he loves her all right." Cash leans against the doorjamb, sidling up. "He's completely smitten. With her beautiful brown eyes. Her vast fortune. Her half-mad, easily influenced mind . . ."

"Wait, I thought—"

"She and James both own Locus Informatics."

I sigh, but it comes out more like a growl. Of course. James and his brother-in-law, working together. I've been totally played. "My father drove for Locus. What a complete coincidence—Locus manages the courts and Benroyal shows up, right after my hearing."

My pacer is quietly laughing at me. "I hate to break it to you, Vanguard, but it's King Charlie's universe, and we just live in it."

I pull out my flex and image-search James and his sister. Oddly, there aren't too many of her. Just a few publicity shots of her on Benroyal's arm, smiling at circuit galas and PR events. Even in the grainy stills, you can see there's something missing. The vacant look in her eyes. I can almost fill in the gaps, imagining the way she might have shined, but the picture won't quite come into focus.

Cash looks over my shoulder. "She looks . . ."

"Like the ghost of someone else." I shiver, remembering her voice in the dark. "Cash, does the word *Sweetwater* mean anything to you?"

"No. Should it?"

"It's nothing . . . nonsense. Just something she said."

I follow him through the living room, which is almost a mirror image of mine, a negative snapshot of my cloud-colored space. But here, there are glass doors beyond the kitchen.

I don't wait for another invitation. I pull open the doors and step outside. A quicksilver band of Pallurium skims the top of a waist-high, transparent railing. Stepping between two lounge chairs, Cash and I stand against the railing and let the air gust over us. It's like we're perched on night's open windowsill, breathing in the light of the stars.

"How'd I draw the short straw on apartments?" I ask.

"I got here first?" He points at the huge black telescope at the end of the patio. "And I like being able to sneak a glimpse of home."

Prince Cashoman. I can't forget that. He hides his accent

well, but it's so obvious that he's Biseran. I glance at his eyes. Dark irises, charcoal with the telltale golden rim.

He knows I was staring. "Some say it makes us less than you. Inferior. The first colonists from Earth called us Black-eyed Devils."

I can't deny it, and I've heard even worse. This one difference in our genetic code makes the Biserans a target. Never mind that no Castran could see so well in the dark. This gift, the unique glimmer and shadow of their eyes—it makes them a people apart. Prince or no prince, it can't be easy for Cash, to live here and deal with those kinds of assumptions. Especially when he headlines every gossip feed. Runaway Royal. Rogue. Gambler. That's all they see in him. For the first time, I wonder if they're wrong. "Some say I'm nothing but south side trash. Who cares what they say?"

"I don't. I've learned not to." He walks over to the telescope. After adjusting the focus, he beckons me closer.

I lean over the scope. The enhanced view is astounding, as good as any satellite image. I see twin orbs—the moon, lustrous and pale, floats next to Cyan-Bisera. Cash's home planet is the brightest jewel in any diamond sky, and even through the lens, I can almost feel its silent pull. "It's so . . . beautiful . . . all that blue water and green mountains and white shores . . . so—"

"Lush."

"Exactly. I know Castra is more . . ." I almost say "civilized" but I know how elitist that would sound. ". . . developed, but still—it's so dry and ugly here. Why would anyone give up . . ."

Silence. The trademark grin vanishes.

"I'm sorry," I say. "I didn't mean—"

"I know exactly what you meant. I'm a coward. A spoiled aristocrat who would rather play pacer than face my responsibilities to a ruined country. Bisera's just a haven for greedy noblemen, dealers, and thieves, and I'm no better."

"I never said I—"

"You didn't have to say anything. I saw it in your eyes the second we met. I guess I hoped you'd be different."

"I was completely blindsided that night, Cash. James hauls me into a black sap den and introduces me to a rusting prince. How was I supposed to look at you?"

"Maybe like you weren't predisposed to hating my guts. Like you didn't assume I was a complete amateur, unworthy of two words. That might've been nice, actually."

"Oh, but you were so warm and welcoming? You should talk, Your Highness. You're the one who could barely be bothered to get up from the table and meet your new driver. You made it pretty clear we ruined your precious twelve-hand streak."

"I was tired. You were a mess."

"I was not a—"

"Look. Just forget it." He invades my personal space again, his smile coming back out of nowhere, this time lopsided and almost contrite. Almost. I hate the way it moves me. Already, he's too good at slipping past my defenses. "I misunderstood you, you misjudged me," he says. "Do-over on first impressions, all right?"

Fair enough. For once, it doesn't hurt to nod in agreement. We're standing shoulder to shoulder, in quiet truce, when he reaches for his flex. After glancing at a text, he quickly stuffs it back into his pocket.

"Who's that? Some other girl waiting to look through your telescope?"

Brazenly, he laughs. "No. If you must know, it was Hank. He asked if you're okay. Should I text him you're all right or would you rather I tell him to double the guard because you're weeping in fear?"

"I'm fine. Obviously, Your Highness."

He texts a quick reply, but makes a show of turning away, just so I can't read it.

"Honestly, Cash. How does someone like you end up friends with one of the guards?" I ask. "Or better yet, how does a prince end up in the Spire at all?"

I'd meant it playfully, but by the look on his face, I can see the question cuts too deep.

"I am a second son." Suddenly, there's a thickness in his voice, a sigh that he can't let go. "After my father was . . . after he died, my older brother, Dak, didn't much want me around."

"Why?"

"It doesn't matter," he says flatly. "Let's just say I'm no longer needed in the palace. So here I am. Under Benroyal's protection. Fifty-six million miles from home."

Protection. A kinder word for prison.

"I'm Benroyal's ward now," he adds. "Have been since I was thirteen. I've apprenticed for three different crews. Cameras and feedcasters always in my face. Bodyguards forever breathing down my neck. Kept me out of the Spire, at least. But two weeks ago, Benroyal calls me back. Tells me he wants me here. Says he's getting a new driver, and that we're going to be a team."

"Two weeks ago? But I was only arrested last—"

"You said as much yourself. You know that arrest was no coincidence. Benroyal gets what he wants. You and I are no exceptions."

I don't answer. My mind turns over his words, but I can't find a single angle that makes any sense. I get why

Benroyal might want to keep Cash—the politics of holding him like some high-stakes marker—but I'm nothing. I'm not royalty. Just a street rat racer who doesn't belong here, least of all on the 210th floor.

"I'm sorry," I say at last. "That I'm the reason he made you come back—"

"It's fine. It's done. Besides, I'm the one who should apologize. I didn't mean to get into it with your friend."

"Bear's just a little protective, that's all. Practically the only friend I've ever had."

"I see. Does your only friend know you're here, with me?"

I fight the stupid blush creeping over my whole body. Suddenly, I feel guilty, as if my two a.m. visit is some kind of terrible betrayal. "No. And he doesn't need to find out either. He wouldn't appreciate—"

"No worries. This will be our secret. I can pretend to hate you in front of him, if you like." He edges closer—the whisper-light scent of balm leaf drifts my way, and all I can do is welcome the sweetness.

Before I can answer, a sharp gust of wind blows my hair back, exposing my neck, the site of my fading hospital scar. He stares at me. I feel his eyes mark the spot his lips once grazed with a warning.

Be careful, he'd whispered.

The shape of his voice, even imagined, makes me suck in a breath. I didn't ask for this. I don't want to feel this way—it's stupid and irrational to let moonlight soften a stranger's face into something more than handsome. I can't look at him anymore. I focus on the railing, where his arm is inches from mine. One careless move and our hands would touch. I can't let that happen. I can't allow him to have this power over me.

The night air is perfect. I look back at the balcony chairs. "Can I just sit here for a while?"

He nods and ducks back into his apartment. He's gone for a minute, and when he returns, I'm already settled into the chair with my eyes closed. I feel a soft touch as Cash tucks a wool blanket around me.

"I can't stay . . ." I whisper.

"Just a little while . . ." He sits beside me. "I won't fall asleep."

But I could fall. Out here, I could easily dream.

CHAPTER FOURTEEN

TOO EARLY, I OPEN MY EYES. I'M IN MY OWN BED, COVERED IN soft wool and the ghost of Cash's scent. But it's Bear who is shaking my arm.

"Hurry and get cleaned up," he says. "They're waiting for you downstairs."

I sit up and we both stare at the smoke-colored blanket tangled around my hips, the one that doesn't belong in my ivory room. He opens his mouth to ask the question, but turns away instead. Bear does not ask, because no matter the explanation, the answer would sting. He isn't one to talk things out, and I'm ashamed to feel so relieved. I don't want to lie to him, but I can't volunteer to torture him with details—how, half-asleep, I let Cash pull me into his arms and carry me here, how I let him lay me down and whisper "Sweet dreams."

That was a mistake, and it won't happen again.

"Who's waiting?"

"Auguste and what's-his-face . . . Dradha."

I'm certain he knows Cash's name well enough, but I let him pretend. "Oh. Practice today?"

Bear shakes his head. "Check your schedule. You've got some hair and makeup drama. Then gear pickup and media training for your first circuit press conference."

I take his advice and glance at the schedule they've loaded onto my card. I keep scrolling, but there seems no end to the events. I've got a handful of days to practice for this season's races, but this morning, there's nothing but makeovers, media training, and other nonsense.

"So basically, today is really going to suck exhaust." I blow at a few flyaway strands of hair.

Bear smiles, tucking them behind my ear. "Pretty much. Sorry, short stuff."

I don't think he's called me short stuff since we were eleven. The memory's a comfort.

"You're coming with me, right?" I ask.

"I'll meet you at the press conference," he says. "Until then, Gil's going to work with me at the track. He says there's room on the crew for an alternate pacer—"

"That's good, isn't it? I could talk to him and tell him that you—"

He shakes his head. "I've got this. I need to do this on my own."

"You don't have anything to prove," I soothe.

"I do—"

"Not to me, you don't."

"But I need to prove it to them. That I can pace you just as well as . . ." Just as his voice edges toward impatience, he doubles back, teasing again. "Just let me do this, short stuff. You go off and get your hair extensions or whatever, and I'll show Gil I can earn my keep."

I nod, then haul myself out of bed like a condemned prisoner. Ridiculously, I groan. "I am not getting hair extensions, Bear."

"I know." He smiles. It's a small thing, but it's enough. I know we'll make it through the next twelve hours.

Goose and I walk into the salon. It's over-the-top, the kind of snooty henhouse I'd never dream of visiting on my own. Stepping inside now is enough of a nightmare to make me cuss under my breath. We pass through a funhouse of booths—the whole place is wall-to-wall mirrors and rich women and mile-high hair—to get to a VIP room in the back, a space that is, today, reserved just for me and the most stubborn hair stylist on the planet. Oh, and Bijan is here too, just to twist the knife. Apparently, not only is she an expert in clothes, she is also a "cosmetics color specialist."

This means she's in charge of lining up lipsticks and dangerous-looking jars of waxy goop. Every time I try to stand up and walk out, Auguste pushes me back into the hydraulic chair.

I look at Penelope, the stylist, who's comparing sample tresses. "You can shake those rattails in my face all you want," I say. "But you are not putting them on my head."

Penelope says nothing, but Bijan purses her pout-perfect, fat-enhanced lips. "We get it, no extensions," she says. "These are designer pigments. We need to decide which color, and then which gloss to brush in."

I stare at the sample strands in Penelope's hand. All are bright shades of copper and ginger. "No way. I'm not going red. Don't try to make me into something I'm not." I shake my head, scuttling out of the chair before Goose can pin me down.

Bijan starts to protest, but he raises a forefinger to silence her. Hand still in the air, he paces back and forth twice before wheeling on me. "Sit," he says.

"I'm not going along with some stupid—"

"Sit." It's nothing less than a command this time.

So I sit.

"Listen, my friends." He circles my chair. "This spitfire

123

girl is right. We are wasting time making her over, when we should be accenting what is already there."

I wince when he pulls and holds up a tangled handful of my hair. "See? Look at this. It is dark, *noire*. All we need to do is finesse this into something . . . more. Make her a Phoenix, yes, but *ma lune et les étoiles*! Save the red for her lips."

He lets my hair fall back onto my shoulders and stares at Penelope. "Cut it. No color, clear gloss. Keep it black."

"Yes, Mr. Chevalier," Penelope and Bijan both answer at once.

Thanks to Goose, by the time they are finished with me, I look a little less like a Sixer doll and a little more like a circuit vixen. My chin-length bob has been shined into a glossy black waterfall and I make them take it easy with the makeup. No lotions or creams. Just a little powder on my pale nose, some black eyeliner, and a dab of velvety lipstick.

I look older, and it's the only thing I like about this whole ordeal.

The color on my lips is a shade between ruby and dried blood. I jokingly suggest they should match it to the exact red in my rig's paint scheme, but Bijan shrieks approval. No doubt, by next week, Benroyal's engineers will have a thick tube of gloppy, custom-made crimson and I'll be a laughingstock among circuit drivers.

No, no, Auguste keeps saying, I am a fierce femme fatale. It sounds dangerous enough, so I'll settle for it.

The final uniform fitting is much easier to endure. Everything is delivered to the back of the salon, and I use an adjacent dressing room. Once I'm alone with my new gear, I allow my giddiness to show. My hands quiver as I fasten each snap and latch and zipper. Unlike the rest of my team's, my new zip-front jumpsuit is black with a stripe of red. My gloves and boots are also black, along with my helmet, which is finished with a flame-colored wing motif. On each side of my head, a wing stretches out, the last golden feathers arcing back. My number is painted on each side as well.

Six. Of course I'm six.

I feel a stab of pain behind my rib cage. It could be my skintight gear, or it could be remorse. I say I don't want to be here, but do I really mean it? Am I so easily bought? With black leather and fireproof suits?

Yes. Maybe I am. I cannot deny the thrill of this moment. I step out of the dressing room. When I look in the full-length flex wall mirror outside my door, the sight makes me gasp.

I am a tiny superhero, a black-booted femme fatale. A real circuit driver.

Auguste will be pleased, I'm sure. But I wonder, if he were here, would my father be proud? Is this fierce-looking creature the girl he wanted me to be? Or was he just as trapped, caught between the sport he loved and the keepers that controlled him?

When I picture my father's face—the sunbaked crow's-feet under his eyes, the perpetual shadow of red-brown whiskers on his jaw—I'm struck by something more than melancholy longing. I'm angry at him for being dead and gone, absent but not invisible to my heart. For leaving me with his flaws—his stupid need to always run, smashing into every wall. Suddenly, the gloves, the clothes—everything is too heavy and stifling hot. I fuss with the straps on my helmet and pry it off just as Goose comes in to check on me.

His hand sweeps over his chest and he feigns a heart attack, as if one look at me had left him a dying man. I tug at my collar and gulp a breath of much-needed air. Auguste starts to laugh. The sound builds and builds until I can almost see tears in his eyes. For a split second, I misread him, and think he is making fun, but then I realize, he is overjoyed, overcome with more than one emotion.

That makes two of us.

"Ah, *ma fille*! You are my greatest triumph, Miss Vanguard. Yes, you will be *une légende*!"

It's only one in the afternoon, but I'm already worn out. I change back into my tee and gray cargoes. For now, I just need some food and room to breathe.

I'm only getting the food.

Auguste and I still have an appointment with Benroyal's PR team. We're in a suite at the Grand Delian, Capitoline's fanciest hotel. The circuit will be hosting this year's first press conference in the ballroom downstairs. All the biggest Castran racers will be there, so we've just enough time to inhale some room service while Benroyal's media goons put me through the paces.

There are a lot of rules, things I have to remember, not just for this press conference, but for pretty much every occasion that takes me outside the Spire. The way they talk, I'm three hours from diving into a public pressure cooker, complete with tabloid reporters, stalker-like fans, and corporate bookmakers starving for insider information.

My role has been all but spelled out: Dazzle the public and above all, perform for the stockholders.

To them, I'm a variable in a spreadsheet. There will always be someone watching, analyzing my every move, waiting for me to win or lose. I'm a name in a bracket, a made-up girl. Property of Benroyal Corp, bought and branded. This, my handlers explain, is the normal price of circuit fame.

For me, there's nothing normal about managing my body language, crafting deflective answers, and staying "on message" eighteen hours a day. I'm not thrilled about the "key takeaways" the PR drones want me to hammer home during the press conference either.

```
1. I'm so grateful Mr. Benroyal discovered
me through Capitoline's UrbanReach youth pro-
gram. As soon as I turned eighteen, I jumped
at the chance to sign with his team.
2. I'm just happy to be here and I'm not wor-
ried about my standings on race day.
3. I've idolized circuit racers all my life,
and I'm honored to work with such a capable
team, especially my crew chief, the legendary
Gil Gates, and my new pacer, Cashoman Dradha.
```

At best, one of these statements is a half-truth. Aside from these answers, I'm not to reveal any more details about my personal life. If anyone asks anything off limits, I'm supposed to grin and make eye contact, all while explaining what a private person I am, and how excited I am to get behind the wheel and let my driving speak for itself. Under no circumstances can I frown or grumble or cuss.

During our practice interviews, I frown and grumble and cuss a lot. Every time I do, I have to backtrack from the beginning and answer the list of questions again. By the fifth time, I surrender and smile until my face feels like it's going to fall off.

"Very good," the evil inquisitors say. "Just like that."

Just like a sellout.

"Are we done now?" I ask. "I'd like to actually have two minutes to chew my food."

They nod, backing away like wild-animal handlers. The thought makes me howl with laughter, and I choke on my rice-leaf wrap. I'll never be completely housebroken, and it makes them afraid.

CHAPTER FIFTEEN

A MOB WAITS FOR US IN THE BALLROOM. TURNS OUT THE media trainers weren't kidding about it being intense. Journalists of every stripe are crammed into this giant hall. On the walls, flex glass panels are framed with gilt scrollwork. Sprays of yellow limonfleur and imported white poppies grace marble-top tables along the periphery of the room. Circuit drivers will be herded onto a dais, three or four at a time, to answer questions. While we wait in the wings, in hallways on either side of the ballroom, live feeds of the action on the floor and the stage flood the screens.

Two minutes until show time.

I look for Eager's face in the crowd, but I don't see my old crew-mate. I'm not the only new driver—on the press conference list, there's at least one name I don't recognize.

Maybe, like me, Eager's another fresh recruit, forced to take an alias. He could be here, somewhere backstage. Surely that ambush was not just for me.

The sight of so many jostling reporters leaves me white-knuckle nervous. In a moment, it will be my turn to run this media gauntlet. Cash and Bear arrive, accompanied by six guards from the Spire. At first, I don't understand why they gape at me like I'm a stranger. But then I remember they've never seen me in this gear before.

With Bear, there's a gasp. I detect the wince under his smile—a part of him is wary of my transformation. Am I still the same girl underneath the black armor? In contrast, Cash is all approval. He bares his teeth and bites his lip, all the while stepping back to get a better look. Without apology, he grins and drinks up the sight of me.

I hear the snap of flex cameras as reporters jostle to capture the moment. I'm sure they'll have plenty to say about the way Cash is checking me out. This could be trouble.

Mercifully, Cash steps back. Bear takes his place beside me. "You look different," he says. "You look . . . dangerous."

"In a good way?" I ask.

Bear touches the Benroyal logo on my collar. "Is this what you want?"

I don't have an answer. I don't know anymore.

I turn into his shoulder. Bear won't let this go, and he's

picked the worst possible moment to hash it out. So many eyes are on us now.

"It's time," Auguste says.

Even as Bear stands aside, my eyes flick to Cash.

"Don't let them push you around too much, Vanguard," he says.

I take a deep breath and let go. My security detail clears a narrow path and I follow them all the way to the stage, and then I'm on my own. By the time I make it up the steps, one of the other drivers has already taken his seat.

I know his red hair and freckles and light blue eyes, at least from feeds, anyway. Cooper Winfield may be past his prime and he may not win many races, but people love to watch him. Who am I kidding? I love to watch this guy.

Coop is the last independent driver, the son of a rig parts salesman who to this day still refuses to go corporate or sell his father's company to any conglomerate. Year after year, the Winfield crew manages to roll out on a shoestring budget, with only one or two cars to crash. Every race day, they face down the moneyed elite, high-tech rigs backed by the most powerful men on the planet. The Sixers bid and make their offers, but Winfield Mechanical always refuses to incorporate or sell out. They race, not for stocks, but purely for the glory. How could I not root for an outfit like that?

The corporates hate him, but the rest of us scream his name, from the stands and from our living rooms. Even when ole Coop finishes in seventh place. And now, as unworthy as I am, he sits at my left. Soon enough, he'll be my rival on the track. For the second time today, my hands tremble.

At my right, there is an empty chair. The placard marking the space reads MAXWELL COURANT. I don't recognize the name, but the placard reveals he's driving for AltaGen, the Sixer medical giant. Maybe it's Eager, or another new recruit, plucked from the streets like me. I'm guessing Max Courant is another silly alias, contrived by the same minds who thought up Phoenix Vanguard, the world's most pretentious-sounding driver.

A hand touches my elbow and I realize Coop is trying to get my attention. He actually wants to shake my hand.

"Hey there," he says, reaching out. "I'm—"

"I know who you are," I blurt. "You're Cooper Winfield and you're my favorite driver and I've watched the last thirty minutes of the '87 Sand Ridge Rally 400 at least a million times and I can't believe I'm sitting here talking to you and—"

"Well there." He's laughing. At me. "Nice to meet you too, young lady."

Mesmerized, I stare back. He is sitting right here. In the

flesh. Shaking my hand. I might actually pass out from the sheer brilliance of this moment.

"Um . . . So you must be . . ." He trails off.

It occurs to me Coop is waiting for me to speak. My jaws flap up and down, but I can't quite spit anything out. If you toss me a headset and put me behind the wheel, I'm never at a loss for words. But two minutes in a camera-filled ballroom and I'm hopelessly mute. Rescuing me, Coop lets go and turns my placard to read my name.

"Phoenix Vanguard," he says. "That's what I thought. So you're the new kid everyone's talking about."

Surely Coop is just blowing exhaust to put me at ease. I've just about worked up the courage to smile and thank him, but a chair-pulling scuffle and bump distract me.

Maxwell has arrived, and he is definitely not Eager. Without an ounce of grace or common courtesy, he's plopped himself into his seat and elbowed my right arm off the table. Before I can get a word in, he stares me down.

Somehow, I know this guy. I may not recognize the bleached hair or the crazy violet contact lenses, but . . . Did he really shave his eyebrows completely off?

"Watch it, will you?" he says, reaching across me for a glass of water. Not the one in front him. Mine.

I know that voice. Even with the forced accent. Maxwell. I turn the name over and over in my mind.

Winfield is too classy to scowl at him, but his high-wattage smile fades a bit. "Guess we can get this show on the road now," he says.

A speaker blares and I hear the moderator's voice. For all I know, they're beaming her in from some better air-conditioned, alternate universe. "Ladies and gentlemen, welcome to this year's pre-series launch. Please text your questions to the registry number for this event, which is now listed on all screens. We will try to get to as many as we can in the next half hour."

With that, there's a flurry of activity as four hundred reporters fumble over their flexes and race to get in their questions first. An eye-in-the-sky-camera, equipped with a laser pointer, is ready to tag the lucky few who submit the ones deemed harmless enough to answer.

After a few moments, the red light shines on a man in the front row. I recognize the silver-haired suit—he's a well-known correspondent for CSF, Castran Sports Feed. "This one's for Winfield," he says. "Coop, there are more new drivers this year than ever before, what do you think? Is this year a game changer?"

"Well now . . ." Coop doesn't miss a beat. "No doubt about it, the lineup's different, but I think the infusion of new blood is great. Keeps me on my toes, that's for sure. But as for the game itself? I don't think the circuit ever really changes. I'm betting there'll be the same old rivalries and smash-ups come Sand Ridge. There'll still be plenty of winners and losers, and I just hope I'm one of the former."

There's lots of murmuring and chuckling from the audience. Coop definitely knows how to work a room. I should be taking notes. I look down at our glass tabletop. Bold as anything, my three "takeaway" talking points blink on and off before my eyes. It's like the PR crew loaded some kind of evil mind control app onto the flex glass. Be a good robot. Stay on message.

The laser chooses the next journalist, a woman with bleach-blond hair piled so high, I can't imagine the next three people behind her can see the stage at all. "Miss Vanguard, can I call you Phoenix?" she says.

Dumbly, I nod.

"Thanks, Phoenix. You're one of the unknowns, the 'new blood,' as Coop would say. So here's my question. As a rookie, how do you expect to compete with seasoned pros like Winfield, Fallon, and Banks?"

I am not a good robot. Seconds tick by, and it's like I'm paralyzed. Stay calm. Stay on message. "I . . . I think . . . I'm . . . justhappytobehereand . . . I'm not worried . . . aboutmystandingsonraceday."

Great. I might as well have just announced, to everyone in this room, that I'm completely bugging out. I tug at my uniform's collar. It feels like three thousand degrees in here. I can't rusting breathe anymore.

The reporter breaks protocol and follows up. "So you don't care if you lose?"

I nearly blurt out "Of course I care, you harpy," but the media training kicks in and I pull myself together. "Absolutely. I'm going to give it everything I've got. I'll do anything I can to win for Mr. Benroyal. I've idolized circuit racers all my life and I'm honored to work with such a capable team, especially my crew chief, Gil Gates, and my new pacer, Casho—"

Just when I'm starting to sound semi-coherent, Maxwell leans forward and talks right over me. "I think what Vanguard is getting around to saying is that she knows it's going to be a rough series for her. We all know she'll be eating my exhaust by the end of every race."

He did not just say that. This mother-rusting sap-hole upstart thinks I'm just going to sit here and let him interrupt with his stupid jaw-jacking? Under the table, my fists curl. My smile must have fallen away, because the tabletop is flashing urgently: Stay calm. Stay on message. BEMUSED. Project BEMUSEMENT.

I try to smile again, but I can't. I glance at the hall, but I can only find Goose and Cash. Bear has his back turned, he's talking to a couple of suits. They start to lead him away, and I'm furious he'd leave me now when I need him most. Cash looks pretty scorched at Courant. "Rust him," he mouths, and shakes his head.

Maxwell opens his trap again. "Here's the thing. While I've been gearing up for this year's series, Vanguard's been . . . well, what do we really know about her, anyway? She was part of the UrbanReach program, right?"

I want to clock this guy, right here and now. They want bemused? I'll show them some bemusement. I'll be-rusting-muse this guy all over the place.

Winfield tries to cut him off with an "excuse me," but Maxwell just keeps flapping his gums. "For all we know, Vanguard's dad is a street cleaner or something. Bet he taught her to drive behind the wheel of a garbage rig."

Garbage rig. I've heard that exact line of trash talk before, not more than one month ago. I know exactly who "Maxwell Courant" is. Put a helmet on his head and slap an eye-patch over his right peeper and he's still that coward Matias Kirk—One Eye—who fled the street race the night I was arrested. Except now I realize he wasn't running away at all that night. He was in on it, from the jump. He was a plant, a rusting informant. The whole race was a setup. Oh, hell no. I will bury him for this.

Winfield and Courant are arguing, reporters are shouting out of turn, but I can't hear them anymore. I look at

Maxwell, and suddenly I'm seven years old, a foster kid standing in the alleyway between the Picker's Grocery and Gold Flake Pawn. Every face I see is a bully, calling me names. And he is the ringleader, the biggest bully of all. In the alley, he drives me into the ground with another open-handed slap, but I just keep getting back up, rising from the dirty asphalt.

I am rising now.

I move out of my seat on the dais, but Coop puts a hand on my wrist to calm me down. I am way past calming down.

Maxwell grins. I see his face plastered across every screen. "So we'll see who flames out on race day."

"Why wait until then?" I ask. Before he can so much as wet his zip-front, I lean over him and grab his prissy yellow collar. Squeezing hard, I go for the throat with my left hand and pull back my right fist.

My hand feels so good slamming into his face. Pity I don't get the full satisfaction of hearing his jaw pop as his lights go out. The thunder on the stairs, the sound of security guards coming for me, drowns out everything else.

CHAPTER SIXTEEN

BACK AT THE SPIRE, AUGUSTE ORDERS EVERYONE OUT. AFTER
slouching onto my couch, I soak my fist in a bowl of anti-
gel. The cool, clear medicine takes the pain and swelling
away.

Ironic, really. Hose up all the sap in the Gap. Refine it,
skim off the fuel, and you're left with two very different
pools of runoff goo. Crystal-clear anti-gel, a regenerative
source of healing, and black sap, the murky narcotic that's
fried far too many brains.

Auguste sits beside me, and we catch the recap feed on
the nearest flex wall. I watch the security team herd me off
the stage and out of the ballroom. Apparently, the media
goons trained me all too well. Even though I was shaky
and scared, that doesn't show up on the feed at all. Shock-

ingly, after the sucker punch to Courant's jaw, I smiled the whole time.

An incoming call preempts the feed. I move to swipe my flex and accept the linkup, but it seems this particular caller doesn't need my permission to hijack my screens. A giant face appears on the wall, canceling the press conference replay.

Rust. Benroyal himself, sitting in the passenger hold of a luxurious vac. Probably flying back to the Spire. "I'm en route," he says. "The gallery—"

"We weren't sure if you'd still want Miss Vanguard to appear tonight," Auguste says. "After what happened at the—"

"The gallery," Benroyal repeats. "Twenty minutes."

"Yes." Auguste nods. "Without delay. I shall—"

"Both of you." And then he's gone. The screen is blank, as milk white as my blood-drained face.

The elevator rises. Up one level, to the floor between my apartment and Benroyal's penthouse. Goose keeps begging me to go back and change into "a more suitable frock," and I keep shaking my head. I should heed his advice, but I'm in no mood to play dress-up tonight. It's bad enough I'll have to smear on makeup and wear dresses outside the

Spire. Besides, if Benroyal's scorched, a silk gown won't protect me. Dirty cargoes are the only armor I've got.

We come to a stop and the elevator opens. The outer lobby is almost identical to mine, only there's one set of heavy wooden doors straight ahead. Two pairs of guards flank the entrance. Hank is one of them.

"Good evening, Mr. Chevalier," Hank says, then nods at me. "Miss Vanguard."

"After you." Auguste urges me forward.

Another guard flashes a flex. The bolts on the double doors open. I'm startled by the mechanical thunderclap. When we step inside, I try not to gasp.

The gallery isn't the usual Sixer space, flex walled and sterile. King Charlie's turned this vast hall into a temple of ancient civilizations, filled with antiques. The walls are swathed in crimson, black, and gold. Overhead, banners hang above the crowd—the red silhouette of Benroyal's lion strikes far above the chatter of guests.

As I follow Auguste, the soles of my boots travel over bare floor and then thick carpets, relics spun from what must be impossibly old wool and silk. Wide-open thresholds surround the airy concourse. There are rooms upon rooms to explore.

All around, Sixers mill in clusters. Women poured into

cocktail dresses. Corporate suits packed into every corner. I scan the room and strain to listen for the threads of conversation. They sip champagne and stare at each other's flex cards, fretting over stock prices and gloating over today's conquests.

Far away, I recognize a face. James. He stands on the fringe, a man apart. After he tosses back a drink, a woman approaches him, her security team hanging back. I've never seen her before.

Slim as a bare branch, she wears black while every other woman in the room is a splash of gaudy color. Her gown makes it seem as if she's gliding across the floor. She turns and I see an unexpected flash of skin. Her dark hair gathered, unadorned, at the nape of her neck.

She is the opposite of me. Elegant.

She pulls James aside, and they dive into what looks like an intense conversation. He doesn't even notice I'm here.

"What is all this?" I ask Goose.

"I told you, *ma chère*. Your after-party. To celebrate today's press conference."

I'm suddenly wishing I'd paid more attention to the schedule on my flex. "Didn't sound like Benroyal was in any mood for a party. Not after what I pulled today."

"Do not worry, spitfire girl. Better to pull yourself

together and hope for the best." I don't think this little pep talk is for me alone.

"Is he here yet?"

"I don't think so. Everyone's still breathing, no?"

Suddenly, the main doors sweep open. The Sixer gossip fades into a tense, closed-mouth hush. King Charlie has arrived. My teeth cold and on edge, I find myself shrinking back, retreating into the crowd before he can pin me in his sights.

No one says a word. Auguste wasn't joking at all. It's as if the revelers need his permission to exhale.

"By all means," Benroyal commands his guests. "Carry on."

The room comes alive again, erupting with murmur and movement. While Auguste has his back turned, I slip into a side room. I feel the change in air pressure. This smaller exhibit is colder, climate controlled to protect the precious relics on display.

I spin slowly, taking in the blood red walls, the endless row of bookshelves, and the spotless glass cases. For a minute or two, I do nothing but stare.

"Take a good look, Phee."

I turn and find myself face-to-face with James. "I didn't hear you come in. Who were you talking to?"

He ignores my question. "Very few are ever allowed up here. Priceless history. Treasures from Earth and Cyan-Bisera. And all of it locked away from the beggars on the street."

There's mockery in his words, but I can't tell whether the grudge is directed at me, the uncultured orphan, or at the tyrant who built this museum only for himself. James is baiting me, waiting for an answer, so I pivot, sweeping away to get a better look at what's on display.

I wander past the musty books, skipping the history lessons they offer. Instead, I focus on the big stuff in the cases.

A sculptured bust. Empty eyes. Chipped nose. Curly locks and full lips carved from stone. *Portrait of Alexander, 340–330 BC, Acropolis Museum, Athens, Earth.*

I don't know who he is, but Alexander was handsome, I'll give him that. I move on to a tapestry mounted on the wall. Ancient Cyanese longships wait to sail away from the ice-kissed fjords of Raupang, ready to cross an endless sea. The detail is so fine, the artist's weave is so vivid, I can make out the faces of the warriors on the decks. I can almost feel the whip of the wind and hear the creak of boats as they drift against their moorings.

Below the framed threads, there's a rough-looking hunk of rock enclosed in a large case. The placard includes a detailed sketch of an outdoor stadium, a setup that looks just like a circuit arena. *Roman Colosseum, Fragment,* AD *80, Metropolitan Museum of Art, New York, Earth.*

The next case is empty except for a tiny pile of ash. And when I stand closer to the display, a hologram beams to life—a three-dimensional image of a faded swath of parchment. When James closes in, I ask, "Why am I looking through armored glass at dust? And a blank piece of paper that doesn't even exist?"

"It's the Magna Carta," he says. "One of Earth's greatest legacies, the roots of a free society."

I blink. "It's a hologram."

James sighs with disapproval. You'd think he was my eighth-year teacher, here to school me. Pity there's nothing to be learned from lying Sixers. "It's a reproduction of something long lost," he says. "Read it."

"I can't. The words are completely faded. There's nothing but digital shadows left."

Clearing his throat, he stares at the case. " 'No freeman shall be taken, imprisoned, disseised, outlawed, banished, or in any way destroyed, nor will We proceed against or prosecute him, except by the lawful judgment of his peers and by the law of the land.' "

The words stir something in me. The urge to press my

fingers against the glass is overwhelming. I lean closer and stare at the illusion. "It doesn't say that. There's nothing there. You're making that up."

James frowns. "Just because the words have faded doesn't mean they're not there, Phee. Hidden away? Forgotten? Yes. But they exist."

On this planet those ideas are a joke. This whole gallery is a joke. There's nothing like this anywhere else. No ancient charters. No storied tapestries. Benroyal hoards this beautiful decay, but down below, on the streets, there's no trace of this history. Our walls are crowded with an ever-changing parade of Sixer ads and corporate feeds, and people like me are tried and convicted in the span of a day for crimes too petty to mention. In my world, there is no room for the Magna Carta.

"What's the point in all this?" I growl, wheeling on him again. "Why does he keep all these—"

Benroyal is standing in the doorway.

"Is it a crime to safeguard such dangerous treasures?" he asks.

I don't answer, but I know he's not just collecting for posterity. People like me were never meant to touch this version of history. The feeds, our schools, our museums all tell a different story. Earth wasn't a cradle of art and civilization. Earth was chaos. A broken hell to escape. Thank your lucky stars for Castra and the companies that built it. Be grateful for what you've been given.

I see it now. This room wasn't built to preserve. It was custom made, for Sixers only, with walls but no windows, a place for ideas to die. South Siders like me—we're not supposed to notice. No "free society" or "lawful judgment" for us.

So softly, Benroyal speaks as if he were the most reasonable man in the world. "All priceless things. All that's one of a kind. Everything in this room is mine."

My right hand twitches at my side. My fingers still ache from punching Courant, but again, they want to curl into fists. "You don't own me."

James is silent, but there's a low rumble of amusement in Benroyal's voice. "I find it perplexing that you should doubt my word," he says. "Especially since you've seen how easily I strike a bargain. Some assets are acquired so cheaply."

Me. Yes. He's right. I was cheap. Weak-willed and pacified by a contract full of lies and empty promises. I'm about to mouth off again, when Auguste interrupts. I've never been so thankful to see him.

He offers Benroyal a glass of wine. Not champagne. Something red, probably a vintage reserved just for him. King Charlie takes the glass and savors the first sip before waving James off. "Go. I have business with Mr. Chevalier and Miss Vanguard."

James seems reluctant to scatter, and I'm not sure why he'd risk his neck to run interference. He opens his mouth, but Benroyal silences him. "Leave us. Why don't you go upstairs and check on my darling wife? Mrs. Benroyal isn't quite up to entertaining tonight."

With that, James leaves Auguste and me to weather Benroyal's wrath alone. "I anticipated crudeness, a certain unpredictability in your appearance today." He takes another drink. "But the press conference was something else altogether, Phee."

Goose slips into damage control mode. Palms out, he tries to spin the ballroom debacle into something less than a PR nightmare for our team. "Yes, yes, I think we can agree, that was not ideal, but—"

"Ideal? Oh, it's more than ideal." Benroyal runs a finger over the nearest case. It's a possessive caress I can almost feel. "Since the press conference, her numbers are through the roof, in all target sub-pops. Non-corporates. Sixteen- to twenty-four-year olds. Circuit diehards. They all love her, Auguste."

"Wait," I say. "What?"

"You see, we've always rated high among our own, but I've never been able to pull support from Castra's very large pool of . . . less fortunate. But 'Phoenix Vanguard' and her renegade theatrics just bought me all of Capitoline."

Benroyal looks at Auguste. "Have you seen the feeds? No one's talking about yesterday's labor riot or rising fuel prices or the latest crisis in the Gap. All eyes are on your rebellious new darling of the circuit." Far too calmly, he turns to me. "I couldn't be more pleased with your performance, Phee."

Another protest. Another bombing. Another twenty-five thousand soldiers deployed and no one cares. I've become Benroyal's PR tool, and the realization makes me want to vomit.

Even now, I see the invisible weight slide from Goose's shoulders. He takes out his handkerchief and mumbles something about the heat, but I'm pretty sure the beads of sweat on his forehead have nothing to do with the meat-locker chill in this room. What would have happened to Goose if King Charlie wasn't so thrilled with my "theatrics"?

So much is on the line. Much, much more than I ever realized. If I don't perform or dazzle the press, I'm not the only one to pay the price. The rest of my team answers too. I didn't give anyone else a second thought when I clocked Maxwell, and that can't happen again. I have to protect the people who look out for me. Even if it hurts. "Where is Bear?" I ask.

"I arranged a little reunion with his parents," Benroyal says. "I'm not entirely heartless."

"Can I go with—"

He clucks his tongue, as if I were a misbehaving child. "Out of the question. You will honor your commitments here."

He might as well have added *or else*. I should be glad for Bear, but the selfish part of me whispers and nags. "Is he coming back?"

"Of course. He's bound to me—and to you, Phee—by contract." He crosses the room and stands before a pair of paintings, a rendering of two Biseran nobles. "But I'll give his parents a few days. Just enough time to drain the venom and convince them this is for the best. It's not that I couldn't deal with them, of course."

"You leave Hal and Mary alone," I half whisper, for once afraid to push too hard. My threats are nothing more than a reflex.

Benroyal's lips twist into something fiercely perfect, an angel's smile, so cold and yet so stunning. "Careful now, Miss Vanguard. I'm in such a cheerful mood, but any more of your temper and I'm liable to void your contract. I'd hate to see you in custody again."

"Yes, yes," Auguste says. "I think Miss Vanguard is a little vexed. We're all tired."

"You may leave, Auguste."

"As you wish." He bows, giving me a final warning glance before slipping from the room. "Good night, Miss Vanguard."

A swallow and a nod. That's all I can manage in return.

Benroyal turns and gestures at the two paintings, skimming his fingers over the first frame. It's a portrait of a beautiful woman, draped in Biseran silk. "Do you know who this is?"

I stare into her face. Dark eyes, rimmed with starlight. Their gleam matches the jeweled sparkle of her crown.

"It's Her Majesty Queen Napoor. Cashoman's mother. It was taken from the palace, just after the war." Benroyal raises his glass to the other piece, a painting of a scowling, spiteful-looking young man. The image doesn't quite match its companion. The colors are muddled somehow. "I commissioned this one for the queen's firstborn son, Prince Dakesh," he adds. "Dak was very pleased to have his royal portrait painted over his late father's canvas. And I was only too happy to help him erase the old king. Pity he was assassinated."

Anger boils in my blood, but I can't answer him, not even for Cash. Not when it could cost me my family.

"It's just as well," he says. "Prince Dak will make a fine

king. Unlike his father, he does what I require and stays out of my affairs in the Gap."

I stare at the painting, into the dark eyes of a treacherous prince. One that Benroyal surely put into power.

"How about you, Miss Vanguard?" Benroyal asks. "Will you do what I require?"

For now, I tell myself. I force a nod.

My silence seems to appease him. "Very good. I think we have an understanding. I will look after the Larssens as long as you play your role. Drive around in little circles, as it were."

"You won't—"

In one swift movement, he raises his free hand. I steel myself for a strike, but instead, he tilts my chin, unbalancing me with nothing more than smooth fingertips. "You will save your little protests for the feeds." He delivers the threat so softly, a gentle purr that paralyzes me.

He might as well have both hands around my throat. I have to buy an inch of breathing room. I need leverage.

There's only one thing I can think of, Benroyal's one weakness. I can still hear her voice in the dark. "I met your wife." I stare. Unblinking. Defiant. "Do your threats work on her?"

For a second, I'm sure I've wounded him. But the soft

flicker of pain in his eyes is gone all too quickly, replaced by animal rage. He is going to shout at me and sentence me to death. The wildest part of me roars: Do it. Kill me. I don't care.

Benroyal's mouth twitches again, his perfect smile falters. For a moment, he studies me, as if there's something in my face that intrigues and repulses him. "This conversation is over." His hand drops and he stalks out of the room.

I brace my back against the wall, letting the terrible shiver ripple through me at last.

CHAPTER SEVENTEEN

I STAND AT THE DOOR, BUT I CAN'T BEAR TO WALK BACK INTO
my new apartment. My flex buzzes. It's James.

> JA: STILL IN THE GALLERY?

> PV: NO.

> JA: YOU ALL RIGHT?

I don't answer. I'm not all right, not by a long shot, but
rust if I'm going to tell him that.

He tries again.

> JA: ANSWER ME. ARE YOU OKAY?

> PV: I'M FANTASTIC.

> PV: WHERE ARE YOU?

> JA: UPSTAIRS.

> PV: GALLERY?

> JA: NO.

> PV: BENROYAL'S PENTHOUSE?

A minute ticks by. No answer. He's there. I know it.

PV: I'M COMING UP.

JA: DO NOT COME UP. I'LL CHECK IN LATER.

Cursing, I shove the flex back in my pocket. If James thinks I'm going to be a good little girl and go to my room, he doesn't know me at all.

I turn to leave, but the bolts on Cash's door snap before I have the chance to duck into the elevator. Bare-chested, he leans against the threshold to his apartment. Probably fresh out of the shower—his hair looks shaggy and wet.

"Back so soon?" he says, relaxed and lazy. "How was the party?"

I hesitate.

"Are you going to just stand there?" he asks when I don't come inside. In the low light, the gold-rimmed irises of Cash's eyes wink like dying stars, black holes that could easily pull me in. His hair. His skin. He is all darkness, and I can't stop myself from staring.

There's a voice in my head warning me to back away from this boy and all the trouble he'll bring, but I take one step. My hands are shaking again.

"Are you okay, Vanguard?" Cash's voice is low and husky. He closes in on me until there's nothing but a breath between us. I tilt away from him. The doors are still open—it's not too late to leave.

"Tell me what's wrong," he says.

"Benroyal . . . This place . . . I'm not myself."

"It's safe. You don't have to be anyone here. Not with me." He grips my arm. If I look him in the eye, I don't know what I'll do. He's so close, and I'm not sure if I want to shove him off his feet or . . . I don't know . . . I don't know . . .

When I face him again, he leans closer. I flinch, as if steeling up for a strike. But then I can't stop myself. I push him, driving him backward across the room. He doesn't resist until we're in his hallway. There, against the obsidian gleam of the wall, he plants his feet and reaches for my arms. I attack first, gripping him by the neck and pulling him down upon me. I kiss him hard, inhaling the warm taste of his lips and damp clean of his skin.

He is just as lost as I am; his arms hold me just as fast. One hand finds the base of my neck, and his other presses into the small of my back, fusing us from collar to hip. I feel the intense warmth of his body and the hard clench of his stomach against mine. Fierce and tight, this hunger coils between us.

I can't pull away, and neither can Cash. We are starving, inhaling quick gasps between kisses that blur my senses. Nothing exists except lips and teeth against feverish skin. His mouth on my neck. My shoulders. The soft underside of my wrists. Again and again, Cash returns to that tender space between my ear and my jaw. Only then does his mouth soften.

I melt too. I relax and breathe with him. We fall against the wall, both of us panting. I'm pressed against him, tangled in his arms. I touch Cash's chest and feel the breakneck thrum of his heartbeat. Its rhythm is the unsteady run, the dockside plunge, the irresistible rush.

Now that I've surrendered to it, guilt floods my system. I look into Cash's eyes, but I see someone else. The boy I pushed away for wanting me the way I wanted Cash.

What have I done?

My fists curl against the smooth muscle of Cash's stomach. I am a selfish, unfeeling monster, a traitor to those I love best. I shift, edging away from Cash, but his hands find my wrists. "Don't go," he begs.

"I'm sorry," I say. I rip free, slipping toward the front door. My senses are drunk, my limbs are sluggish and unwilling, but I'm no less determined to leave. "I can't do this."

Cash is just as quick to follow. Even as his eyes plead, he doesn't try to block my way. "Is it me? Did I do something wrong? I thought you wanted me to—"

"It's not you," I answer. "It's . . . I can't—"

"It's him, isn't it?"

He knows.

"I'm sorry." I drag myself out and through the front door. The pained look on Cash's face nearly destroys me. He stands with open, empty hands. I know he's wondering why he is not enough to keep me here. I can't bring myself to tell him that's it's me. I'm the one who is unworthy.

Cash doesn't follow me. And I can't be alone in this empty place. James is upstairs, in Benroyal's penthouse, and like it or not, he's going to let me in. The look on Benroyal's face when I mentioned his wife was the only thing that rattled him. She's somewhere up there, unstable and full of secrets, and I want to know why she came into my room.

She tried to tell me something. Maybe it was nonsense gibberish. Or maybe those mad whispers in the dark are something Benroyal doesn't want me to hear.

In the elevator, I swipe the button for the top, the 213th floor. The second I touch the penthouse icon, it glows red, blinking on and off. An automated female voice answers in a monotone that's both polite and terrifying. "Restricted access. Please authenticate security clearance."

My fingers twitch as I reach into my pocket, finding the corner of the stolen flex. I swipe it against the panel.

"Welcome," the voice says. "Gold Security Clearance. Surveillance deactivated."

The number turns green and I barely have time to stuff the flex into my pocket before the elevator stops again. I step out, scanning the hall for guards. And of course I find one. He stands beside the penthouse doors. Benroyal's crest is inlaid from hinge to handle, every detail carved into solid gold. The lion seems to stare me down, its mouth open in a savage, silent roar.

"Good evening, Miss Vanguard," he says. There's a waver of shock under the polite facade. Bet nobody comes up here without permission or an escort. "How can I assist you?"

"James—Mr. Anderssen—told me to come up."

"No one said anything about that."

I shrug. "Call him. I'm sure he'll be thrilled you're wasting his time when he's waiting for me."

The bluff's a stupid gamble, but it's enough to get me inside. Now I just have to pray James doesn't toss me out before I sniff out what's spooking his sister.

The doors close behind me. The foyer's yet another great hall, decorated with the same nod to a history I don't know. Everything in this enormous apartment—every vase, every rug, every chair—looks like the last of its kind, so beautiful and forgotten.

I'm halfway down the corridor when I hear a crash. It's her. With her back to me, Benroyal's wife moves behind the last open threshold. I didn't get much of a look, but she had something in her hand.

Voices. James. She shouts and he pleads. I can't make out the words over the smash of more crystal, but it's obvious she's completely gone, unreachable in lunatic rage. I can't see either of them now. His voice drops and she quiets. I creep forward, unable to stop myself. But when James appears in the doorway, his jaw slack with surprise, I freeze.

Startled, I let him drive me back. He pounces—the tiger's keeper, moving in when someone's too close to the cage. But I wonder which of us is behind the bars.

"I told you not to come here. How did you get in?"

"I wanted to talk to you."

I try to get around James, but he's too quick "Don't you move," he snaps. "And stay out until I deal with this. Then I'll deal with you." He backs into the room. The door slams in my face.

I'm pretty sure I know who he's protecting now, and it's not me or his sister. I backtrack, ignoring his orders to stay put. There's no way I'm standing here like a scolded child when I could be snooping around. Back in the main hall, I spy another set of double doors. I flex my way in and turn in to a wide corridor. I stop at a stone archway. One look and I know this has to be Benroyal's study.

There's a fireplace opposite the arch. Blue flames dance, wasting their sap-fueled warmth. Outside, it's scorching hot, but King Charlie keeps the hearth fires burning, probably just for show. I step inside, letting the flex walls of Benroyal's inner sanctum hem me in. Quick and quiet, I explore.

The walls are crowded with interactive feeds screens—one touch and the images pop out, three-dimensional pictures floating in the air, ready to be examined, manipulated, enlarged. It's almost impossible to focus with so much to look at—I'm not here to goggle at circuit trophies, but I'd be lying if I said the row of engraved Corporate Cups above the fireplace don't turn my head. Instead, I fight the urge to drool over them and go straight to his desk.

So many old books. *Life of Alexander* sits on the edge while another volume is open and waiting. I lean over, catching the title in the upper margin. *The Glory of Rome: A History*. I flip through it until a familiar illustration catches my eye. For the second time tonight, I see an image that mirrors the circuit track. A giant stone arena, carved to pack in thousands of fans. There's a footnote under the pen-and-ink sketch.

The Colosseum

"The people that once bestowed commands, consulships, legions, and all else, now meddle no more and long eagerly for just two things—bread and circuses."
—Juvenal, AD 100

I don't understand Benroyal's obsession with Earth's history, but still my breath catches in my throat. I turn the chapter back, my ears pricked, waiting to hear something in the crackling of dead pages—the whisper of ghosts, the echo of the arena. The Colosseum. The circuit. There's a connection between them, and I can almost read the link.

I step away from the book. On the wall, a giant flex map draws my eye. It's a floor-to-ceiling rendering of Castra, every ocean and continent vividly detailed in digital paint.

As I run my hand from Mid-iron to the far western coast, more feeds and photos pop up—Benroyal's factories, villas, fuel sap stations. I swipe to get a better look at my home, the city he all but owns. Capitoline, a three-dimensional grid of streets and landmarks, unfurls over the map. The second I reach out and touch the tip of the Spire, my pocket buzzes. I pull out the stolen flex, only to find it glowing with blinking text.

SAFE MODE: ON

DATA SYNC: OFF

I can only guess this flex is a key card, a remote control for the room. I run my thumb over the SAFE MODE toggle, to switch it to OFF, but the flex asks for a passcode I don't have.

PASSCODE:

— — — — — — — — — —

I'm not risking a wrong answer. It's only when I turn to leave that it occurs to me. The fragile creature in the dark, trying to give me this card . . . You have to remember. Remember it's . . .

Sweetwater.

I text the letters into the blanks. Before I can react, a smooth Pallurium door slams into place, closing the archway. The shock and noise is enough to unbalance me. As I teeter against the edge of the desk, the blue flames die and the lights dim. On the walls, new images flicker into place, filling every screen. I gasp at the pictures. This isn't Benroyal's study.

It's the devil's war room.

CHAPTER EIGHTEEN

SAFE MODE MIGHT HAVE CLOAKED THIS ROOM'S SECRETS, BUT now I see them all in the silvery dark. The news screens are gone, replaced by surveillance feeds. All around me, I stare at IP soldiers patrolling refinery fields, aerial shots of buildings, hundreds of other satellite streams. In horror, I recognize one of the feeds—there's a camera trained on the back door to the Larssens' clinic. I whirl and scan the rest, looking for a shot of their apartment, but thankfully, I see none.

Benroyal's watching everything—our planets, the cities, the Mains. When I touch the Spire again, gleaming red lines ripple out over the streets, crisscrossing Capitoline and beyond like infected veins. I press my fingers against the grid to see what lifeblood pulses at our feet. My breath catches at the answer, what Benroyal's wife tried to tell me.

They cook it themselves.

Black sap. Thanks to Benroyal, the drug flows every-where, carried by his own transport rigs. Screens pop up over the mapped routes and show me everything happening from here to the Gap. Benroyal's refineries. His labs. They aren't just handling fuel. Live feeds show pipes spewing murky, scorched liquid into vials. Workers in hazmat suits carry trays and boxes, loading the drug into interstellar vacs.

Ships headed for Castra.

I trace the lines on the maps and press my thumb against the web of tangled intersections. Benroyal has distribution centers all over the place, and most of them are pushing black sap right through Capitoline. I try to take all the images in, but there's so much more, hundreds of icons and flex documents—lists of dealers, distribution orders, import manifests.

It's easy to connect the dots when the pictures spiral out in such straight and terrible lines. Cash's people aren't to blame for the black sap trade. While we're busy pointing fingers at Cyanese "terrorists" and Biseran dealers, Benroyal is hard at work. He takes the dregs of his own fuel sap, and instead of destroying it, he's running it straight through the heart of my city. No wonder the DP aren't making that many drug arrests. Benroyal Corp pays them well enough to make sure they don't.

We buy every half-truth and every product Benroyal pushes while he grows richer by the second. We cower while his hired guns pretend to police the streets. We watch his IP soldiers perfect the charade, as they "protect" us from drug dealers and terrorists in the Gap, when they're really protecting his product.

We are all King Charlie's fools.

Breathe. Grab the flex. Swipe into Safe Mode.

Run.

I bolt from the apartment without even looking for James. I slow down only to get by the guard at the penthouse doors. He calls out, asking again if I need any assistance, but I close the elevator without answering. After slamming my fist against the ground-level icon, I sink to the floor and pull my knees to my chest.

I've made a deal with a monster. His brand is tattooed on my shoulder. The thought pushes me over the edge. I kick the wall like an animal, trapped in Benroyal's cage.

Only when I have no more fight or breath do I pull myself to my feet again. The encrypted flex promised deactivated surveillance, but what happens if Benroyal finds out what I've seen? What happens if he doesn't?

What the rust am I going to do, keep racing and pretend I don't know he's shipping out enough black sap to deep-fry an entire generation? Look the other way while the feeds blame Bisera and Cyan for the constant threat of more war?

Benroyal is so clever at this game. War is a brilliant distraction, and there's profit in holding the Gap and poisoning the throwaway poor. Cash and I, so many of our people are hooked on his mind-killing sludge. I can imagine Benroyal's twisted logic. Keep the strong ones, put them on the payroll. The rest . . . who cares?

Lifting my head, I force a slow exhale. I watch the numbers blink as I reach the ground level. I need advice from someone I can trust. There's only one place to run now.

I'm ready to bolt for the lobby doors, but the scene outside the elevator stops me in my tracks. There's a crowd of Sixers down here, milling around, saying their good-byes. To Benroyal, who's circled by smiling guests.

Traitorous son of a jackal. That smug look on his rusting face. The adrenaline buzz hits me like a storm surge, feeding my blood with rage and numbing my brain. I stalk out of the elevator, ready to kick his teeth in, to spit in his eye and expose him, no matter what it costs me. I slam into someone. It's the woman from the gallery. The stranger who pulled James aside.

Her bodyguards start to pull me back, but she calls them off with a wave of her hand. Unfazed, she holds me at arm's length, studying me.

My eyes flick past her shoulder. Benroyal's still absorbed in conversation. My pulse rockets up, but I'm still dazed.

"Apologies," she says calmly. "I don't believe we've been introduced. My name is Grace Yamada."

Yamada. As in . . . "Yamada-Maddox?" I blurt. I've run headlong into the planet's most powerful banker. It's a wonder one of her bodyguards hasn't already stunned me. Or maybe they have, and that's why my brain can't quite sync up with my mouth.

She nods. "And you are Miss Vanguard."

"I . . . I—" I stutter.

"Take a breath," she commands.

I can't help but obey. Benroyal's turned away from us now. This time, when my eyes sweep the room, logic kicks in, anchoring me in place. In the Spire, amidst this crowd, there's nothing I can do. If I confront him here, I'm dead. I'd be dragged away before I landed a single blow. A new anger blooms. The cruelty of reason. I wish I'd never run into Grace Yamada.

"I just need to get out of here," I croak.

She nods, then signals her entourage. Instantly, her bodyguards surround us. She takes my arm and suddenly,

I'm gliding alongside her. "Let's go for a walk," she says.

She steers me, and seconds later, we're walking through the first set of doors, shielded by her escort. We breeze past several pairs of Benroyal's guards. Alert at their posts, they watch me, but no one makes a move.

I feel my pace quickening, but she holds me back. "Don't run," she says softly. "Head high. Back straight. Prove you have permission to leave. You're only going for a walk."

And just like that, we reach the last set of doors. No blocked exits. No shouts for me to halt, but the silence is more terrifying. I sense it's no mistake, that I haven't engineered some brilliant escape. The animal part of my brain hums in alarm. This woman is not your friend. None of them are. They are letting you leave. This is a trap.

After the front doors slide open, I wait for a struggle that doesn't come. Once we're outside, Grace Yamada lets go of my arm. I drift beyond her, but she is very still, like a carved goddess who's rooted to the steps. A sharp breeze lashes through my hair, and I could almost believe she is one, the force of nature who willed it.

I pull myself together. "Thanks for getting me out of there."

"I find it hard to breathe in the Spire." She looks down at me, then gestures toward the sculpture garden separating us from the street. "But I'm sure there's at least an hour's worth of fresh air out there."

"Why are you helping me?"

There's something both casual and dangerous about her smile. It could harbor sympathy. Or it could hide a death threat. "Sometimes it's good to take a walk. Fresh air clears the head. Stops girls from making very foolish mistakes. The clever ones, at least." Smoothing the drape of her gown, she turns away, then signals her men back inside.

And with that, she's gone. Back inside with the rest of the Sixers. The night air was her gift, so I risk a breath and take it.

Quickly, I make my way through the sculpture garden. Abstract shapes—sun-bleached and sterile—loom like the giant bones of ancient things, skeletal creatures long dead and drained of marrow. Above, the Spire rises like the blade that pierced and slaughtered them all.

It's quiet. The only sounds are of my quick footsteps and the rush of wind as it gusts against stone and metal and glass. Down the Mains, I spy the Sixer playgrounds—all the standard clubs—like so many splashes of light in the dark.

I'm so far from the grubby food carts and the black-market back rooms on the south side of Capitoline. Here, the facades are all the same. Every sidewalk is smooth and unstained. Each sign and corporate logo promises the unique, the exotic, but it's all an engineered ruse. No one but Benroyal and his elite friends taste anything unique.

I figure once the Sixers run their focus groups and test their assembly lines, there's nothing left but the illusion of choice. This is why it must be so easy to hook people on toxic black sap. We're dying to see something original, even if the tripped-out mind movies erode our memories and rot out our brains. And that's the only choice Benroyal wants to give us—we can accept dull, prepackaged lives or we can die slow deaths, poor and drug-addicted. I want to break something. Get behind the wheel and tear these streets apart.

I step closer to the curb and snag a passing cab.

"Twenty-first and Mercer."

I knock on the apartment door. Mary answers, bleary-eyed and in her scruffy gray bathrobe. I'd forgotten it's pushing midnight. Here I am, on her doorstep, wild-eyed and huffing after running up five flights of stairs. "I'm sorry," I gasp. "Is Bear here?"

"Phee!" She pulls me close, more tightly than she ever has before. The gesture breaks something in me and I'm not a circuit racer or a jail-break runaway. I'm just Hal and Mary's daughter. Suddenly, I'm stringing words together without making much sense.

"I . . . I had to come home . . . I've seen it . . . He's making it himself and I don't know—"

"Who is it?" Hal staggers into the living room. The second he lays eyes on me, it's over and done. He practically tackles Mary and me, guiding us both inside. I break loose, scrambling past them to get through the hallway and into Bear's room.

I swipe the light on, but he's not here. His bed is made, empty. "Where is Bear?" I ask. Hal shuffles me back and guides me to the sofa, my favorite lump of cushions in the whole world. I sink into its red raggedy softness.

Hal and Mary sit beside me. The fact that they still haven't answered my question makes me uneasy. "Where is he?"

Mary cuts in. "What were you thinking, street racing in town? We've been so worried, Phee. Hal's been at wit's end since you were picked up. Are you hurt? Are you all right? What has Benroyal done to you?"

"I'm . . ." They are keeping something from me. "Where is he? Where is Bear?"

Mary looks away. Hal is quiet. Tense.

"He's at Jason Eager's house." Mary's voice limps along. "He and a few of Benny Eno's boys are keeping vigil."

I blink. "Keeping vigil for what?"

"Jason Eager's gone. TransCorp offered him a circuit

deal, but he wouldn't have it," Hal answers. "He didn't—"

"You know how TransCorp laid off Eager's daddy?" Mary says. "How his mother marched against them before last month's strike? Jason didn't want anything to do with a Sixer contract. When he didn't sign, the court recalled him on new charges. They said he resisted arrest and tried to pull a DP's gun," Mary says. "They shot him, Phee."

I curl into myself, sinking further into the couch. Poor Eager, my crew-mate, the boy who never said a bad word about anyone, hardly a line of real trash talk. We'll never see his crooked smile again. I think of loyal Bear, who must be comforting Jason's family tonight. I can only imagine how badly he took the news. I need to share this grief with my brother.

Hal says quietly, "Has Benroyal let you go?"

"No, he definitely did not let me go."

Mary pulls her robe tight. "How did you get here?"

"I walked out. I don't know what's going to happen." I take a deep breath. Another nervous glance around the room. "I took an all-access flex from Benroyal's wife."

"Wait," Hal says. "What?"

"Well, really from a guard, but I scammed my way into Benroyal's study and saw everything. He's using his own fuel runoff to cook black sap and he's shipping it every-where and now I'm—"

"Slow down. Black sap?" Mary gapes. "You're sure, I mean, absolutely sure of it?"

I nod. There's realness, a feeling of safety in our apartment that gives me a scrap of courage. "Positive. I know what I saw." I tell them about the cameras and distribution routes I uncovered.

Hal drags his hand through his hair, something I've seen Bear do a thousand times. "Phee, this is . . . Who saw you? Who knows what you saw?"

"I don't know. The flex gave me access, supposedly disabled surveillance, but I don't trust Benroyal. At least a couple of guards know I was in his penthouse tonight. Grace Yamada walked me outside, helped me get past the guards. I didn't tell her anything, but—"

"Oh Phee. Don't you say another word. Not to her. Not to anyone." Mary presses the heels of her hands into her eyes. "If Benroyal's really behind the black sap, your life's not worth two credits once he finds out."

"I know. That's why you have to get out of Capitoline. Benroyal's got eyes on the clinic. Just take Bear and get out. Settle someplace outside another city, Dalmark or Midiron, maybe."

"We're not going anywhere." Hal stiffens, then squeezes an arm around my shoulder. "Not without you. You're our daughter."

"He'll kill you," I say. "If I step out of line, it's not just me who'll pay for it."

Mary sighs, then puts on that deep-thinking face, the one she wears when treating an incurable disease. Her blue eyes are bright with worry.

"I'm sorry." My voice almost cracks. "If I hadn't taken that race, the DP wouldn't have picked us up and come to shake down the clinic and I never would have—"

"I can't do this, Phee. Ever since we heard about Jason Eager, we . . ." Her eyes flick to the door. "I can't handle losing you or Bear. How could you be so reckless?"

The sharp edge in her scolding cuts too deep.

Tearing up, she cups my cheek. "What's done is done. And now we're just going to have to manage this. Hal and I will think of something."

"There has to be a way to expose Benroyal without putting you in danger. I have to tell someone."

Her hand drops. She jerks her head toward the door. "Who're you going to tell? The DP? The feedcasters? The prime minister? Out there, you tell anyone, and you're as good as dead."

"There has to be someone."

"You don't breathe a word of this to anyone, Phee. Not to anyone outside of this room. Not even Bear."

"I can't keep something like this from him."

Mary turns on me, shoulders squared, as fierce as I've ever seen her. "Anyone who knows is at risk. The less you tell Bear, the safer he'll be. I won't have my son beaten and interrogated by the DP. And I won't see you cut down like Jason Eager. For now, while we sort this out, you're going to forget what you saw and that's the end of it."

Before I can argue, the Larssens' front door bursts open.

CHAPTER NINETEEN

THE SIGHT OF THE FLIMSY DOOR, TORN FROM ITS HINGES BY six of Benroyal's guards, pushes me into fight or flight. I lurch from my seat, but Hal beats me to the punch. He shoves me back, ready to hold off anyone that advances.

"Get out of my house."

The guards ignore him. The first two, a hulking pair in black, make a move to toss him out of the way. I fly against them, but my fists are no match for these men in their bulletproof vests. So easily, they pin my arms behind my back while Hal and Mary struggle to fend off the remaining goons. I watch as one of them puts Hal in a chokehold, pressing a deactivated stun stick against his throat.

"Stop it!" I scream. "I'll go! Let them be and I'll do whatever you want."

The brute pinning my arm relaxes his grip. He nods at the rest of his team. "All right. Let's move out."

As they drag me away, I dig in my heels to buy one more moment. "I won't be there to pay my respects," I call back. "But tell Eager's mom I'm sorry."

I can't keep up with the officers' pace as they hustle me down five flights. Overpowered by their jackboot stomp, I give up, limp and spineless, my feet sliding against the landings. This was a trap. They know where I've been and what I've seen. They let me walk out, just so they could take me down for violating some rule or contract clause.

How long before they kill me? Will there be some pretense of arrest, like Eager's fall? Or will they just haul me into the alley and shoot me in the back of the head?

I stumble on the last riser. I feel the jolt and bounce of my misstep all the way from my heel to my jaw. My teeth clack against the inside of my cheek, and a trickle of my blood lashes against my tongue, sharpening something in me—a last gasp of courage, of desperation, of longing to taste freedom before the bullet's call. In the split second of confusion, I twist and slip the guards' hold. I'm off the leash and through the exit doors, only fingertips beyond their reach.

The spectacle beyond the curb stops me in my tracks. A

row of DP speeders. An Onyx from the Spire. Three other armored rigs, lights flashing. A score of silent officers in riot gear. And they are not alone.

Old Mr. Fontanata and his daughter watch from their opposite stoop. Lang Metter stands in the threshold of his shop, Gold Flake Pawn. It's late, but my neighbors hover in their doorways and lean from open windows. Lang's middle son, Rip, makes a move. Even as Benroyal's guards catch up and lay hands on me again, he dares to approach, stepping off the curb and into the street.

"Step back," a DP barks through a wrist amp. "Do not advance."

The door to my building clangs open. I twist and catch a glimpse of Hal and Mary. Several DPs have to hold them back.

"All civilians back inside," the leader commands, but no one retreats. Strangers appear in doorways. Lang moves onto the street to join his son.

"I said get back!" The officer pulls his gun, gliding his thumb to deactivate the safety. I gasp and taste the charge in the air, scanning the taut uncertainty in the faces of my neighbors. Heat shimmers from the sap-stained pavement while we dance on the brutal edge between indecision and resistance, doomed at every tilt.

I think of last month's strike, and the riots that trailed

it. One shot fired into a crowd of protesters was all it took to spark a raging fire. So much smoke and south side blood. Tonight, I know my life's not worth the burning. "Please . . ." I collapse into myself, falling pliant and slack. "Call them off and I'll—"

Lights blaze across my field of vision. Another Onyx roars through a gap in the DPs' line and slams to a stop in our path. Its doors fly open, and Hank is beside me. In two blinks, he's flanked the guards and pulled me loose. James is at his side.

"Are you hurt, Miss Vanguard?" Hank asks.

I don't know what to say.

"What in the name of Castra do you think you are doing?" James yells at the guards, then wheels on the lead DP officer. "Stand down and tell me what's going on before I have you all charged and reassigned for desert watch."

The tallest guard, the one who'd put Hal in a chokehold, shrugs. "She was unescorted and hadn't returned by midnight, so we—"

"They took her," Mary shouts. "Burst into our apartment and dragged her into the street."

"Are you insane?" Hank asks the guard. "All this for a girl breaking curfew?"

"Hey, they called us in." The DP is quick to shift the

blame. He points a finger at Benroyal's guards. "Said she broke a contract clause and that they might need some help to bring her in."

Even though it's not fixed on me, James's sneer is a little terrifying. "Well, aren't you something, Miss Vanguard. You stay out half an hour past curfew and apparently, it takes six grown men and two armored squads to fetch you and bring you back home." Again, he turns on the DP commander. "Who authorized this . . . constellation of sheer recklessness and stupidity?"

One of the guards owns up, meekly raising his palm.

"Does Mr. Benroyal know about this?"

"No, but we have standing orders to make sure she doesn't go out after her curfew."

"Then pray I don't regale him with the details." James pivots. "Hank, flex me this imbecile's contract number. The rest of you jokers say good night and pack it in, before I call Mr. Benroyal and tell him you very nearly damaged one of his most valuable assets, inviting a full-scale riot in the process."

No one's said anything about the stolen flex or what I saw in Benroyal's study. I sway as the waves of adrenaline panic ebb. They aren't here to silence me. I think. I hope.

There's a long string of "yes, sirs" and half-hearted apologies before James waves everyone off. I give in to the collective exhale as the neighbors retreat. Hal and Mary approach, but James steps between us.

"Please return to your apartment, Mr. and Mrs. Larssen." He pretends it's a request. "I'll send someone to replace your door, and I promise no further harm will come to you."

"What about Phee?" Mary asks.

"I'll see her back to the Spire."

I shudder.

He turns and makes his way toward the Onyx, confident I'll follow. I look back at Hal and Mary.

"Good night," I tell them at last. "Take care."

We speed away and I collapse. The driver's screen is up, and Hank drives us past empty blitz ball courts and dim warehouses and trailing flex banners that blink with share prices and circuit odds. Cash's image appears. It's a handsome shot of him at a circuit event, but a tabloid headline's splashed over it, ruining his smolder.

I hardly recognize myself when my picture flashes next to his. It's from today's press conference, and a close-up of our team logo links Cash and me. I close my eyes until Benroyal's lion is out of sight.

I don't know why King Charlie has me on such a tight leash, but this has been the longest rusting night of my life.

My lids twitch and my whole body burns with exhaustion. Like an overspent fuel cell, I'm scorched and drained. James can stare and fuss at me all he wants—I've got nothing left to give.

"You can thank Cash," James says. "If he hadn't guessed where you bolted, I might not have been able to intervene in time. Let's not mention the fact that you defied me outright. I told you to stay put and you didn't. I don't even want to think about what would've happened if I hadn't found you. No one's saying you can't go out, but you can't break curfew like that again, Phee. Next time, take an escort."

I sigh. "I'm not an 'asset.'"

"Yes, you are. To Benroyal, everything and everyone is either an asset or an obstacle. And you're one of his most important holdings now." He thrusts an oversized flex into my face. "Read it. Look what they're saying about you. Phoenix Vanguard: Racing's New Rebel, Circuit Renegade, Applause for Sucker Punch."

A cold and oily nausea slithers through me as the words sink in, even as I fight the smile tugging at the corners of my mouth. Inside me, there's a space that craves this approval, but swallowing it whole, it all goes down so wrong.

James must sense I've reached my limit. He pulls the

flex away. "You're not just some street rat anymore. Be careful, Phee. That's all I'm asking. Why did you run off like that?"

I can't tell him the truth. James might've saved me this time, but I can't forget he's King Charlie's right-hand man.

"Grace Yamada. I ran into her. She led me outside and told me to get some fresh air. So I did."

"You've been talking to Grace?" he barks. "Tell me you haven't been talking to Grace Yamada."

"Stop bugging out. She helped me get out of the Spire and I caught a cab. She was nice."

James sighs and pinches his forehead. "Grace Yamada is a lot of things, but she is not nice. Furthermore, you cannot just follow her out of the Spire, breaking your curfew every time you feel like it." There's real fear in his eyes now. All this scolding is just a smokescreen.

"Why do you care so much? What's your play?"

"This isn't a game. I need you to lay low and stay out of trouble. It's crucial you do your job and do it well. I need you to win."

"Sure." I turn away, resting my head against the window glass. I'm too tired to make a fist or roll my eyes or even raise my voice. "Shut up and drive. I get it. Your bet's on me. I need to score high so you can rake in the shares."

"You think you know everything? You see through me so well? You can't even begin to grasp everything that's at play and how high the stakes are for me right now. I am not the villain, Phee. Maybe I'm the one person who's not. I'm trying to protect you."

"Protect me? Why should I trust you, Mr. Locus Informatics? I'm nothing but Benroyal's property to you. Something you can use."

"You are my concern, Phee." James pulls off his frames and the mask slips—I catch the pinch of weariness and alarm. "You'll just have to get used to that."

"Then convince me you're really not the villain here. You act like Benroyal's errand boy, playing fetch for the biggest lying Sixer on Castra."

"You think I like taking orders from that—" James cuts himself off, but I'm not fooled. Even his quietest voice presses like a blade against the throat. "While Charles Benroyal's great-grandfather was peddling tear gas and stun sticks, mine was collapsing the space between stars. My family built Locus to bridge gaps. To move information from one world to another. We pioneered interstellar communication, flex tech, infinite data highways. You think I've enjoyed watching Benroyal dismantle the heart and soul of my company, turning Locus into just another cog in his machine?"

"Then why don't you stop him?"

"Four minutes. My sister is four minutes older than I am. The firstborn heir. That gives her fifty-one percent of Locus, and leaves me with forty-nine. Which makes it all too easy for Benroyal to declare his pretty little wife incompetent, take control of her shares, and twist Locus into whatever he wants. My family's company became a rent-a-judge, insta-trial punchline, and I had to stand by and watch. Think you hate King Charlie?" he says through his teeth. "You don't know the meaning . . . No one wants to take him down more than I do. And right now, I'd say that makes me the best friend you've got."

"Some friend. The kind who offers prison or the Spire."

"I didn't have a choice."

"Spare me your act. You don't—"

"Once word got out that Tommy Van Zant's daughter was winning on the streets, it was over and done." He pauses. "Your father was the greatest driver the circuit has ever seen. People loved him like no other, Phee. Benroyal knows that's in your blood."

My hands are shaking, but I can't bear to tell James how much it burns to hear my father's name. "Don't tell me about my—"

"Your father was more than a driver for Locus. He was a good man. I couldn't stop Benroyal from forcing you to sign with him, but I'll do what I can to protect you. I owe Tommy that much."

"Your company, your family used him," I spit. "I don't know how you did it, whether it was the pressure or the contract or your stupid rules, but somehow it was enough to break him. Because of Locus, my dad walked away from me, from everything, fell off the face of the planet . . . Or maybe he didn't walk away at all. Maybe you erased him."

"No, Phee. I would never . . ." The look on his face—the accusation cut him to the heart.

But it doesn't matter that I believe him. I can't stop myself anymore. I can't resist dealing someone else a taste of the pain. "Oh, you're so sorry now. My father is gone, and now you feel so rusting guilty. Yet you want me to be grateful, that you would finally remember his poor orphaned daughter. Thank you for looking out for me. Thank you so much for the life sentence."

He looks away. "Hate me. Go ahead. I'm not blameless. But if you want to stay alive long enough to outlast Benroyal, you need to listen to me. Stay out of trouble. Live by his rules and do whatever he asks until I tell you otherwise."

I don't answer. I'm caught like a dune bird, tangled up in the poacher's snare. Tell what I've seen, and I'm dead. Play along, and I might as well be. "Let's say I shut up and drive. Be a good robot. Do everything you ask. How does that do anything but win for Benroyal?"

"You're not the only one who hates him. You think people like me, like Grace Yamada, are going to sit around and wait for the day Benroyal either eliminates us, or folds us all into his own private empire? There are plans in motion. Not all of us are as evil as you think."

"Right. I'm supposed to blindly trust you, even when I'm pretty sure this has nothing to do with protecting me, and everything to do with protecting your precious company. I do as you say, but of course, you only tell me what you think I need to know, which is basically nothing. Is that it? How's that work?"

"It works like this: Show me you're more than a reckless, foolish, careless girl and then we'll talk. Perhaps I cannot trust you."

We are silent all the way back to the Spire.

CHAPTER TWENTY

THE MORNING AFTER MY MIDNIGHT FIELD TRIP, THERE'S no inquisition, no mention of breaking curfew. An early wake-up call is my only punishment. If Benroyal knows what I saw last night, he's sure not letting on.

Even so, for most of the morning, I watch my back like I'm in custody again. It doesn't help that Bear's still gone, and I don't loosen up at all until I arrive at Benroyal HQ for practice. For Hal and Mary's sake, there's nothing to do now but stay silent and play my part with gritted teeth. James would be so pleased.

But I won't stay silent for long. Maybe I can't tell James the truth, but there might be one man I can reach. I look over the guest list for tomorrow's exhibition race and trace my finger over his title. Esteemed Chamberman Toby Abasi.

If the Larssens taught me anything, it's that a vote for most Chamber or Assembly members is nothing more than a vote for one corporation over another. But if there's anyone with enough power who hasn't been bought, it's Abasi. If I can get to him, I'm almost certain he'd help me stop Benroyal.

After the exhibition, we've got a handful of days until our first official race. I know this, because about every twenty minutes or so, Goose walks by me and Dev and Gil and Banjo and everyone else on our crew to remind us.

The hangar is buzzing. Everyone is anxious to start running speed trials and simulations, and at ten a.m. or so, Gil tells me my rig is ready for practice.

It feels too good to jump in again. After I strap in and pull on my helmet, I wait for Cash's voice to come over the headset. In an open-air booth, he's high above the track, ready to scout for me. For the first time, he'll be my pacer.

All morning, Cash and I have been playing a stupid game of let's-avoid-each-other-and-pretend-nothing-happened-last-night. It's awkward and dumb, and neither of us is very good at it.

He rumbles through my headset. "You ready for this?"

"Thanks for ratting me out last night." Even as the words come, I curse myself. It's a false and selfish play, goading him just so I can hear his voice.

But he is silent. Either he's scorched, or he knows how ridiculous I really am. One minute I'm trash-talking him, the next I'm all over him like he's never been kissed before. Even now, a part of me wants to blurt out an apology and tell him how much just seeing him sends a twitchy rush of feel-good chemicals into every cell of my body, but it's a safe bet that there are other members of our crew listening in.

And after the way I acted last night, I'm pretty sure he's washed his hands of me anyway.

Through the headset, I hear him clear his throat. "Okay, once you start your engine, the simulation will begin. You'll have about thirty seconds to pull into pole position before the race starts. You're going to see a sap-load of extra visuals, not just your virtual controls. Through your visor, you'll see a lot of other rigs, cars that aren't really there, even an occasional pileup or caution flag."

"Got it. I'm supposed to pretend this is real and work my way around them."

"Yeah, but we're not just going for speed, Phee. This is about strategy and precision. I'll watch for target markers on the track surface. When I tell you there's an arrow flashing on a particular position on the track, you'll need to adjust your route. Just like in a real race, you'll pick up extra points running over those markers."

I think the holographic markers are lame, but that's how the circuit is run, so I can't argue. If I were in charge, I'd make every rally strictly a free-for-all. Who cares about points? To me, the only thing that matters is who finishes first and who sucks exhaust.

"Still with me?" Cash says.

"Yeah. I'm with you." Already, my blood is pumping. I'm ready to tear up this track.

"Good. Pay attention to what the rig is telling you too, okay?"

Gil's voice cuts in. "Cash is right, Phee. The goal is to hit it as hard as you can without blowing out your tank, your engine, or your tires. If you need to pit, say so and we'll set you up. I listen in most of the time, but Cash can also relay your feedback, so we can figure out when to bring you in and when to keep you running. You ready, spitfire girl?"

It seems Goose's term of endearment for me has gotten around. "Yes, sir. Absolutely."

"Let's fire it up, then."

And so it begins. After switching on the hyper screens, I punch the ignition, roll out, and wait for the first green flag to fall. When it does, I pick up speed and make the first turn. I'm off to a pretty good start and just when I think I've got this down, I get sucked into the second turn magnetic wall. I have to burn my first fuel trigger to launch away and I end up smashing into an imaginary car in the process. If this had been a real race, I'd have knocked both our rigs sideways.

"You've got speed, Phee," Gil coaches me. "But that isn't always what wins the race. You're going to have to learn when to rein it in or the other cars are going to gang up and force you into the wall every time. Right now, Cash isn't saying much. He's letting you get a feel for the track. But trust me, girl, soon enough he's going to start giving you what for."

"I'm here," Cash says. "When you need me, I'll read the pace and help you through the rough stuff."

I could get all huffy about the way they're babying me, but I'm not completely witless. Every member of the circuit team serves a purpose. Rallies and races aren't just won behind the wheel; they're won by a whole crew of tire haulers and mechanics and grunts, out front and behind the pit wall. It's my job to run like hell, but it's also my job now to listen and learn.

I speed up until everything outside the track blurs into nothing more than streaks of color. After I rack up more laps, Cash starts to coach more, and we pick up target points right and left.

Bear and I always won out by exploiting our opposite strengths. Foresight and reflex, channeled together. He found the safest routes, and I found a way to tear through them. But with Cash, it's different. Not a second of caution between us. His instincts mirror mine so closely, it's rusting scary. We're syncing up like we're wired, his impulses sending a charge through my limbs. The matchup brings an incredible rush, but there's also a warning whisper in my blood. So alike, we must share the same blind spots.

Just when it looks like I'll take the lead, the simulation throws an obstacle my way. Two virtual cars smash across the other side of the track. A yellow caution flag blinks through my visor. Now would be a great time to pit and not lose any ground.

"You're fine on fuel, but how's she running?" Gil asks. "We need to make any adjustments?"

There's not much to complain about; this thing runs like a dream. "It's still a little tight, but maybe I'm just used to my Talon."

A third crew member cuts in. "Phee's got that reckless streak, she likes it loose around the turns. Maybe adjust the spring rate?"

I'd recognize that voice anywhere, especially through my headset. "Bear! You're here!"

"Uh-huh."

This race is over, at least for me. Foot to the floor, I ignore the caution flag and bullet around the backstretch, only to slam on the brakes once I get close enough to pit road. After swerving and roaring to a stop by my rig's designated stall, I punch the release on my six-point and jump out of the car.

Bear's standing behind the pit wall with the rest of my crew, so I toss off my helmet and climb over. Once I scramble to the other side, I tackle him. I can tell he's glad to see me, but also horrified at my heart-stopping finish. I look back and see there are only a few inches between the car and the pit wall—I nearly slammed into it.

"I'm sorry," I blurt out to Gil, who's clearly close to a heart attack thanks to my careless stop. "I'm just—"

"Glad to see you too." Bear touches my cheek, then squeezes me tight. He's wearing his old clothes and when I take in a deep breath, I smell Mary's kitchen. It's enough to overpower even the stench of my sweat-soaked gear. The scent of burned buttered toast makes me want to cry. I'm reminded once more of the life I've signed away.

I let go of him just in time to force my tears to stay put. I can't lose it or tell him what happened last night. "I'm so glad you're safe."

"I could say the same about you," Bear says.

Sunlight haloes his face. I look at him, and it's like drinking in blue skies and fresh air. "How'd you get here so fast? Thought you'd be gone for days."

"Benroyal's people told me I could have a week off, but I couldn't stay away."

"Bear! You should've stayed with them as long as you could."

"Didn't you want me to come back?" he asks. "I was worried about you, Phee. I thought you needed me. Don't you need me to pace you and practice before tomorrow's exhibition?"

"Of course I need you, Bear." I'd forgotten we were going to have to work this out. Cash is experienced, practically a circuit pro. There's no way I can push him aside, and I'm not willing to toss Bear away either. For now, I need to ease Bear's mind. "I'll always need you. You'll always be my pacer."

From the corner of my eye, I see Cash has already made his way back down into the pit. Just in time to hear me. He turns and stalks away, and deep down, I know I've brought this all on myself. First I kiss-attack him, then bolt. Now, the second Bear shows up, I all but dismiss him from his job, a job he rocked for me. We were good together, even in our first practice. Even after last night.

"Cash, wait," I call after him.

But he doesn't stop, not even for a second. He pretends he can't hear me, and I can't blame him at all.

CHAPTER TWENTY-ONE

MY FIRST RACE DAY, AND LATE-AFTERNOON SUN BAKES the track. There's little breeze, and the heat tastes like fuel and grit. Gil tells me not to worry about today's exhibition. For the Castran Classic, it'll be me running alongside five other rigs for a mere twenty laps. No one expects any clashes or bumps, just a nice clean show to give the circuit's biggest VIPs a look at the competition. We don't even have to leave Benroyal's arena. King Charlie's hosting it here.

Outside, while my crew adjusts my rig and the officials check their work, I flick through pit rosters and driver profiles and guest RSVPs on my flex. I double-check the guest list and suite numbers.

Abasi's listed as a top-tier guest, along with just about

every other significant Chamber or Assembly member. He'll be to the left of Benroyal's personal suite, sitting with James and Prime Minister Prejean. I'm surprised. Since Abasi's shown no love for the circuit, or, for that matter, our prime minister, I can't imagine why they'd want him so close. I look up into the stands, but it's too far and there's no way to see through the boxes' mirrored glass.

"Hey." I push the flex back into Bear's hands. "I'll be right back."

He frowns. "Wait. We need to walk through strategy one more time. It's almost go time, Phee. They're going to let the feedcasters in here in less than fifteen minutes. We really should be—"

"I'm just . . ." I trail off. I hate lying to Bear, yet I find myself doing it more and more. "It's nothing. Call it nerves. Gotta unzip and park it one last time before the race. I'll be back in a minute, I promise."

The boy I used to know would step aside. He'd shrug like my exit was nothing. Instead, Bear crosses his arms and stares me down. Because he knows. Better than anyone, Bear can spot my little tics and tells. I'm a map he memorized a long time ago. I turn away so he can't look at me anymore.

I duck inside and take the long way around the track, avoiding the strand of locker rooms and team pit stalls. After I've skirted most of the action, I take a service elevator up to the top tier of spectator boxes—the warren of ridiculously plush suites reserved for Benroyal and the rest of Castra's finest.

In this hallway, the walls are a mosaic. Tiny bits of flex glass are fused against one another, rimmed with light. Images fade in and out—a history of the circuit glows in a parade of color. I see the first drivers, colonials racing over hundreds of miles to plant their flags on new land. The old routes evolve into high-profile rallies. The corporates devour the sport and institute the first oval course. Sleek rigs careen round and round, going nowhere.

Overhead, a lineup of legendary drivers. My father's portrait, his profile half lit. The final panorama is of the Sixer emblems. Benroyal's lion rises and overshadows everything else.

To reach Abasi's suite, I have to push through a cluster of Sixer underlings placing circuit bets for their bosses. The scene here is far posher, but the action isn't so different from what happens in the bettors' stalls at Benny Eno's garage. Slick bookies scan the wagers, offering odds while calculating their cut of the credits and stocks. Whatever happens today, I hope my driving costs them all a fortune.

A pair of DP guards flank Abasi's box. When I try to stroll in, they stop me. "I'm sorry, Miss Vanguard, but you're not allowed in here. Gold security clearance only."

Instinctively, I touch my hip. My fingers graze the pocket where I've tucked the stolen flex. Oh, I'm gold clearance, all right. They just don't know it.

I scan the crowd inside the room. Abasi's on the far side, surrounded by well-heeled politicians and their aides. I may not have the clout to get in, but I'm sure as sap not getting turned away without catching his attention. The minute I lean forward to get a better look, the DPs react.

"Hey!" I say. The guard pushes me and pins my arms behind my back. I've got maybe two seconds before his wingman pulls his weapon. A little too loudly, I growl, "Keep your paws off me!"

A murmur ripples through the box and out into the hallway. A pair of bodyguards rush out of the suite, followed by Grace Yamada.

"Stand down," she commands the officers.

She is ice-water calm. Only the barest trace of irritation flickers over her face, and I'm not sure whether she's annoyed more with me or the DPs.

She waves the guards off. They withdraw and take their places at the door. Grace Yamada turns to me. "How can I help you, Miss Vanguard?"

When I hesitate, she tilts her head, leaning enough that I can almost whisper in her ear.

"I was hoping for a moment with Chamberman Abasi."

"That would not be wise, Miss Van Zant."

She knows my real name. The sound of it is a warning, a hammer tap to the sternum. "Perhaps another time," she adds. "I could arrange another hour of fresh air and we could discuss—"

There's something about her that demands respect, yet at the same time leaves me unbalanced. Grace Yamada is no one to be trifled with. "Please. I have to see him."

She turns away, and my courage fails. I pivot to leave, but she calls over her shoulder. "Wait here."

So I wait. A minute, ten minutes. I don't know. I'm cutting it too close to race time. I'm just about to leave, edging past her bodyguards, when someone taps my shoulder, startling me.

The old man's not as tall as I'd expected. "Chamberman Abasi?"

Kindly, he nods. "Toby, I insist. Your friend Grace said you wished to see me?"

My gaze flicks over the hallway. A lone aide trails us, but unlike Ms. Yamada, Abasi didn't bring a pack of bodyguards to shield us. We are surrounded by Sixers, exposed on every side. All this scheming to get here, and now I don't know what to say. I'm not equipped to play the spy. Nervously, I reach into my pocket. "I . . . I have something for you . . . information about—"

Abasi cuts me off with a warning look. His gaze flicks up. No longer than an eye blink, but I catch the signal. Surveillance. Of course. "I'm very glad to meet you, Miss Vanguard. Very glad. In fact, quite honestly, the only reason I came at all was to watch your debut." He touches my shoulder until my hand drops. "But I am afraid I cannot accept any campaign contributions today. Alas, circuit rules. I would never encourage you to break them."

"But—"

His smile is old parchment. On his face, a hundred lines, creased and inked. He reaches into his own pocket and pulls out a flex. "But perhaps there is one thing you could do for me?"

I nod.

"My niece, Amisa, would be very disappointed if she found out I met you and did not ask for an autograph. Here, I have today's race schedule, with your picture. Would you be so kind as to personalize a message for her? Here, let me spell her name for you." He taps on the flex before handing it me.

TA: **THIS CARD IS SECURE. TELL ME WHAT YOU WANTED TO**
SAY. TEXT QUICKLY.

Shaking, I hold his flex and leave the only message I can.

PV: **BLACK SAP. BENROYAL IS BEHIND IT ALL.**

"Your niece is beautiful. I hope she likes the autograph,"
I say.

Abasi looks over my shoulder. I finish texting.

PV: **EVIDENCE. I CAN GET YOU EVERYTHING.**

"Thank you, Miss Vanguard," he says, taking back the
flex. Casually, he swipes it clean. Like me, he knows how
to smile for the cameras. "I know Amisa will be thrilled.
Of course, she'll want to meet you someday soon. I'll be
in touch."

Still on edge, I'm down the stairs, round the track, and
almost to the pit stalls when I hear the two voices outside
the pre-race commotion. Instead of turning the last corner,
I press my back against the wall.

"She deserves to know up front."

"No, absolutely not."

My brain blinks and I know the voices. Cash and James.
Infuriating, these two. Thick as thieves.

James's voice drops to a whisper. I have to concentrate
to hear him over the buzz and clang in the pits. "If you tell
her, she'll go guns out and get herself killed. I know you've

grown partial to her, but this isn't your call. I promised to watch out for her, and right now, that means she's out. I can't risk it."

"Risk what?" I round the corner, almost colliding with Cash. Of course I don't do the smart thing and keep eaves-dropping. Of course my anger and pride get the best of me. Again. "What are you two jaw-jacking about behind my back?"

James looks stricken, then irritated. He's not used to being caught by surprise. Cash is unreadable. Silent and cool.

"Gil's been looking for you for the last ten minutes," James says, already advancing. "Where have you been?"

"I was looking for someone. Actually, it's none of your business."

"Did you find him?" Cash asks, but there's no trace of the usual swagger.

"No, I didn't. You mind telling me what's going on? What don't you think I need to know?"

James grabs me by the arm and drags me toward the team stalls. I thrash, but he's a lot stronger than he looks. "You are going to report to your crew and get ready to race this instant."

"Let me go." I twist out of his grip and blaze past the first stall, the one with AltaGen's purple logo plastered all over it. Courant is there, grinning as I stalk away. I'm nothing more than a girl on a leash in front of my fellow drivers.

James doesn't follow, but Cash slips beside me, easily keeping up.

"What is going on?" I say. "Don't pretend you're not hiding something from me."

"Look." He sounds more weary than annoyed. "I'm going to hang back tonight. Give Bear a chance to pace you."

"Stop avoiding the question. What were you and James talking about?"

"Nothing. Who were you looking for?"

"No one. Nothing. Tell me, Dradha."

He sighs. "It's Maxwell Courant. He and the rest of the Sixer drivers are out to put you in your place. Don't expect to get very far tonight, Phee. James didn't want you to worry about it beforehand. Are you happy now?"

We both stop in our tracks, but I don't answer. I stare back, certain he's thrown out an obvious truth to distract me. Cash and I both have our secrets, and I guess neither of us is ready to come clean.

"No, I'm not happy, Cash. I'm not happy at all."

Goose is furious. While I was shaking hands with Abasi, I missed the pre-race photo op. By the time Cash and I wander back, it's already time to roll out.

"I told them your absence was planned," Goose says, smoothing the lapel of his crimson jacket. "That you prefer to make your statement behind the wheel rather than in front of the cameras, but I won't make excuses for you again, spitfire girl. You had better impress them tonight."

"Don't worry," I lie, "I've got this. Where's Bear?"

"Dependable, that boy. Already at his post." He scowls at Cash. "I suggest you join him."

Scolded, we take our places. While Cash scrambles to the pacers' deck, I climb behind the wheel and gear up while my crew makes final adjustments and rolls me onto the track. It's just an exhibition, I tell myself. Twenty laps. We're not supposed to break a sweat or even pull a fuel trigger. My game plan is to slide behind the front-runner until the last second, then break loose just before the finish line.

Hundreds of white flags ring the arena. They're supposed to remind us of the brave pioneers who raced to claim Castra, but in the wind, the banners snap like a thousand surrenders. There's no one in the stands save for a handful of feedcast crews. And, of course, the corporates who hold our contracts. Far above, they watch with a few of their favorite puppets, the politicians who carry out their will. So it's weirdly silent beyond the rhythmic snarl of six engines.

We're not a full lineup. I don't even get to drive against Cooper Winfield today. This is strictly a Sixer affair, and I couldn't feel more out of place. While my custom ride is sleek and snub-nosed, their rigs are all muscle and curve. If this were a knife-fight, blade against blade, I brought the stiletto and they're swinging battle axes.

Staggered into our starting positions, we wait, draped in our corporate colors. I race for the crimson. Max Courant in purple for AltaGen. Bobby Banks Jr. in brown for Agri-tech. Will Balfour in orange for Yamada-Maddox. Scott Kimbrough in emerald for Locus Informatics. I wince. It's the deepest cut to see Marcus Fallon at the end of the row. It should be Jason Eager in TransCorp's deep blue uniform instead of Fallon, a black-hearted driver who's come out of retirement to take his place.

Every rig snarls, ready to run. Aggression ripples through the air; I taste its heat and fury. Cash was right. My rivals are out for my blood. And I cannot let them have it tonight. Not because James wants me to win, but because I can never stomach losing.

The pace car leads us off. We crawl once around the track. Five seconds until the starting flag drops. I take a deep breath and . . .

Rust. This isn't a race. It's an ambush.

CHAPTER TWENTY-TWO

LONG AFTER EVERYONE HAS LEFT MY APARTMENT IN THE
Spire, after Bear has gone to bed, I sink into the cloud-
cushioned sofa and try to reconstruct the colossal failure
otherwise known as today's exhibition. My first race and
I choked. Wait. *Choked* implies initial success followed by
catastrophic loss.

In my case, I blew it right from the start. Maxwell and
the other cars moved as a synchronized unit at every turn,
completely boxing me in for twenty laps. Bear did everything he could, brilliantly anticipating the split-second
gaps, but I just couldn't bust loose.

Technically, I finished in fifth place, but the other drivers
made their point. They showed me they could pin me in
place for an entire race. And the worst of it? Agritech's one

of Benroyal's biggest rivals, and I tasted plenty of Bobby Banks Jr.'s exhaust. He made sure I stared at the back end of his mud-brown rig the whole time.

The whole ordeal was beyond humiliating, and there's no way I'm letting it happen again. I thumb my flex and summon a search screen.

Tommy Van Zant.

I flick through official photos and clips until I find my favorite. It's a two-minute feed of the final laps of the 2380 Sand Ridge 400, the race that made my father a legend. That day, he became a six-time Corporate Cup series champion. He set the record no one has ever broken.

I lean back and watch the last seconds. He's driving for Locus, of course; his emerald rig's leading the pack once more. Unlike me, no matter how hard the other drivers push him, he always shakes them off. On victory lane, he pulls off his helmet, closes his eyes, and smiles against the sun. I lean forward, longing to taste that glory.

There's another clip, one I can hardly bear to watch tonight. After his last mountain rally in 2381, my father collects his trophy but doesn't grin. When the helmet comes off, his wild brown hair falls over his face, half obscuring weary eyes. The race is over, but he looks as if every prize is lost and every route forever closed.

I'm starting to understand the temptation to drop off

the face of the planet. Is this what finally broke him down? Was it the pressure of the circuit, the demands of the Sixers, or something else? I swipe the screen clear and search again.

It's a familiar game. I try a dozen search terms, but each variation is just as useless.

Tommy Van Zant Wife

Tommy Van Zant Girlfriend

Tommy Van Zant Family

Thomas Van Zant Personal Life

Of course, I get a million hits, more than I could read in a lifetime. But none of them tell me what I want to know. There isn't a single picture of anyone who looks remotely like the woman on my father's old flex. It's as if my mother never existed. I've never understood why.

As my eyes move over the image results, my mind slips into that secret place. I invent my mother, re-imagining her as someone I never lost. She is beautifully alive, luminous and full of laughter. I take the best of Mary—owl-wise wit and loyal nerve—until the picture blurs into something I can almost hold. I conjure the best mother I never had. It hurts, but I do it because I can't resist pressing my thumb against the bruise.

Footsteps in the hall. Quickly, I call up the Castran Sports Feed, letting it run on every wall.

Bear shuffles into the living room. "Can't sleep?"

When I don't answer, he sits and throws an arm around my shoulder. He pulls me closer, and I relax into his warmth, cozy and snug and a little less gloomy.

"I let you down tonight," he says.

"You didn't, Bear. You watched out for me at every turn. It's not your fault. They were gunning for us, and I didn't have my head in the game before the race. Cash tried to warn me, and I didn't listen."

He tenses at Dradha's name. I feel the wince.

"I have to win the next one," I say.

"Do you?" He withdraws, putting on a sleepy frown. "For Benroyal?"

"Not for him. Or James or anyone else. I just can't stand losing."

"Then we'll practice." When he slides his strong hands down my arms, the rift is almost gone. "Win or lose, I'm here."

"I know." It pains me to see him this worried. With a look, he summons the tenderest part of me, the vulnerable girl no one else is allowed to see. Suddenly, I need him to smile again. "Remember the plan? How we were going to—"

He obliges, half grinning at memories. "I haven't forgotten. Our own garage. Our own crew. Winning every—"

"Street race from Capitoline to Piper Dunes." Even as I finish his sentence, I know the dream is gone. It died the moment the DP picked us up. Through the prickle of unshed tears, I look into his eyes and see an altered future. I mourn the one we've lost. "That's over now. We can't go back."

"I don't care. No matter what happens, no matter where we end up. Nothing's going to change between us."

But something has changed.

He folds me close and I listen to the drumbeat of his heart. Its steady rhythm always quiets the keening in my blood, but this time, the surrender feels too much like drowning. I pull away, dazed and more uncertain than I've ever been.

Bear misreads my wide-eyed stare. "No one's going to hurt you. I won't ever let that happen."

"It's not that," I answer. "The drivers and feedcasters can do their worst. I'm not afraid of them."

"What is it, then?"

"I don't know." I lie because I'm not brave enough to whisper the truth.

I'm afraid of hurting you, Bear.

Bear watches me for a moment before settling back, and I wonder if he's as scared as I am. I try to pinpoint the moment things shifted, but so many edges overlap, a hundred memories slipping against one another. We are six and eleven and then thirteen, knee-deep in mischief and forever inseparable.

I can try to pretend I've always bloomed the same shade for Bear, but my love for him has deepened over the years. It has, and no matter how many times I call him my brother, I can't deny the subtle drift. It's as if our routes were always angled to converge, and I've never resisted the slow pull. Until now.

I pull back to look at him. We are frozen, staring at each other.

It's Bear who reaches first. He brushes away a strand of my hair, then cradles my jaw in his hands. He leans forward, moving so slowly, like a ship rowing to shore against the tide. A few seconds more, and our lips will touch, but the kiss meant to bring us closer looms like something dangerous and sharp, something that, if mishandled, might cut the cord between us.

I focus, tuning out the feeds, ignoring everything but him. The familiar exhale. The gentle weight of his touch. Even now, the way his eyes call to me. I have my answer, insistent and clear. He sees me as he always has, his to hold and protect. And even if I'm not sure anymore, even if that's not what I . . .

He is the boy I'm supposed to love.

I swallow, then break away, shattering the moment. Confused, I pull him close again, burying my forehead against his shoulder, and it's then I feel the quiet shudder. I hear it in his voice, even as he tries to pretend I haven't sunk another dagger into his heart.

"Hey," he whispers. "It's okay. I didn't mean to—"

"I'm sorry," I say, my voice two seconds from cracking. "It's just . . . I'm just a little worn out."

"I know. Be quiet. Go to sleep."

He shifts, and puts some space between us. We both pretend it's okay, that the distance doesn't matter.

"You don't have to stay." I pull a blanket to my chin.

Bear doesn't answer. As we sit shoulder to shoulder, I silence the voices in my head and in my heart, and focus on the chatter of the feeds. I pretend to watch the exhibition recap as talking heads parse and analyze the gory details of my first defeat.

". . . You certainly called it, Jack. One week on the circuit, and the other teams have already put the new kid in her place. After tonight, you have to wonder if Phoenix Vanguard can ever live up to all the hype . . ."

CHAPTER TWENTY-THREE

THE MORNING-AFTER MOOD IN THE HANGAR IS PRETTY somber, like it's not just me who tossed and turned all night. Although everyone's going about their usual business, running tire tests and detailing rigs, they might as well be tiptoeing around me. Sure, I get a few smiles and tired "good mornings," but I can read the hush. My less than stellar debut has done nothing for morale. And I don't even want to think about how scorched Benroyal must be right now.

After sitting behind the wheel for a new six-point harness adjustment, there's nothing for me to do until Gil is ready to put me back on the practice track. Right now, his office door is closed—Goose has arrived, and I'm pretty sure they're having it out.

Cash and Bear are busy, hauling extra fuel for Banjo. So, flex in hand, I lean against the far wall. I check for messages and scroll through feeds, anxious for a sign that Abasi's doing something—anything—about Benroyal's black sap empire. I know I can't expect a lone politician to perform miracles overnight, but even so, there are no rumors of an investigation. On the feeds, there's nothing but more rumblings about Cyanese terrorist groups hiding out in the Pearl Strand.

Hold tight, Mary'd said. Wait and see. I didn't honor my promise and now I'm just praying my family won't pay for it.

"Attention! Attention!" Goose's thick accent cuts through the murmur in the hangar. With Gil at his side, he stalks to the center of the room and stands in front of my rig. After waving all of us over, he silences my crew. "Mr. Benroyal has made a few adjustments to Miss Vanguard's schedule. In order to better support our new driver, he has canceled all her public appearances for the next few days. That is to say—"

"What that means, boys," Gil interrupts, pacing like an IP sergeant inspecting field troops, "is that you'd all better clear your schedules and gear up to win. Until the next race, it's going to be sixteen-hour days and short suppers with no time to spare. And anyone who wants to whine about it, you

217

can call your momma and tell her I've got you degreasing parts and sweeping up for the rest of the season."

No one else says a word. Not a single groan. The only sound is the hustle of footsteps as people get back to work. Satisfied, Goose leaves. When Gil starts to follow, I grab his arm. "They're all going to hate me now," I say. "For losing and for doubling their work."

Gil grins so easily, sidestepping like there's no reason to panic. "C'mon back to my office."

Gil's space is more modest than it should be, a small room tucked behind the far end of the hangar. Even here, the sharp, oily tang of fuel sap hangs in the air. The photos on his wall screens crowd and overlap, tilted at odd angles—if I squint, the effect is old-fashioned, like the walls are actually papered over with a thousand circuit memories. Pit rosters. Stat sheets. Victory shots.

There are so many of my father.

Gil touches one of them, a promo for my dad's last race, the treacherous mountain rally on Cyan-Bisera. Out front, my dad leans against the hood of his emerald rig. Behind him, the horizon's dusk-purpled summit.

"I knew your daddy," Gil says.

I don't even try to play it cool. "How'd you know?"

"Please." Gil snorts. "That Vanguard nonsense is strictly for tourists. I know why you're here. Benroyal's smart. Of course he'd want the next Van Zant. And even if I hadn't been briefed on your bloodline, I'd have figured it out. Benny Eno flexed over enough footage—you drive just like your dad. Fierce and a little foolish. But it works."

"Benny sold me out?" I blurt, too scorched to control a gasp.

He huffs a little, like he's disappointed I hadn't caught on more quickly. "I wouldn't call it that. Call it business. Survival. You think things would've ended well for him— or for you—if he'd tried to resist? This way, Benny gets to keep his garage, I get a scrawny little thing bursting with raw, reckless talent. And you get to win."

"Except I've already lost."

"You didn't let me finish," he says, sidestepping again. "I'm the one who scouted your dad. Back in '69, he'd just started racing cars. You know those slow-start, smoke-belching junkers that passed for rigs on Earth?"

I nod. My father used to show me pictures. The cars were small and fragile-looking, yet much less sleek than the vehicles we race.

"See, I'm the one who brought Tommy from Earth to Castra in the first place," Gil says. "Back when you could still get off that forsaken rock."

"But you weren't on his team. I thought you crewed for—"

"Yamada-Maddox. Yeah, I did. It was good, a lot of early wins. Magnus Shirkey raced for me and brought home three Corporate Cups. But I scouted for everybody back then. Sport was different. Tommy signed on just in time to watch everything change."

Gil's talking, but it's Benny I hear. How many times have I heard him rant about the old days, when he crewed "real" rallies? About the sellout drift, the way the circuit evolved from a breakneck rush into a stockholder's game?

"Two real rallies," Gil fusses. "That's all we got left anymore. Used to be a race wasn't a race unless it was three days over a long stretch of unforgiving country. Drivers cutting through the old pioneer routes. Now it's nothing but arenas and chasing your own exhaust for the cameras. Your daddy hated those oval courses as much as I do."

I nod. He did. I've seen every one of his old interviews a thousand times. Mouthed off about the round and round tracks every chance he could.

"You hate 'em too, don't you, spitfire?"

"What happened to him?" I ask.

He cuts me off, palms raised. "You're hoping I've got answers, but I don't. Sure, I watched him tote you to every event, but I can't pretend we were ever that close. Not really. Never could understand why a man would walk away like that." He is lost for a moment, as if staring right through the screens.

I was too young to remember, and it's a strange thing to watch him wonder. I hadn't let myself do it for a long time. Seemed pointless, like questioning something that's always been. The desert is hot. The moon shines at midnight. My dad is gone. But lately, I've been brooding over it more and more.

Gil turns and looks me straight in the eye. "What really gets me, a man like your daddy—winning every race, raking it all in for Sixers? For the life of me, I can't figure out why they'd let him walk away at all."

I wince. The sting of anger. It's a needle-prick stab in the throat. I know what Gil's implying—that my father didn't just leave, that he was somehow pushed out or eliminated. But am I ready to believe that? That some corporate engineered his "disappearance" for failing to perform? Or more likely, for failing to lose?

Yes. I am. I live in a world where assets are acquired and liquidated every day. Suddenly, I don't want to be in this room anymore, with all these pictures on the wall. "Was there something else you wanted to talk to me about?"

Gil stiffens up a little. I've yanked him back into the present. "Benroyal pulled your bid for the Biseran mountain rally. You'll still get a little point-to-point experience at the end of the season, but you're looking at nothing but round and round for the duration."

I don't answer because I know the score. I didn't place well in the exhibition, and Benroyal would sooner pull me than let me embarrass him during the biggest prestige race of the year. I won't get to compete off-planet. Not this year.

"You got anything to say about that? You just going to lie down and give up your bid?"

I know Gil's trying to provoke me so I'll work harder to win. Of course I hate losing. But for the first time, my will to compete falters. Everything that's happened in the week since signing my contract. Benroyal's secret game. James's constant scolding. Now my father. How can I make myself score for these liars?

When I don't answer, Gil shakes his head and whistles through gap teeth. "You said the crew's gonna hate you now for losing. But that ain't hardly the truth, is it? You didn't lose. We lost. And they'll only hate you if you work half as hard. Give it everything you've got, and they will too."

Yes. Gil, Banjo, all of them. Even Cash. Win or lose, like it or not, our fates are bound together now. I can't forget that. I open my mouth to promise my best, but Gil's already walking away.

"Don't tell me, spitfire girl. Show me. See you on the track in twenty minutes."

Back in the hangar, I look around. Bear is still moving fuel. Far behind him, Cash looks over his shoulder and then quickly slips into the exit corridor. I can't believe he'd bail at a time like this.

I don't want to draw Bear's attention, so I skirt the edge of the shop. I catch up with Cash before he can turn the last corner. "Where are you going?"

"I have business on the south side. I'll be back for evening practice."

He opens the last door and steps outside. I have to double-time it to keep up, and I can hardly breathe in the noon-day heat. "What kind of business? How can you just leave when we're so far behind?"

"I need to take care of something."

He's not even flustered that I caught him slinking away, and his noncommittal shrug completely sets me off. The anger makes me careless. I choose the worst words, the ones I know will twist the knife. "Too long since you've been at the tables? That's the real reason you're leaving, isn't it, so you can sneak off to your little sap house and gamble on Benroyal credit?"

"Look, Vanguard—"

I shut him down. "No, you look. How many guards will it take to bring you back in?"

That scorches him well enough. He gets right up in my exhaust. "Right. You'd like to think that, wouldn't you? Makes it that much easier to write me off, doesn't it? Just keep pushing me away, Phee."

"Who's pushing who here? You're the one who's running off when your crew needs you."

"I realize that, but I can't—"

"When I need you."

"I know." He stops himself, clamping his jaw. "I'm sorry. But there are things about me you don't have the first clue about. The circuit isn't my whole life. I'm not here just to—"

I see it in his eyes. He's arguing with himself as much as with me. I watch him struggle, and it's like looking in a mirror. Underneath it all, we're both divided and volatile. At war with ourselves half the time.

"Talk to me," I beg. "Where are you going?"

"I can't tell you. And it wouldn't matter even if I could. You'd still think I'm just off to gamble and waste your time. But I'm not. I'm not how the feeds make me out, Phee. You don't understand what it's like for me to live here." His voice wavers, and I know he's about to lose control.

Cash takes me by the arms. The move is rough and desperate, but if I shake him off, he'll be the one to break. "Every day, I wake up knowing that my own brother helped Benroyal murder my father. He was a good king, Phee. My father never stopped trying to protect my people, and he died for it. Knifed in the back for control of the Gap. A million more barrels of sap. That's all his life was worth. I won't ever let that go. I can't. I just want . . ."

"Tell me," I whisper.

"I want you and me . . . everyone to stop living off scraps. To stop accepting the only choices given. I'm tired of living in fear. It's exhausting, and I don't want to do it anymore. I just want—"

I finish for him. "A real life."

He nods. "A new world."

The words finally sink in, tasting black and hopeless. Now I'm the one who's shaking. Pulling away, I retreat— an inch, a mile. "Impossible. We can never have that, Cash. Never. Not as long as we live in the Spire. It hurts too much to dream."

He lets go. "I guess that's the difference between you and me. I don't want to live without that ache. I have to believe in impossible things."

Before I can reply, I hear the hum of an engine. An Onyx pulls into the lot and heads straight for us. Cash waves it over. Through the windshield, I spy Hank driving, with three other guards riding inside. Their caps are pulled low enough to shadow their faces, but I'm pretty sure two

of them are Biseran, and the guy in the back looks . . .
Cyanese? Which makes no sense. I can't imagine Benroyal
would hire these guys as security.

"I have to go," Cash says, stalking toward the rig. "I'm
sorry."

"Where are you going? Who are they?"

"I told you. I can't talk about this right now."

When he reaches for the passenger-side door, I slide
between him and the rig. "Don't do this, Cash. You can't
just run off and leave me hanging."

One of the men inside the Onyx rolls down a window
and raises an eyebrow at Cash. "C'mon, let's blaze already."

"Just a minute." Cash turns to me. "People are counting
on me. For sun's sake, trust me. Just this once. Please."

Before I have the chance to argue, my flex buzzes. It's
Bear.

BL: YOUR RIG'S ON THE STARTING LINE. GIL'S WAITING.
WHERE ARE YOU???

Rust. I can't stay out here and hold Cash hostage, no matter how much I'd like to blow off practice to get answers.
People are counting on me too.

I move out of his way, but he stops me. No taunt or
smirk in his eyes. No more walls, only honest truce. "I'll
make you a deal, Vanguard," he says. "Cover for me, then I
swear I'll tell you everything."

CHAPTER TWENTY-FOUR

AFTERNOON PRACTICE IS BRUTAL. FOR THREE HOURS, I DRIVE with my foot to the floor, my jaw set, my mind spinning through every backstretch turn. Cash is gone, but Bear and I are *perfect*. He's all business today, focused and confident, while I punish my rig, tearing through routes like my hair's on fire.

Turns out when I'm on edge, we light up the scoreboard. I finish first, beating out every virtual rival, but I couldn't care less. I'm mad and confused, but most of all, worried about Cash.

I roar into the pit stall for the last time. Bear grins at me and stops for a triumphant high five before he hits the showers. After he leaves, I rip off my helmet and pull Goose aside. "Take me to the sap house."

"What? You have practice again in two hours. Until then, you need to rest."

"Get a rig, call a guard, whatever," I say. "But get me over there. I need to see Cash. Please, Auguste."

He frowns, deliberates for a moment. "We'll pick him up? Bring him back for practice?"

"That's the idea."

"All right, ma chère. But if you tell Gil I let—"

"Thank you, Auguste. Thank you, I mean it."

"Quick, quick. Let's go. You can thank me later," he says. "When you make it back on time."

As usual, it doesn't take much to get Auguste to stay in the Onyx, but I can tell he's mortified I'm going in alone. I stalk through the chophouse and burst into the noisy kitchen. Sure, I get a few double-takes. I'm pretty certain it's not every day a girl passes by in a Benroyal zip-front, still sweaty and all geared up. I head straight for the back-room entrance, but this time it's locked.

I give the handle a shake, then pound on the door. No answer.

"Cash, I know you're back there," I shout, slamming my fist. "Let me in or I'll—"

A bolt snaps. The door opens six inches. I spy a face. Hank. He stares at me.

"Open up," I say, wedging my foot in the crack.

"You shouldn't be here."

"Neither should you. Open up."

"Sorry. No can do." He smiles, as if he's enjoying his gig as bodyguard-turned-bouncer a little too much. He is different here, every trace of "yes, ma'am" is gone.

I roll my eyes. "Look. I'm not going anywhere. Either you let me in, or I go back to the rig and tell Auguste that maybe he should go ahead and let someone at the Spire know that His Highness is down here, doing who knows—"

Hank yanks me inside and bolts the door behind us. He drags me down the darkened hallway. "Hey," I say. "You don't have to—"

He shakes his head, unrelenting in his pace, half mumbling the whole way. "I keep telling him you're more trouble than you're worth. You just had to come down here. I swear, he's going to kill me when he finds out I let you in."

"We'll see about that," I say as he practically carries me through the last doorway. Unceremoniously, he lets go and I stumble inside. By the time I look up, the crowded room is already hushed. From around the table, a dozen faces stare back.

Standing in the middle, leaning over a holographic map, not a stack of cards, is Cash. Too quickly, the Cyanese woman next to him swipes the tabletop clean. Some of the others take a step forward, but Cash stays them with a hand.

He gapes at me. "What are you doing here?"

Suddenly, my mouth goes dry. I hadn't exactly planned out what I was going to say once I got here, and I certainly don't know what the rust to do now that I've caught him, I don't know, planning a field trip? Presiding over the Castran Geographical Society? "I . . . Auguste and I," I sputter. "We're here to bring you back for practice."

I've seen Cash irritated before, but I've never seen him quite as scorched as he is now. I'm surprised he doesn't come straight across the table. Instead, he rounds the crowd and drags me back into the hall.

I shake him off, once, twice, but no, he's still all over me, steering us into another room. "What is with you and Hank? I think it would be great if you two would quit manhandling me!"

Inside the dim and empty space, he slams the door behind us. Alone, we stand toe to toe. "Oh really? Because here's what I'm thinking. I'm thinking I will personally toss you over my shoulder and carry you out like a sack of ochre-root if you ever sneak in here again."

"You wouldn't."

"Oh, I would," he says. "I can't believe you did this. You put me at risk coming down here unannounced."

"How is that, exactly? What are you doing down here?"

"I can't tell you." He paces. "I told James I wouldn't."

"Enough." He tries to tilt away from me, but I grab his arm and reel him back. "No more bull-sap, Cash. There are no cameras here. No guards or feedcasters or anyone else. It's just you and me, so you've run out of excuses. What the rust is going on?"

"You want the truth?" he taunts. "The truth is, every morning, I get up and pretend this is my life. I smile and bow and work the circuit like a good little prince. I let King Charlie put his boot on my neck, because all the while, I am sharpening the blade, waiting for the right moment to rise up and cut him down. I am a rebel and a spy, and I have been one for the last sixteen months and twenty-one days. I will never stop trying to avenge my father's murder. I will never stop until men like Benroyal are exposed. I will never stop fighting for my planet and yours. That is what is going on, Phee."

The shock of everything he's just said hits me like a body blow. When I look up at Cash, most of the anger in his eyes has drained away. "That's a lot to take in," I say quietly.

"I'm sorry." He has the nerve to almost smile. "But you kinda forced my hand."

I nod dumbly. And nod some more. I straighten up and

try to collect my wits. "So when you say rebel and spy, what does that mean, exactly?"

"It means I am actively supporting the rebellion against my brother's rule, and working against Benroyal by passing along information about his illegal black sap labs."

"Wait. You know about the labs?"

"Of course I know. How do you know about them?"

"I snuck into Benroyal's study and I saw what he's doing. Yesterday, at the race, I told Chamberman Abasi."

Cash frowns. "I wish you hadn't."

"Why?"

"Abasi can't do a thing. At least not yet. He's a good man, but your government's too far gone with every politician and soldier on Benroyal's payroll. You can't take King Charlie down from the outside right now. You have to beat him at his own game, from the inside. That's what we're trying to do, Phee. You thought I was coming here to gamble, but every time, I was really meeting allies, Castrans, Biseran, Cyanese, basically anyone who's sympathetic to the cause. And I'm also working with . . ." He stops himself, as if he's not sure I'm ready for this.

"Who?"

"Not all the Sixers are as bad as you think. Some of them despise Benroyal as much we do. James and—"

"Grace Yamada."

When he steps back, he's more than surprised. He's impressed. "How did you . . . Has she approached you?"

"No. But we've met. She helped me out once. Okay, maybe more than once. But how can you possibly trust a pair of Sixers, Cash? Maybe they're on board to cut down a rival, but you don't seriously think they'd be in this to do the right thing."

"You're wrong. James isn't like the others. We're working on something big."

"On what?"

"A huge circuit bet on the Biseran mountain rally. A double-cross that will cripple King Charlie and get me back on my home planet. My people need me, Phee. If I don't step up and fight, no one will. I've been wanting to tell you, but James wanted me to hang tight."

The door opens, and it's Hank. "Auguste is in the kitchen. I don't know how long I can stall him. You better get out there."

"This isn't over," I say to Cash. "If this is for real, I want in."

He nurses another half smile, this one a shade more devious. "Oh, this is for real, Vanguard. Win the next race, and I'll be begging for your help."

CHAPTER TWENTY-FIVE

I AM ALONE, STANDING IN AN AIR-CONDITIONED ROOM underneath Sand Ridge Speedway. Cash and Bear and the rest of the crew have done their best, working their exhausts off to get me here. This is it. The Sand Ridge 400. My first real series race.

After zipping into my gear, I stand and face the full-length mirror and mark the changes in my reflection. Grueling hours of physical conditioning have made me stronger and leaner than I've ever been in my life. I hardly look like a street rat anymore.

The last few days have been all practice, all the time, and with no extra time outside the Spire, I've been forced to focus on the circuit and nothing else. The endless laps have eased the restlessness, slaking my thirst for fuel-triggered speed, and now I hope I'm ready for whatever happens today.

Someone knocks on my door. "Come in."

It's Bear, dressed in the Benroyal crimson. Like the rest of the crew's, his uniform is the reverse image of mine— red zip-front, black stripe. He's carrying a huge arrangement of flowers, red and white poppies, tipped in gold. He finds a place for them on the already crowded counter.

"Who are those from?" I ask.

He shrugs. "Not sure. Just arrived. Auguste asked me to bring them down."

I peek at the flex tag in the crystalline vase, the one half hidden by leaves.

Good luck today. Amina looks forward to meeting you. Tomorrow's gala.

Best wishes, Toby

Shaken, I take a second look at the gaudy poppies. Abasi wants to talk, and I don't know whether I'm more relieved or terrified. Cash and I have been careful not to talk in the Spire, but if Benroyal finds out what he's up to or what I've already told Abasi, the Larssens are at risk. I can't afford to lose my family. Today I'd better perform, and not just for James. I'd rusting better well give King Charlie every reason to trust me.

Misreading my nerves, Bear moves behind me and puts his hands on my shoulders. "It's time. You ready?"

I nod. "I hope so."

He tugs me closer, his strong arms encircling my waist. I inhale the crisp, clean scent of freshly scrubbed six-foot boy. "You and me, just like always," he says.

I don't answer. We've agreed to headset both Cash and Bear, but I can't help chasing this fear that soon I'll be caught between two voices. They are so different, with strengths that clash like bumper to steel. For now I have no choice. When the first flag drops, we'll have to make the best of it. I need them both.

"Let's go," I say.

His arms drop. I take in one last breath of chilled air on the way out the door.

After the elevator takes us up two levels, and the doors open, I feel the hum of the arena. The deep, relentless beat of drums vibrates through the sandstone risers. The anxious buzz of one hundred thousand fans washes over me. By the time Bear and I reach the blinding sunlit peak, the sound crowds out almost everything else.

I am afraid. I am ecstatic. I'm alive and ready to drink everything in. The light, the heat, the roar—it's all my adrenaline elixir.

Bear takes my hand for a moment before walking away.

He must join Cash on the pacers' deck and I must stand beside my rivals. I make my way to the drivers' stall and take my place in the lineup so every feed can get one last shot of us all together. I stand between Coop Winfield and Bobby Banks Jr. Coop is handsome for his age, matching his rig in head-to-toe silver.

That's more than I can say for smart-mouthed, scowling Banks, who always wears mud-colored gear for Agritech. It's a shame looks don't count for laps. If they did, Banks wouldn't be so high in the standings. I'll still have to watch out for Marcus Fallon too. He's preening at the end of the row, smoothing his hands over his deep blue TransCorp jumpsuit before giving everyone a thumbs-up.

Last to arrive, even after me, is stupid, arrogant Maxwell Courant. I'm not supposed to scowl in front of the cameras, but I make sure he hears the snarl under my smile. His rig's got a new paint scheme. The purple AltaGen car now has flames and dragons and lightning bolts. It's got to be the most ridiculous thing I've ever seen.

There are many others; I know every name and face, every corporate logo. I could rattle off their stats, but the numbers don't matter now. It's time to show them I'm not still that nothing girl who's easy to beat. When the reporters ask if I'm nervous, I say I don't care about the outcome, that I'm just happy to get my chance. Of course, my answer is a lie.

I have to place today.

After the last photos are taken, we scatter. I jog over to my crew. As I grab my helmet, Gil walks over and puts his arm around me. "I don't want you to get killed out there or anything." He lifts my chin and looks me straight in the eye. "But this time you've got to tear it up, kid. You have to."

I nod, but I'm already too lit up and edgy to say anything more. I jump into my rig. Once I get settled in and start my engine, the jitters fade. It's always like this. I always feel wired, too punch drunk to tie my own shoes right before a race. But the second I'm strapped into the six-point, when they connect fresh air hoses to my helmet and suit, it's like I fall into a stone-cold, chilled zone. Suddenly, I'm steady, and nothing exists beyond the growl of my engine and the sound of my heartbeat in my ears. There is the road and my rig, but nothing else.

Overhead, open-air sky bridges cross over the track at various points. Each bridge is two levels. The top deck is the pacers' domain. Cash and Bear are both somewhere up there—their eagle eyes will probably be my saving grace at more than one point in this three-hour race. Below the pacers, on the lower decks, the most daring, hardcore fans lean over the railing to watch the spectacle below. Circuit fans call this level the spark zone. When there's a serious smashup on the track, it's not uncommon for debris to fly up and take someone out.

Finally, the drums stop beating and the announcer's voice fills the speedway. When he calls my name, my likeness flashes across the flex boards and I can't help but savor the crowd's response. They thunder and howl and stomp their feet, just as they would for any other circuit driver. I swallow hard, tasting the moment, so hot and sharp and sweet. I can almost believe I belong here.

Right now, maybe I want to.

We roll onto the track and take our positions. By some miracle, I managed to take second in the qualifiers. My fastest lap scores me the outside pole, the outside end of the first row. Banks, to no one's surprise, took the pole position, opposite me on the inside of the track. Winfield is right behind me. Unfortunately, Courant is too.

I hate starting out near the wall. Somehow, I'll have to figure out a way to move inside or there will be trouble. I know Maxwell will be gunning to smash me up.

The pace rig leads us around the track for one warm-up lap. The screens mark the climb of RPMs, but it feels like we're crawling.

Everything I've done in my life has led to this day, this hour, this moment. We round the last turn, the front stretch looms before me. I take a deep breath and wait for the green flag. The announcer rallies the crowd. I hear the roar of one hundred thousand fans and a dozen engines.

Let's go . . . let's go . . . let's go . . . The flag drops and I punch the accelerator. We're off, flying up the track. The scream of my engine resurrects me. I'm slammed against the seat; every cell in my body wakes and sings with forward movement.

Within seconds, all the rigs are pushing hard. This time I know what to expect, and I rip forward before they can pin me down. We're snapping at each other's heels at maximum speeds. Banks and I are still out front, holding back the tide of rivals. The intensity is like nothing I've ever known.

"You hanging in there?" Bear asks.

I don't answer. I need to get my bearings first before I can run my mouth. There's so much going on, and everything is a series of blurs and turns. It takes every bit of my attention to keep all four tires on the road.

"Looking good, Phee," Cash says. "Stay loose, I'll find you an inside route."

"She needs to watch out for Winfield. If she clears low, he'll—"

"I've got Winfield," Cash says. "I know his pacer. Winfield will move over if she laps him."

"I'm right here, guys," I growl. "Don't talk over me."

They both chime in at the same time. "Sorry."

I roll my shoulders and settle in. Speed is not an issue. I just burned my first fuel trigger to stay out front, but now I have a bigger problem. Banks and Winfield and I are moving so fast, we're about to lap the pack. We're all going to get stuck behind the rest of the rigs.

And that gives Courant and Fallon a chance to catch up. I'm forced to brake hard as we hit the lock-jam horde of cars. Several cars have already formed draft lines to cut through the air, but there are plenty of them all over the track. I have to find a route, or I'm stuck sucking the exhaust of my slowest rivals again. Every time I try to nudge one way or another, a pack of steel jackals blocks my escape. Banks has made more progress—these same rigs move over for him. If I don't watch it, he'll break completely loose and leave me in the dust.

"Which way?" I shout through the headset.

"Go low, pass Balfour," Cash says. "If he doesn't move, give him a nudge."

Bear cuts in. "Wait. I see a hole. If she goes high, she can—"

"If she . . . if you go high, Phee," Cash corrects himself. "Kimbrough and Courant will force you into the wall. Don't do it."

Cash is right. I can't get sucked into the second- or third-turn mag wall. I pass Balfour. I don't make it past Kim-brough, but at least I was able to make a little headway. I'm going to have to battle for position an inch at a time, I guess.

This is going to be a long race.

Lucky for me, the first time I need to pit for fuel and new wheels, we get a caution flag. Halfway through the race, Balfour hits another rig and spins out of control. When the yellow flag slows everyone down to clean up the track, I race down the pit lane, tires scorched and smoking.

My crew is beyond fierce—in just under ten seconds, Dev gets my car off the ground, Corky and Josh haul the tires, and Billy and Arad put new ones on. At the same time, Banjo reloads my tank and triggers, locking in new ninety-pound sap cells without wasting a drop. Every move-ment is streamlined, synchronized, and choreographed. In the time it takes to suck in a deep breath, they've got me ready to run again.

Rust. The green flag just dropped, letting everyone regain top speeds. The rest of the cars still on the track roar past while I'm still in the pit stall. There goes my lead.

"All clear, all clear. Go, go, go!" Gil signals. And I'm off, punching the accelerator so hard I almost clip Winfield's back end as I screech back onto the track. My engine snarls as I push hard to catch up with the rest of the pack. When I get there, I'm stuck in the middle draft line of cars. Fallon and Banks are out front while Courant and three of his corporate cronies have me—and Winfield—boxed in on all sides.

I am so done eating Maxwell's exhaust. There's no way to go low. Nobody inside the track is going to let me in. We're down to the last critical laps of the race and if I don't make a move, I won't place at all today.

"Bonus target, high on the next turn," Bear says. "Extra points might save you if you don't finish first."

"Yeah," I shout. "I'm going for it!"

"Phee, wait," Cash says. "I'm working out a route, something with Winfield's pacer. Just hang in there for one more lap."

I don't have time for one more. I nudge Courant. His ugly rig coasts forward just enough to buy me room to pass. When I break high, I realize my mistake. Courant is in league with too many of these sap-holes. Banks moves over to block me, and the yellow rig behind me bumps my tail, driving me farther out. I clamp my jaw shut against the earsplitting shriek of metal on metal as I'm shoved against the wall. I swerve, but it's too late. I'm fully into the turn and magnetic forces are dragging me to a stop.

I yell through my headset, "Mother-rusting son of a—"

"Trigger!" Cash shouts back. "Now!"

I'm already on it. My fist punched the console before the words made it out of Cash's mouth. "You tell every one of those pacers up there that their slow-hauling drivers better move out of the way or I will smoke them into the ground!"

"Take it easy," Bear says. "Stay focused. Try moving on the—"

Cash interrupts. "No, stay in the middle. Next turn, go low. Winfield's got your back."

"Who says he won't leave her hanging out to dry?" Bear growls.

"He won't," Cash snaps. "I know what I'm talking about!"

I've hit my limit. The track's become a white-knuckle blur and my air hoses aren't working right. It's so scorching hot in here, I think the soles of my feet probably have second-degree burns. And if my pacers don't stop bickering, I'm going to explode.

I take Cash's advice and move toward the inside of the track. I'm able to pull up on Banks, and Winfield moves forward with me, absorbing the space on my right between me and Courant. We four are flying high, leading the pack.

Banks pulls a trigger, but I can't understand why he'd waste the burst. We have three laps to go and he's just going to rocket forward, only to get stuck behind the cars we've already lapped. Now Winfield and I are forced to burn a trigger too, just to battle for lead position.

Courant ducks behind us and we're all trapped at the tail of the slowest group again. Another lap. Two more to go. Every time I move one way or another, Courant and the rest shuffle and dance, pinning me in second place behind Banks. Maxwell makes his move and whips around me.

Cash and Bear argue about routes, and I can't take it anymore—my brain is stringing together the curse words I don't have time to scream. Time has run out. I've only got one more rusting lap. I could win this, if only Courant's gang weren't closed in on every side, all up in my exhaust.

I stare through the windshield. That's it. "I am not looking up the tailpipes of this purple clown car for one more second," I say.

I lurch forward, giving Courant a warning nudge. He surges forward, breaking from the pack. That's all I need to pass Banks and bust through the rest of the herd. I bump and bang against half a dozen cars—each bone-rattling scrape shoves one more out of the way. Once I clear the lagging horde, I quickly catch up to Maxwell, but he swerves on the second turn, blocking my attempt to take the lead.

I know Bear can read my mind. "Phee, don't do it . . ."

I wait until we're deep in the backstretch. The sky-bridged finish line is seconds away and I'm desperate to earn my place on victory lane. Old habits die hard. I reach for a mechanical trigger stick that isn't there. When I don't find it, I slam my fist against the console, launching two fuel triggers at once.

I'm the assassin's bullet again, and I've found my mark. My rig rockets against Courant, launching him against the straightaway wall. For him, this race is over. I grip the wheel, using muscles I never knew I had, grasping for the strength to keep Benroyal's precious rig on the road. I fishtail and spin sideways, barely recovering.

Stay on the track. Stay on the track. Stay on the track.

Finish line. I can't believe it. I've actually. . . .

Phee! Watch out! Stop!

I don't know if it's Cash's or Bear's or the one in my head, but the voice comes too late. I didn't see the jam of lapped cars leaving the track. I can't even slam on my brakes.

Smash. Tumble. Burn.

I hit hard, so hard and it hurts and I think . . . *yes, I'm going to die.*

CHAPTER TWENTY-SIX

I'M ON FIRE.

Smoke everywhere. I'm shattered and shaken, battered and stunned. I can't make sense of this input. I think my rig flipped, maybe once, maybe a thousand times. Blood is rushing to my head; I claw at the straps of my harness. What happened? Which way is up?

Which way is out?

Static fuzzes and pops in my ears and I don't know if it's just my ruined headset or my exploded skull. It's like I'm not really here, this isn't really happening.

I'm hanging upside down and I have to get out. I pummel my fists against my chest until I find the six-point's quick release. It's a fight for inches and gasps of air. Something slices through my suit and tears into my shoulder on the way out, but I'm feeling no pain. It takes me six lifetimes to crawl out and roll onto the scorched ground. After scraping my forearms across the track, I'm on my knees, rising up.

When I stand, the static gradually fades. I'm unsteady, close to blacking out. My blood rushes back too fast. One second I'm blind and the next, I'm squinting against the light. There's a ringing in my ears. Even though I can't hear anything, I can feel the roar from the stands; the rumble pulses through me. Sightless, I should fall, but the energy of the crowd nourishes me. My eyes adjust. I see the blur of faces, the flames on the track, the smoke billowing from my ruined rig. People surround me. My crew. Gil pushes through and shoulders my weight. I lean on him, limping away from the wreck. All the while, he's talking to me, but my brain isn't ready to process his questions.

"If I'd have just had . . . that wouldn't have happened if . . . I need . . ." I shout and sputter. "GET ME A REAL THROTTLE STICK, GIL!"

There must be a microphone in my face. The booming volume of my voice makes me stumble, falling against my crew. Even as it echoes, I hear the mob's answer. Thousands of voices. In the stands, they are calling my name, shouting and chanting and cheering for me.

PHOENIX. PHOENIX. PHOENIX. PHOENIX.

I'm alive and everything is burning bright. Everything is beautiful.

They vac me to Capitoline General North, the same hospital I woke up in after my arrest. When I begged the medics to let Bear or Cash ride along, they ignored me. The emergency crew wouldn't let anyone else on board, not even Goose. Although the flight rattled my teeth, I feel fine. I don't know why they're getting all dramatic. I wrecked. I rolled. I survived. End of story.

At least Benroyal hasn't come to check on me. Since I'm alive and not permanently disfigured, I guess he can't be bothered. I'm not complaining, either. He's just about the last person I want to see right now.

Dr. Menar, his personal physician, says I've got a mild concussion and a bruised rib. My whole backside—from tailbone to toes—is laced with heat rash, but that's not really an issue. Pretty much every driver overheats during the race, even when they don't flame out in a spectacular wreck. My car's Pallurium roll cage saved my limbs, and my fireproof gear saved my skin. I'm lucky I don't have serious burns. After they wrap my ribs, a soak in a tub of anti-gel will sort me out. I'll be as good as new.

The uni-vac crew already cut me out of my zip-front and now I'm forced to wear one of those horrible gowns again. I lie facedown on the exam table.

"Hold still," he says, looking me over.

I cuss him out when he cleans the deep gash on my left shoulder, the place the twisted metal cut when I crawled out of my ruined rig. He holds up a mirror to show me the ugly slash down the middle of my corporate tattoo. The Phoenix-winged crest is diagonally cut, completely sliced in two.

"This is our most serious problem," the doctor says. "I recommend an artificial graft. After six weeks, the skin will be ready for a new mark."

If King Charlie and his team of corporate vultures think I'm going to accept a patch of synthetic skin and a fresh brand, they're crazy. "Get out," I yell at Menar. "I don't care about the scar. Let Mary stitch me up."

I'm on the verge of bugging out when Goose arrives. He fusses and frets over me before pleading my case to Dr. Menar.

"Do as she asks. Today has been stressful enough. We will worry about the brand later."

Menar frowns. "I should check with—"

Auguste stiffens, then sniffs, as if he has caught a whiff

of something especially rank. "Mr. Benroyal does not wish to be bothered with such matters. I am in charge of Miss Vanguard's well-being. Are you deaf? Why are you still standing there? Go do as she asks!"

To my surprise, Menar shuffles off, and Goose leaves instructions with the hospital staff to attend to my every whim. Apparently, I'm a valuable asset and the powers that be will appease me as long it leaves me more docile. It's a load of sap, but I've never been more grateful to my manager.

Bear's mom arrives half an hour later to patch me up.

For the first time in weeks, we've got the chance to talk freely, but Mary is quiet and tense. A quick, careful embrace and she starts to gather what she needs to treat me. Somehow, I thought seeing her would ease the pain of this forced separation. Instead, I sense the gulf all the more. The cage's latch still holds. This close, I'm just reaching through the bars.

"Has there been any trouble? How are you? How's Hal?"

After holding her hands under the sterilizer panel, Mary swabs the area around the wound. "Better than you. We watched the live feed. Those last few seconds nearly gave Hal a heart attack. 'Would it kill her to be a little more careful?' he says."

"I'm sorry." Bracing for another scold, I change the subject. "I need to tell you something. About Chamberman Abasi."

"Abasi? He's been arrested." She leans over my shoulder to shoot it up with local anesthetic. Wasting no time, she grabs the threaded needle. "Today. Just before the race."

"What?" I cringe when she plunges under the skin. "How—"

"Rumor is he was gathering evidence for some kind of public inquiry against Benroyal. Next thing we know, he's charged with treason."

"I told him the truth. I met him at my first race, and he was going to help."

Mary flinches. Too many emotions flash over her face. Betrayal. Anger. Fear. Resignation.

"I'm sorry," I say. "I thought he could do something."

"He tried, I suppose." She takes a weary breath. Her lips pull into a taut line of concentration as she begins to stitch me up again. "But he might as well have signed his own death warrant."

The tears come fast, burning down my cheeks.

"It hurts. I know." Mary wipes them away with a scrap of sterile gauze. As if I'm crying over the cut on my shoulder and not the brutal slash of bad news.

"Listen to me," I say. "You have to leave Capitoline. Now. If he has Abasi, Benroyal will interrogate him until he finds out who betrayed him. There has to be someplace you can go."

Mary shakes her head. "Not without you. Not without my son."

"I can get Bear's contract canceled. It's my fault he got caught, but Benroyal will let him go if he thinks—"

As she pulls the last stitch, there's a ragged edge in her voice. "Don't take the blame for Bear's part in this. He made his choice, just as sure as you made yours. I wish Bear hadn't followed you, but that's the way it is. That's my son. He loves you, Phee, maybe more than anything." This time, it's her eyes that shine with tears. "It's no crime to love him differently." Finishing up, she splays her fingers under the sterilizer and the bloodstains instantly disappear. "You think I don't know both your hearts like the lines on these rough old hands? For years, I've watched your feelings lag behind his, never quite catching up. And you've done nothing but bury your head in the dunes, denying the difference. You have a right to choose your own road, Phee. Maybe it's high time you did."

"I never wanted to hurt him. I've been trying to spare him."

"I have to wonder, Phee," she says. "Who are you really sparing?"

My throat tightens. I'm desperate to throw my arms

around her again, but somehow I can't. In this fragile place, I know we'd both splinter and crack. "I'm afraid of so many things."

"You're stronger than you think, Phee. And you can't give up. The DP can't arrest everyone. Benroyal can't silence every voice. One day, you may find you're not his pawn after all."

"How can you believe that? I already signed my life away and I'm just—"

"I watched the end of that race. I saw the faces in the crowd," she says. "You're one of our own. At every turn, the Sixer drivers tried to box you in, but for one glorious moment, you broke loose. The people in the stands, they are battered and bruised, cornered every day by a powerful few. Today, if only for a few seconds, you gave them a taste of something different."

She comes around to face me, cupping my chin in her hand. "You made them roar."

I feel the ache that Cash holds on to, the heart-tug thread of impossible dreams. Before I can answer, Menar comes into the room to check on us. I'm told it's time for me to rest and that Mary's cab is waiting. After we say our good-byes, I watch her leave. I brood over everything she's said long after the pain in my shoulder fades.

CHAPTER TWENTY-SEVEN

BACK AT THE SPIRE, I SEE MY KEEPERS HAVE ALREADY BEEN here. In my master bath, I find a deep metal tub filled with anti-gel. Menar told me to soak for half an hour, and I'm not about to argue with that. Even if it can't numb the grief-sick ache in my bones, the clear goo will heal my burns and erase my bruises in no time.

Crazy how the different by-products of fuel sap can have such opposite effects. Black sap is every addict's favorite brain-burning fix, while pure anti-gel is every doctor's cooling remedy. No wonder everyone fights for control of the Gap. The treacherous canyon is the universe's largest reservoir of priceless ooze. We need the sap for energy, escape, and life.

Hal and Mary would have to scrape and save for a year

to afford this much anti-gel. I suppose I could thank Benroyal's refineries for the supply. Or I could curse him for hoarding it all for himself. And I'm definitely more the cursing type.

My flex blinks with a message from him. *Well done*, he texts. *You prove a valuable investment.* Digits, a parade of too many zeroes, flash below his words. I'm worth quite the hefty bonus today, and if he knows what I've done behind his back, he's not letting on. I scowl and toss the flex onto the nearest counter.

Before climbing into the tub, I strip down to my shorts and the compression wrap around my chest. The tight bandage makes an ugly tube top. Then I sink into the vat of soothing miracle sludge. The medicine seeps through my scorched skin and tired bones. The longer I sit, the more I edge toward sleep. I hadn't realized how exhausted I really am—the race and all its aftermath pushed me to the limit. Now I feel the downward slide, my pulse falls into a lazy rhythm.

A quiet knock. I'm so relaxed, it takes me a moment to remember how to speak. "Come in."

He opens the door. I don't have to turn around and look. I know it's him by the sound of his footsteps.

"They keep telling me you're okay and I need to let you rest, but I couldn't stay away," he says.

"It's all right, Bear. Honestly, I'm fine."

He kneels near the edge of the tub. "Are you? How bad is it?"

"It's nothing. A cut and a few bruises."

He sweeps my hair back and rests his hand at the nape of my neck while he looks at my shoulder. The anti-gel has done its job, chilling my skin. Bear's touch feels shockingly warm. I shiver.

"Did I hurt you?" he asks.

I shake my head. "You could never hurt me, Bear."

He stares off into space and doesn't answer for a long time. I'm not giving him the right answers.

"It scares me, Phee," he finally says. "You push so hard. It's like you're not afraid to die, like your life's not worth anything."

"It isn't."

"It is to me." He looks away again. I hear the choke in his voice. "One day you'll go too far and I'll lose you."

I can see it all over his face. Bear cares more deeply for me than anyone I've ever known. Running down the alleyways of Mercer Street, Bear wanted to shield me from every bully and every danger. The games we played, he always wanted to let me win.

I want to tell him he won't lose me, and that everything is fine, but all I can do is close my eyes and try not to lose it. He kneels, then kisses the skin above my stitches. The touch of his lips is feather light. I should welcome the tenderness, but instead I feel vulnerable and exposed. How can I tell him I see another face in my dreams? How can I tell him I'm falling fast?

Mary is right. I have been sparing myself, lying to hold him here and forcing him to play second-best. If it weren't for me, Bear would have a real chance at escape. He wouldn't be a prisoner in the Spire. I pivot and face him, my hands gripping the edge of the tub. The gel is non-stick, so it leaves no residue on the compression wrap or my bare skin. I suck in a breath as the air hits my back like an icy gust. It takes every bit of strength to look up into Bear's wide, anxious eyes, but I remember what Mary said to me. "I'm not the one for you." I shake my head slowly. "I'm not."

He slumps, falling on his heels. "That's not true."

I climb out of the tub and pull on a robe. This will destroy us. If he cannot be more than he is to me now, I will lose him completely. I could be selfish and keep him close. I could give him just enough.

Never. I would die for Bear.

I have to tell him, even if it tears us apart. When he stands up, I step closer. "It is true, Bear. I don't deserve you. I don't."

I reach to touch his face, but he grabs my wrist and pulls me against him. There is so much strength just under the surface. I feel the tension as I brush against his body. It's taking every scrap of restraint he possesses to be gentle.

"No. Don't say that. I love you, Phee. Don't you understand?" He cradles my cheeks. "I love you. Every time you get in that rig, a part of me stops breathing. I can't stand the thought of you getting hurt. Every time I see him look at you, I can't take it. I want to . . ."

I pull away. "Bear, don't."

He tries to choke back angry tears, but it's useless, they slide down his face. Each one is an accusation, piercing me. "And every time I see you look at him, it kills me. Why don't you look at me that way? Why can't I be enough?"

We are both crying now. This time, it's me who reaches out. I wrap my arms around Bear and hold him tighter than ever before. "I'm sorry. It's me. I do love you. I love you so much it hurts. But it's not the same. We can't be together the way you want. You're my—"

He stiffens and pushes me away, holding me at arm's length. "I don't want to be your brother." Bringing me back, he fists his hands through my hair and kisses me hard, with all the fury he's been hiding inside. "I want this. Everything. All of you."

I'm shaking and confused and out of control. My pulse

is pounding out a million different signals and part of me despairs at what I'm giving up: a perfect, dazzling boy whose soul burns so bright, kindling only for me. But even now, my soul cries out for something else. "I can't," I manage. "I can't give you everything. I don't—"

"I know. That's why I have to leave."

"Bear, no, wait. Where are you going?"

He turns his back on me.

After he slams the door, I hear him collapse against the other side of it. Seconds later, I know he's gone, tearing through the apartment. When the front doors latch behind him, I stumble to the bed, clutching a pillow to muffle my sobs. He is not coming back.

CHAPTER TWENTY-EIGHT

BY SUNRISE, I'M STILL WOUND IN THE SAME SLEEPLESS KNOT.
The morning light and all its warmth . . . it hurts, and it's not
just the headache brewing behind my eyes. When I open
them, I see a message from Benroyal on the opposite flex wall.

> Barrett has requested a temporary release. As long
> as your performance is satisfactory, he is free from
> contractual obligation until further notice. I will take
> good care of the Larssens should you honor our
> agreement.

The pain in my head makes me crumple; I'm a rag
wrung out for the last drops. Bear is gone, maybe for good. I
pushed him away, and it's probably what Benroyal wanted
in the first place. I can read between the lines on the screen.
I know what King Charlie will do if I step out of line.
For Bear's sake—for Hal and Mary too—I'd better keep

winning. The message disappears and a new alert pops up.

An invitation blinks inside one square on a grid. I'm staring at a huge monthly calendar with too many appointments and scheduled appearances. I glance at the entries for today.

```
11:30 a.m. Follow-up exam, Benroyal Clinic
1:00 p.m. Race debrief (flex interface, sat-
ellite link)
4:30 p.m. Stylists arrive, hair and makeup
6:30 p.m. Gala photography, full crew, sculp-
ture garden
8:00 p.m. 50th Annual Grand Circuit Gala,
Anderssen Estate
```

According to the clock on the screen, it's already 10:38 a.m. and I so don't want to get out of bed today, let alone play dress-up and attend the party at James's house. I glance back at the schedule and curse my keepers. I will have to smile today, even though it hurts to breathe.

I hadn't noticed before, but there are several ribbon-wrapped boxes perched on the settee at the end of my bed. The Benroyal logo is embossed in gold on each lid. I scoot forward and eyeball each of the packages. Might as well get this out of the way. I sigh, ripping open the biggest box.

After pawing through sheets of sparkling gold tissue paper, I hold up the dress.

Ugh. I am so not this girl. This mountain of silk or taffeta or who-knows-what will bury me. The black, strapless bodice isn't too awful. It's plain at least. But the skirt. It's all crimson ruffles and flounces, and I think there's actually a rusting train on this thing. I heave the dress on the floor, cringing as it collapses into a monstrous heap, a bleeding stain on the snow-white rug.

I open the other boxes, but of course there are no alternate choices, only shoes and jewelry and some kind of pushup I-don't-know-what-to-call-it thing.

I stare down at the dress again. The ruffles on the gossamer skirt look flimsy enough. Forget the stylists. I'm going to have to simplify this look.

In my room, Penelope, the hair stylist, quietly works on me, but Bijan is crying. Actual tears.

When she sees what I did, how I tore up the dress, she bugs out. I ripped all the whisper-light flounces off and then when that wasn't enough, with a kitchen knife, I cut the bodice loose from the gown. Sure, I knew it would scorch her off, along with the rest of my keepers. That was kinda the whole point.

But now I almost feel bad. Bijan is devastated. She really believed in this dress, with all its false promises, now shredded and strewn on the floor. I can't help but both pity and despise her for it. Anyone who believes the right shoes and the perfect shade of silk make one girl worth more than another is a fool.

"This is a Mondrian!" she howls at me, holding up the shredded remnants of the skirt. "It's an original. Worth over ten thousand credits."

I smile at the loss. It's only an infinitesimal dent in Benroyal's fortune, but it's a start. "So now it's a Vanguard original," I say.

Penelope holds her breath and ducks behind the curtain of her thick auburn hair. Her grin is buttoned up, she's too afraid to laugh at my joke. But of course, I can't hold back. A snorty cackle escapes, nearly pushing her over the edge. She turns away, then digs through her makeup kit to find something to conceal the bruising around my stitches.

"I cannot believe you did this, Phoenix," Bijan hisses.

A new headache begins to flare. "Look. I'll still wear the black bustier thing. And I'll wear the shoes, even though I think the heels are overkill."

"But—"

"Look. You're lucky I'm wearing half your ugly dress."

Penelope tries to apply more blush to my cheeks, but I bat her hand away. I stalk to my bed and snatch up the pair of ruby satin shorts I found in my closet earlier. They're dressy and stiff, like something I might sport at a Sixer club. As if I'd ever go to one. "I'll wear these." I grin.

The color drains from Bijan's wrinkle-free face. She brings her wrist to her forehead. I've pushed her over the edge. I think she might actually faint.

Bijan sniffs. "We'll see about this. Wait until I tell Mr. Chevalier."

"You do that," I tell her. She can squawk at Goose all she wants. After yesterday's race, I'm pretty sure I can get away with wearing whatever I want. Victory is the best leverage.

This evening, the sculpture garden is crawling with Benroyal's people. There are photographers, lighting technicians, and, of course, a squad of bodyguards. When I show up, no one says a word or offers directions. Either the worker bees are ignoring me, or I'm not conspicuous enough to catch their notice.

I drift around, wondering if I missed something on the schedule entry. Maybe I got the time wrong. Only when I wander to the far eastern corner of the garden do I finally spy Goose and the rest of the entourage. My crew is all dressed up, standing between the tallest statues, two bone-pale obelisks casting long shadows at dusk.

I barely recognize my pit crew; these sharply dressed guys in ties and tailored suits look nothing like the sweaty, sap-sticky grunts I've come to know on the track. Before me, a sea of Benroyal crests. The familiar insignia is embroi-

dered on everyone's breast pocket. Gil always looks digni-
fied, of course, but I've never even seen Banjo without a
hat before tonight. It's hard to believe how well he and the
rest of the crew clean up. They all look pretty slick.

As I approach, Goose frowns. "Bijan tells me you did
not like the dress she chose."

"That's right." He'll get no apology from me.

He gives me the once-over, shakes his head disapprov-
ingly, then pulls a handkerchief from his jacket pocket. He
dabs the gilt-edged cloth against his forehead. "I hope your
ensemble is worth it, spitfire girl. It will be the talk of the
gala. Pray they don't skewer us on tonight's feeds."

As he leads me toward the rest of my team, the crowd
parts and I see Cash.

I stare at him, standing before me in clothes that are cut
so finely for his frame, in shades of darkness that match him
all too well. Everyone else wears a white shirt and a gold
tie under their black tuxedoes, but not Cash. Everything he
wears is black, even the ebony thread of Benroyal's mark,
save for the long slash of red silk knotted at his throat.

Part of me is too numb and broken and scarred, too
wounded to even speak to him, yet my feet keep moving
forward until we're face-to-face.

"You look more yourself tonight," Cash says.

I take a step back. I look down at myself, at my ridiculous heels, my skinny legs, and my ragged-edged bodice. I'm a counterfeit girl, posing in expensive scraps. Suddenly, I wish I'd hidden underneath Bijan's flouncy dress. I could have disappeared in the endless tiers and ruffles.

"I look like—"

"You look perfect," he says, offering his arm. "We match."

I nod and take hold of him, looping my arm through his. As we walk toward the gathering photographers, somehow, I sense Cash is right. And it has nothing to do with the colors we wear.

The annual circuit gala rotates among the Sixers—it's held at a different estate each year. James's home is a desert palace, a hulking villa carved from rosy sandstone. While the front end of the property faces a distant Capitoline skyline, the patios and pools on the other side of the house encroach on the barren foothills of the Sand Ridge Mountains.

As uniformed servants usher us through the massive front doors, the rest of my team scatters. The stone and timbered ballroom is packed. There are people—circuit crews and celebrities and Sixers—everywhere. Guards in black uniforms surround Castra's most powerful. The men laugh too loudly while the women twitch and smile, their hair piled just so, their curves artificially sculpted by corset or by knife. In all their finery, they are butterflies, pinned in place for tonight's display.

Cash snags a bloodred Biseran poppy from a center-piece on an entryway table and tucks the stem through the buttonhole on his lapel. On anyone else, the black-hearted flower would look pretentious. Tonight, on Cash, it's perfect.

"Are you all right?" he asks. "Want to find a quiet corner?"

Before I can answer, a spoon ringing against a glass silences the crowd. Heads turn. It's Prime Minister Prejean, the gray-haired puppet who signs anything the Sixers put in front of him. "Ladies and gentlemen," he says. "If I might have your attention, I'd like to make a toast."

A ripple of approval—raised glasses and scattered applause—moves through the room.

"Friends, I'm sure you've heard of Tobias Abasi's arrest. He'll soon stand trial for his crimes, of that you can be sure."

More applause.

"Thanks to the diligence of our Domestic Patrol"—his voice rises over the buzzing crowd—"Abasi's ties to terrorist groups have been brought to light at last. Even now his accomplices are being rooted out. I think we can all sleep more soundly, knowing that no sinister plots threaten us tonight. I ask you all to raise your glass to peace."

"To peace!" All around me, people are actually cheering. I can't tell if they are blind to all the lies or if they are one more part of the conspiracy. I'm not sure which possibility is more terrifying.

Another voice calls out for a second toast. I turn and wince at the smiling glint of teeth. Charles Benroyal pours another glass of champagne. "To prosperity!"

The mob repeats his cry.

In the cluster of faces, something else catches my eye. The sweep of long dark hair, a flash of pale skin. She's lucid and smiling tonight, no longer a wraith in the dark.

I freeze. How did I not see it before?

Her hair isn't wild anymore, but pulled up, revealing her delicate features. Despite her rail-thin frame, in the light, I recognize the wisp of a woman drowning in a bustled gown of emerald satin. She is so far away, but when she turns . . . the flicker of life in her eyes, the high cheekbones and the oval face. Long ago, a younger image of her was burned into my memory. She is Benroyal's wife.

And she is my mother.

I let go of Cash's hand and stumble forward, ready to plow my way to the other side of the room. I'm tripping up in these heels, so I claw at the straps and peel them off.

Several people are looking at me now. A servant with a tray of champagne touches his earpiece.

"Phee, wait," Cash says. "Don't." He reaches for me, but I dodge him.

I don't have time to explain myself. I have to get to her, right now. I'm just about to push my way into the ballroom when another hand grabs my wounded shoulder. The vise grip makes me wince.

"Let me go," I say, turning back. It's James, with a pair of tuxedoed henchmen at his heels.

"Phee, don't do this," he says. "Not here."

I ignore the warning and surge against his hold. "Let me go!"

It's no use. James's men flank me and quietly lift me an inch or two off the ground, just enough to sweep me away from the crowd.

When we reach the hallway, Cash rushes us, pulling them off. But when I try to spin away, he grabs my wrist.

"Let me go, Cash!"

"Fine." He hooks an arm around my waist. "Have it your way."

One quick signal from James, and the guards escort us down a side hallway, into another room. I writhe and curse, but no one follows us. No one seems to notice I've just been kidnapped.

CHAPTER TWENTY-NINE

A TWO-SECOND GLANCE AT THE WOOD-PANELED ROOM TELLS me this must be James's private office. The guards shut the door after we stumble in, but it's Cash who blocks it. He's the only thing between me and an exit, and I don't know whether to shove him away or bury my head in his chest.

"I have to see her." I choke.

Cash shakes his head, then closes in until our foreheads touch. "You're fearless, Phee. But you're not invincible."

I pull away the second I see James. All the anger comes rushing back.

"I can explain, Phee," he says. "Just calm down and hear me out."

"I'll calm down when you call off your dogs."

James dismisses the guards. As soon as they exit, I lunge at him, but Cash intervenes again. This time he doesn't reach for me, only stands in my way. "Listen. It's okay. I'm here. I'm on your side."

It's his calm that reaches me. My fingertips curl against the smooth lapel of his coat, and when I look down, I realize—all this struggle, and he carried my shoes. I'd like to disappear in his protective shadow, but he can't help me right now. I need to face this myself.

"Cash, would you excuse us for a moment?" James asks calmly. "I need a word with my niece."

When Cash looks at me, all I can manage is a shaky half nod. He steps into the hall and closes the door. James paces the floor, saying nothing.

"Tell me what happened to my mother," I spit.

"I'm sorry."

"I don't want your apology. I want the truth."

Finally, his eyes flash just as hot. "You don't want the truth. You want a fairy tale. You want me to tell you everything? This one doesn't end well."

"My parents—"

He cuts me off. "Once there was a heartless, selfish girl who had everything and nothing. She promised to marry a wicked king, but someone else came along and opened her eyes, if only for a season. She fell in love with a reckless boy from Earth and followed him along the circuit." He mocks, and I can't look at him. Not when his eyes are this brutal storm of shame and despair. "When she found out she was having his child, the boy begged her to stay and keep their daughter. But the wicked king lured the girl back with all the traps that once held her, money and dresses and a palace filled with black sap. And she became his wife, broken and lost, the queen of everything and nothing."

The tears slide down my face. "You're a monster. That's my mother."

"My sister, Joanna, is an addict. And Benroyal is the monster." The storm breaks and he sinks, as if he's carried the truth for so long, it's worn him down to the bones. "Your parents never had a chance."

"Benroyal—"

"He was never going to let her go."

"You're lying."

He shakes his head. "By the stars, I wish I was."

"My whole life, and I never . . . How could you hide this?"

"My sister's always been unruly, and my family was used to cleaning up after scandal. Her pregnancy, the relationship with your father, it was gossip and rumor, just another secret to manage. Joanna's on vacation. Up the coast. Nine months of excuses and then you didn't exist and neither did Tommy."

"She gave me up? To my father?"

He nods. "As for Benroyal, all he had to do was bide his time. Wait for her to come crawling back, hungry for the black sap he'd always given her before. He'd been supplying her with his own product for years, since she was nineteen and at his side at every party. When Tommy came along, again and again, he tried to get her to quit for good. He pleaded, but that was never going to happen. So he took you, the best part of her, the only thing he could."

I press the heels of my hands into my eyes, as if I could somehow erase this. A new headache begins to rage behind my temples.

"The circuit pulled your dad back to the track," James continues. "And King Charlie got what he wanted—my sister and her fortune. For a while, that was enough. Until Tommy's winning streak lasted too long. Every race, Benroyal came out the loser. Your father might as well have worn a target on his back."

The dots connect like points on a route. "He murdered my father."

James nods.

"How long have you known? About his black sap empire? About my mother and my father and everything else? How long have you known and done nothing?"

"I am doing something. Listen to me, Phee, I'm—"

I throw up a hand to shut him up, but a sickening flush

creeps over me. I cross the room and sag against the edge of James's desk. The tears keep coming and coming, and I'm too far gone to stop them now.

"I'm sorry," James says. "I didn't know about the hit on your dad until it was too late and Tommy was already dead. I did the only thing I could. I took you and made sure you'd be safe."

"You lied to me, James. All these years and you never . . ." The dry-heave gnaw in my gut radiates and expands, pulsing through me like an infection. I want to scream, to hurt someone, to make him feel just as terrible and used. "I hate you."

"I know."

I bury my head in my hands, digging my nails into my forehead much harder than I should. There's a vase on James's desk, inches from my right hip. It's all I can do not to lash out and throw it across the room.

"I want to talk to her. Right now." I move to bolt again. "And Benroyal is going to answer for all he's done."

When I shove James out the way, he grabs my wrists. I try to pry myself loose, but he'd sooner bruise himself than let me go. "If you cause a scene, if he finds out you know the truth, you know he'll have you arrested. He'll order your throat slit without thinking twice. But not before he's murdered everyone you care about. Bear, his parents. I'm not letting you back in that ballroom, not when a thousand times over I've vowed to keep you safe from Benroyal."

"Then I guess it's fair to say you failed. Arresting me for street racing and offering me his contract hasn't exactly kept him away."

His hands drop. "Phee, listen to me. I've told you, that wasn't my doing. The second Benroyal heard Tommy Van Zant's girl was actually winning on the streets, the snare was set. The ambush, the arrest, the hospital, it was all a game to put his mark on your shoulder so he could control you and keep you close. You keep finishing first, he wins. You die on the track, then all the better. Either way, he gets what he wants."

Of course. His world, his game. I should have known all along.

I think of that night, and the morning after when I woke up at CG North instead of in the south side hell-hole of Mercer St. Hospital. Even then, I wondered. Just not enough to get anywhere near the brutal truth: that Benroyal put me there to have his own people patch up his newest prize, his precious little driver. His step-daughter, no less. The thought brings another dry heave.

"Why go to all the trouble, James? I'm nothing to him. Nothing. Another obstacle, just like my father."

James takes off his glasses. "You are far from noth-ing. You are my sister's only child. My own blood. The sole heir to the second-largest fortune on three planets."

I blink and let that sink in. No. I can't be a Sixer. I can't hear this.

He grips my shoulders. "You need to process this. If something happens to us, when Joanna and I are gone, the estate, our shares, Locus Informatics, every Anderssen holding, Benroyal gets nothing. It all goes to you."

As I pull away, the shock bullets through me, leaving me more uncertain than I've ever been. Every word out of James's mouth robs something from me, breaking me down into someone else, a girl I don't want to know. "Benroyal's whole scheme was just to—"

James finishes my thought. "Keep you driving in circles, advancing his cause, winning for him while he manipulates your mother and spends your inheritance."

I swallow. I shouldn't be standing here. "Why didn't he just kill me?"

"Benroyal's no fool. It was a brilliant move to pick you up. Think about it, Phee. Yesterday's race was just a taste. Imagine the prestige and power that victory alone bought him. You're the perfect weapon, the upstart, the hard-luck renegade poised to win hearts and score stocks."

"And what does that say about you, James? You just stood by and watched."

"I protected you."

"Right. Did you whisk me away to your summer home? Pay a team of nannies to care for me and raise me as your own? No, you just threw me away."

"I did what I had to do, to keep you safe."

I stab a forefinger into his chest. "Bull-sap. You talk about Benroyal and all that he's done, but you're just another Sixer, no better than anyone in that ballroom. You're my uncle and you never even tried to help me, not when I was abandoned, not when I was given to the state."

"If I'd have kept you," he says, "Benroyal would've gone after you until you were dead or locked away like your mother. This was the price I paid to keep you alive, Phee. He let you go, he let me put you into the system and I thought it'd be enough, that as long as you didn't know your mother, he'd leave you alone."

"How could you possibly think he'd keep his word?"

"I . . . thought putting you outside Sixer society would make you invisible somehow, insignificant enough to escape his notice. I sealed your records. I couldn't erase your memory of your father, but I wiped every clue, every trace of gossip off the flex networks and the feeds until your mother's true identity was less than a rumor, forgotten by even the nursemaids who cared for you in that orphanage."

"But you were never there for me."

James is done listening to my accusations. "I watched and

I waited. I checked the Larssens' background the day you met Bear and he begged to take you home. I made sure their request to adopt you was fast-tracked and approved."

"Hal and Mary knew?"

He shakes his head. "They knew about Tommy. There was no getting around that. Not with a little brown-eyed girl still calling her daddy's name. But no one could know about my sister, not even you. Don't blame the Larssens. They were the one true thing in your life, and I'm glad they were the ones to take you in."

"Go to hell."

"You can curse me. Hate me. Whatever suits you. I accept that. But know that I did it all to give you a chance at a life of your own, far from Benroyal's reach."

"Trouble is, James, no one's out of his reach." I walk toward the door. "We both know that well enough."

"Phee, wait," James says.

"Don't worry, I won't betray you and get us all killed. I won't say a word. I just can't listen to you anymore."

I open the door, only to find Cash waiting outside.

He steps back in, closing it behind us. "Don't go out there like this. Please."

"You don't understand, Cash. I've lost everything. I never knew my mother, and now here she is. I was only five years old when my dad—"

"He murdered my father too."

I stop. Cash's pain is my own. Benroyal killed them both, and kept us both alive to use us. I feel the blood rushing to my temples; its pulse turns my grief into something angry and sharp.

I turn back and look at James. "I can't afford to trust another Sixer."

"I've spent years plotting against Benroyal," he snaps. "Thrown every resource I have into stopping him. You think the insurgents in the Gap are really 'terrorists'? Please. I'm the one funding the rebels, feeding them every bit of intel we can get our hands on, so they can burn down his labs and push him out of the Gap. I'm the one trying to help Cash's cause and get him back home. Go ahead and call me a selfish Sixer," James says. "But I'm not waiting around for the day Benroyal's crest replaces the stars on every Castran flag."

For the first time, I take a breath before mouthing off. I stand very still, letting the angry rattle and whir of my brain wind down into a quieter hum. I'm strangely in control by the time I finally speak again. "You should've told me from the start. We could've exposed him."

"No. You saw what happened to Abasi. Grace told me you got to him. Right now it's too dangerous on Castra for you and anyone else who knows. You go public here and you're dead before a single feed breaks the story. But we can outsmart him."

"How?"

"If Benroyal believes in you," James answers. "If you convince him to put you back in the Biseran mountain rally. If we get him to bet on you and put enough Locus shares on the line, we can take him. Losing my company will weaken him. It'll take the courts and the flex networks out of his control."

"But we have to get off this planet. I have to get back home," Cash pleads. "You can throw the mountain rally. We can both escape Benroyal, once and for all."

"I'll set it all up," James says. "I'll help you."

"What? Leave Castra for good?" I gape at him. "You think I'd leave my world behind—my whole family—just so you can win a bet and get your precious company back?"

"It's not like that," Cash says. "It's not about money. This is about taking a stand. My people are crying out for revolution, and Castra's on the brink of civil war. But there doesn't have to be bloodshed, Phee. This is our chance. We can take Benroyal down without firing a single shot."

There's a knock at the door. The sharp rap is loud enough to startle us all. James talks fast. "Go to the third floor, and wait for me in the Emerald Suite. The house is secure, but I don't want anyone getting suspicious."

"What about Benroyal's security detail?" Cash asks.

James turns on me. "Tell no one about any of this. Take a bottle of champagne. Pretend you're sneaking off together or something, so they won't ask any questions. I'll handle Auguste. You both should stay the night anyway. Tomorrow, we can talk more freely."

After we nod, James touches his hand to his heart and looks at Cash. "Bidram arras noc," he says.

I don't understand the words, but before I can say anything else, there's another knock. James crosses the room and opens the door. It's Hank.

"Mr. Anderssen? Mr. Benroyal would like to see you on the terrace. Alone."

After James follows Hank and clears out of the office, we wait a few minutes, just long enough to pull ourselves together. I lean against the desk and Cash kneels at my feet. Tenderly, like a storyfeed prince, he slips my heels back onto my feet and fastens the tiny buckles.

"What did he say to you before he left?" I ask. "Bidram . . . what was that?"

"It's Biseran. Very old, a half-forgotten greeting." Cash stands up, his hand brushing against my leg. A warm shiver rolls through me as fingers graze bare skin.

"Bidram arras noc. It translates as 'May life be full,' but

the words mean so much more. It's a signal used by the old palace guard. To say it means 'I am your friend,' 'I am on your side' . . . 'I stand with you.' "

I concentrate on the comforting shape of the words as Cash takes my hand and leads us into the hallway. The party is in full swing now. Twice as many Sixers have arrived in the last hour. As we push through them, Cash and I put on our game faces, false smiles and laughing eyes. With each step, I scan the crowd to search for my mother's face, but she's not here. Right now, it's all I can do not to break away and look for her. Despite everything, I need to see her again.

Here and there, Cash nods at a familiar face, another driver or a member of our team, but he keeps us on the periphery of the stone-walled ballroom. We pass a well-stocked bar and he grabs a bottle of champagne. His other arm slips around my waist and we move through the crowd.

On the third floor, we bump into a security guard from the Spire, the one who drove us here. "Can I assist you? The party is downstairs."

Cash shakes his head. "She's had a little too much to drink. I'm just babysitting."

"Let me take over, then." The guard makes a move, trying to pry me away and shoulder my weight. "I'll find

Mr. Chevalier. We'll make sure she gets home safely."

When I flinch and back away, he reaches for his earpiece. The motion rockets my pulse into the panic zone. I pretend I'm drunk, having the time of my life. I laugh too loud and tug on his arm. "We just need some time alone. You don't need to call anyone. Cash can take care of me, okay?"

He stares at us.

"It's fine," Cash says. "Ask James. He knows we're up here."

When Cash invokes my uncle's name, the guard straightens up. "Yes, Your Highness. Have a nice evening."

He turns to leave, but glances back one last time, just as Cash opens the doors to the Emerald Suite. He must have caught a split second of fear in my eyes. "Are you sure you're all right?"

I do the only thing I can think of. I wrap my arms around Cash and pull him against me. In the threshold, I kiss him so hard, it hurts.

When the guard finally turns away, I slam the doors behind us.

CHAPTER THIRTY

THE EMERALD SUITE IS NOTHING LIKE THE REST OF THE
house. Panels of green silk cover the walls. The space is
filled with dark wood furniture, antiques that are elegantly
carved and arranged just so. In the center of the room, a
four-poster bed is draped in a luxe, gilt-edged fabric, in
shades of emerald velvet and satin.

The guard is gone, the doors are shut. We're alone. Even
though I don't have to pretend anymore, I don't want to
stop.

And neither does Cash.

He crashes into me and we fall against the doors. I'm
rattled, shaken. Adrenaline still bullets through my veins,
but Cash's touch—his hands, his lips—makes my body forget everything else.

I push back, pulling off his jacket. The bottle of champagne drops from his hand and thumps, rolling on the carpet. While he claws at the knot of his tie, I fumble with the buttons of his shirt, tearing at the fabric, this flimsy barrier between us. Finally, he's untangled, his ruined clothes tossed aside.

I keep advancing, driving him to the bed. As we tumble onto the green, I roll over and pull him on top of me. My senses are heightened, drunk with input, but I still can't get enough. The salty taste of his throat. The sweet smell of his dark, tangled hair. The crush of his body against mine.

There is nothing beyond this. I want to close my fists around the moment. When I draw another kiss from his lips, he groans softly. I know we've reached a threshold. From here, there's no turning back.

I don't care anymore. Outside these doors, we are both watched. Our lives are controlled. We may never get this chance again.

When I reach for Cash's belt, my knuckles brush the bare skin below his navel. He shudders as I unfasten the buckle, but he stops me. "I . . . We . . . Not like this . . ."

He's so lost—his voice husky and filled with want. I know it takes all his strength to fight me off, and I can't figure out why he won't give in. When I reach for his belt again, he pulls my wrists away, rolling us onto our sides.

"You've been through so much tonight and I want you to be sure," he says. "This is real for me, Phee."

"Cash, I am sure," I lie.

"It feels like I'm taking advantage. You just lost Bear and—"

Bear. The sound of his name rushes through me like the wind on the dunes, bringing the sting back to my lids. I wonder how it's possible to be this hollowed out and still hurt. The feeling lingers and presses, a knife's-edge pain I need to escape. "I just . . ." I falter. "What if tomorrow—"

Cash silences me with the deepest kiss. When he pulls back, I glance away. If I look in those black-flame eyes again, I know I won't be able to stop myself from tearing through his defenses. Is he right? Am I out of my head, too shaken to think straight?

Maybe I don't want to be rational. Tonight, maybe I just want to lose my mind.

I'm about to pull him closer and wear him down, when my eyes focus on the opposite wall. There's an oil painting of a lady in emerald. The lavish train of her gown trails behind her. Her eyes aren't yet haunted, and her cheeks are still apple-bright with happiness. She is young and beautiful, and I am so angry now, so angry, I want to tear this portrait from the wall and rip it to shreds.

I bolt upright and reach for the vase of white poppies on the bedside table. I can't stop myself. I hurl it against the painting. I lean over Cash, shielding him from the shatter of delicate crystal, but he reacts just as quickly. He pulls me away from the edge of the bed.

"Phee, what happened?" he asks. "What is it?"

I curl into him. "That's my mother. I hate her. What she's become. I hate what Benroyal's done to me."

"I know."

"Why didn't you tell me, Cash? Why did you keep that from me?"

He holds me, kissing my temples and caressing my hair until I'm quiet and still, my teary rage melted. "I wanted to tell you. But James begged me to wait. He was certain you'd run off and confront Benroyal and get yourself killed, and I couldn't let him hurt you anymore."

"I don't think I can do this. I can't race for him. I won't just smile and pretend I don't know."

Cash sits up, resting on his elbow. "But what if that was the one thing you could do to stop him?"

"Benroyal pulled my bid."

"I have to find a way to get to Cyan-Bisera. My country needs me, Phee, and your circuit transport could be our ticket out. No more contracts. We could be free."

"Cash, if you turn on Benroyal, you're as good as dead."

"I can't stay here and watch Bisera suffer while I cower in his shadow."

"But if you go back home, your brother will hunt you down and—"

"I'm no safer here," he interrupts. "Every day, Benroyal gets a little closer to the truth. One way or another, he'll find out I've already betrayed him. And I can't turn my back on my home, Phee. My people are either rounded up to work in the mines or left starving, while my brother taxes them to death. You think I'd just stand by and watch my planet wither away, stripped and exploited, until there's nothing left to fight for? I've waited long enough. I have to go back. Come with me."

"What about my family?"

There's more urgency in his voice now than ever before. "Bring them. Take your family and get them out. James can't protect them here."

Cash tugs me closer. I want to believe. I want the chance to answer this longing for something more. My whole life, I've done nothing but thrash and rage, racing hard, but getting nowhere. I had no thoughts beyond myself. No faith in a greater cause. There was only survival. Now am I even capable of imagining a different world, a future in which I have another choice? How can I risk everything—my life, my family, home—for a dream that still feels so impossible?

Castra is all I have. It's all I've ever known.

"I can't lose you," Cash whispers. "Promise I won't have to."

I close my eyes, but I don't have an answer.

I wake up tangled around Cash. He's still deep asleep, sprawled underneath the coverlet of our bed in the Emerald Suite. I climb out of it as quietly as I can.

In the morning light, my improvised party threads feel all wrong. Right now, I'd kill for some casual clothes.

I steal Cash's black shirt and wrap it around me, but for shoes, I've only got the high heels. Barefoot, I'm careful on the way out of the room. I avoid the shattered vase, the withered white petals and broken shards. I creep through the hall and drift down three flights of stairs.

The house is hushed yet alive. Uniformed servants carry away the evidence of the gala. They scrub stone floors and sweep up all the half-empty glasses. Last night's guests—either they are all asleep or James has already chased them away.

A maid passes by with an armful of wine-stained tablecloths. "Excuse me," I say to her. "I'm looking for James."

"Mr. Anderssen takes his breakfast in the sunroom."

She's gone before I can ask her where that is. The sunroom must face the mountains, so I head for the opposite end of the place, hoping I'll run into it.

I'm just about to give up when I stumble into an alcove that's really a stairwell. Turns out there's another floor below the main level, built into the sloping back end of the property. I find James sitting at a giant flex table. The outside wall is one long seamless panel of glass. Early-morning light fills the space and transforms the Sand Ridge Mountains into molten summits of fire and gold. I can't call it breathtaking or spectacular; those words just aren't good enough.

"Morning, Phee," James says.

He doesn't match the view. I've never seen him with a hair out of place before, yet now his dark mop is a wild mess. He's still wearing last night's clothes, a wrinkled shirt and black pants. As I move closer, I see his gray eyes are bloodshot and underscored by dark circles.

"What happened to you?" I sit beside him.

Propping his elbows on the table, James cradles his head. "It's been a long night."

The flex glass is covered with screens and scattered papers. Maps, photographs, and documents bleed into each other, covering every inch of the tabletop. "I can see that. What is it?" I ask. "Benroyal?"

He laughs, but there's no humor in it. "It's always Benroyal."

"What did he want last night? Did he—"

"Benroyal came to me because he's unhappy with the attacks and the growing unrest in Capitoline. There've been too many labor riots, more hijacked transports, more bombings near the Gap, and of course, he has no idea that—"

"You're responsible," I finish.

He nods. "We've been busy. Grace launders the money, funnels it to the rebels, while Cash and I focus on intelligence leaks. We pass along everything we can to Cash's allies—to Castran protesters and Biseran loyalists and sometimes, even the Cyanese."

"Wait. You're in league with the Cyanese?"

"No. Forget everything you think you know. They are not the enemy. Cyan's been secretly arming Biseran rebels for years, almost since the end of the Thirty Years' War. Where do you think all my money goes?"

"So you're telling me decades of bad blood between Cyan and Bisera, and all is forgiven? The Cyanese are actually helping Cash's people?"

He shakes his head. "Never trust the feeds, Phee. That brand of history is a lie. Men like Benroyal have always been the real force behind the conflict. The war was nothing more than a distraction—the division made it all too easy for King Charlie to march his soldiers in to 'protect' the Gap. Can you imagine Cyan and Bisera as allies, two independent nations defending their own planet from the kind of corporations who'd like to mine their world to extinction?"

"How inconvenient."

"Exactly. Benroyal and his kind have always worked to keep the Cyanese and the Biseran at each other's throats. But he's gone too far."

"What did he say last night? Does he know what you and Cash have been doing?"

"No. He doesn't know we're involved. At least not yet. I've covered our tracks well enough for now. Benroyal came to me because he wants me to deal with the rebels and ferret out traitors. He's testing my loyalty. He wants me to take care of it."

I saw what happened to Toby Abasi. "So basically, this is your worst nightmare."

"We've always been careful, but somehow Benroyal's gotten a list of Cash's closest allies." He points to the rogue's gallery of faces displayed on the flex glass. I recognize several of the head shots, the men and women I saw in the back room of the south side chophouse.

James swipes the pictures, enlarging them. "These are

the men and women who've engineered every lab raid and miner's rescue. If they're rounded up and interrogated . . ."

He doesn't have to finish his sentence. I know what Benroyal will do with them. And what he'll do to Cash. "And Cash's older brother—"

"Prince Dakesh is no better. Given the chance, he'd like nothing better than to slit Cash's throat. The only thing stopping him is their mother's bargain. After the king's assassination, Queen Napoor agreed Cash would stay out of the way, living under Benroyal's protection. In return, Dak took control, which is what Benroyal wanted all along. Cash's brother is only too happy to turn a blind eye to what's going on in the Gap. As long as Benroyal keeps giving him a cut. Three percent of the drug trade. That's how cheaply he's bought."

My empty stomach roils. Am I so different? My price was even less. All it took was the chance to drive a fancy car. I slump back into my chair.

"We need your help," James says. "I didn't want to pull you in. I thought I could manage this without putting you at risk, but time is running out. It won't be long before Benroyal links the names on that list to Cash and finds out what you know. But Cash has friends on his planet who can protect you both. The Biseran rally is our only chance."

"What do you expect me to do?"

"I expect you to survive. To save Cash, and escape a life-time in the Spire. Benroyal assumes you'll keep winning, but you can cripple him. You can throw that race and hit him hard enough to hurt."

Outside the window, the sun rises over the Sand Ridge Mountains. The light burns through me. "But where would I go?" I ask. "Where would I live?"

"There are a hundred places to hide on Cyan-Bisera and thousands of allies to shelter you. The Cyanese Mountains. The Pearl Strand. Raupang. Manjor. You'll be safe there until things shake out here on Castra and Cash takes his father's throne."

"I'd be at the mercy of rebels I've never even met."

"You won't be at anyone's mercy. Not anymore. You'll live as you wish, free to take control of your inheritance and use it as you please. The future of Locus should be in your hands, not Benroyal's. I want you to think about that, Phee."

I've done nothing but think about it since last night, but I don't answer. I stare at the screens on James's table. Two maps overlap, one of Castra and one of Cyan Bisera. Castra's little more than sea foam and sand, but as I look, I feel the pang. It's a faded world he's asking me to give up, but it's the only one I've ever known.

I glance at the deeper hues on Cyan-Bisera. Rich green

and cobalt overshadow Castra's moon-bright shores. The glimmer of dawn touches the glass, and I stare into the shine until my eyes lose focus and the vision blurs. Two planets, superimposed, Benroyal's lion painted under each compass rose.

James touches my shoulder. "If Benroyal hunts down the contacts on that list, Cash will die. He'll be executed for treason."

I lean over the table, holding my head in my hands. "Tell me what I have to do."

Breakfast in the sunroom is quiet. Cash is still asleep, and all I can do is pick at my food as the sun climbs behind the flex glass wall. James has a full plate of castraberry tarts, but even he's only sipping coffee. He's on his third cup when the wall blinks, alerting him to an incoming transmission. When he accepts the link-up, the wall frosts into a giant screen, and Cooper Winfield appears.

Coop's smile is a mile wide. "Good morning, Miss Vanguard."

The familiar nervousness kicks in. I nod.

"Morning, Coop," James says. "This feed's secure. Phee and I are ready to talk business."

I nod once more. It's the press conference all over again. I can't seem to get my mouth to work around Winfield.

Coop looks at me. "James had a tempting proposition for me, but he wasn't sure if you'd be on board."

I hesitate. "On board with . . ."

Coop grins all the wider. "Sticking it to King Charlie, of course."

I nod a third time. Because right now, apparently, I'm pretty much incapable of doing anything else.

"Phee," James says. "What we'd like to talk about—"

Coop raises a hand and cuts in. "James here has half convinced me to finally incorporate, put my whole operation on the line against three percent of Locus stock. A big bet. Me against you in the Biseran rally. I win, Benroyal loses, James buys back the wagered shares from me at ten times the price, through Ms. Yamada, of course, and you walk away free and clear. Free and clear and far away, to hear James tell it. Winfield Mechanical survives to fight another day, and King Charlie takes a fall. I reckon that's about right?"

James nods. "That's right."

"Is that how you see it, Miss Vanguard? I hear you gave up your bid. You gonna be able to convince Benroyal to put you back in?"

I clear my throat, finally mustering the nerve to speak. "Yes, sir. I can. I will."

"That's all well and good, but what you're asking . . . it's a mighty big risk. How can I be sure this deal won't backfire on me? There'll be a dozen other rigs in that race, and I can't afford to just hand my company over."

"It's a straight-up wager. You against Phee. Whoever finishes first. Who actually places first and wins out is irrelevant. We've discussed this before. I'll sign a guarantee against your losses. I'm offering to pay you outright, the full value of your entire company, should something fall through. And that's not going to happen, Coop. Phee will not cross that finish line."

"All right," Coop answers. "Let's talk, then."

James nods. "Here's the deal, Coop. This is going to take more than a little finesse, and even then, I'm not sure Benroyal will go for it at all. It's a gamble, and the key is to make it seem like he's—"

"Driving the whole thing," Coop interrupts. "He's got to feel he's on top of things, all the time, during negotiations. I understand."

"Exactly." James takes a sip of coffee, then puts the cup aside. "So here's what I'm thinking. When your broker offers the bet, have him ask for ten percent of Benroyal Corp."

"Ten percent?" Coop actually snorts. "That's outrageous, and you don't even want his stock to begin with. Benroyal'll take a look at that offer and laugh."

"It is outrageous. That's the point. Right from the start, he'll think you're only interested in buying into his company. And the ten percent is just to throw him off. He knows Winfield Mechanical isn't worth more than four percent of Benroyal shares, no offense, but your offer will smell like blood in the water. He'll think Winfield Mechanical is desperate for credits."

Coop laughs. "I am desperate for credits. I can barely hold on to the company as it is. Why do you think I'm even considering this?"

"All the better." James takes off his frames and rubs at bloodshot eyes. "Desperate men make stupid deals. Let him think he's got the upper hand. If he senses he does, it'll make the bet irresistible. Of course, after you offer the ten percent, they'll refuse, and they'll probably offer something equally ridiculous, say, a half percent of Benroyal Corp. And that's when you ask for Locus. Tell him if you can't have the Benroyal shares you want, you won't settle for less than six percent of Locus."

"He won't give me that, either," Coop says. "James, you know he won't."

"He won't," James answers matter-of-factly. "He probably won't give you more than one percent. But try your luck, and ask for four."

"And if he doesn't go for it?" Coop asks.

"No deal if he won't bet at least three percent. And I need that three percent, Coop. I've got to have more shares than Benroyal."

"I understand," Coop says.

Listening to them talk stocks is like watching two dune-shadowed jackals ready to pounce. Only this time, I'm afraid for them—Benroyal is no unsuspecting prey. He's the one used to tearing his enemies apart, and I'm no match for him when it comes to shares and percentages. Outside my rig, I might as well be helpless. "What's my part in this?" I ask.

"The best part," James says. "After you get in that race, all you have to do is die."

CHAPTER THIRTY-ONE

HANK IS SILENT, STOIC AS I STAND IN THE ELEVATOR AND watch the numbers climb. The blinking floors on the glass. The ticking clock on my flex. Time. There's just not enough.

If I pull this off, Winfield will have to scramble to get Benroyal to take an impossibly desperate bet, and my crew will have six days to pack everything up for an off-planet race, the biggest rally of the season. And I will have a couple of hours to leave the Spire, slipping away to Mercer Street in order to convince Bear and his parents to leave everything behind.

Now I'm left with a handful of seconds before the elevator doors open. We arrive, and they part.

"After you, Miss Vanguard," Hank says.

A pair of Benroyal's men flank the lion on the penthouse doors.

"Miss Vanguard's here to see Mr. Benroyal," Hank says. "She has an appointment."

The first guard touches his earpiece. After listening for a moment, he flexes the doors open and waves me in.

"I'll wait for you here," Hank says.

The lock clicks behind me. It's quiet. No sign of my mother or the servants who keep this place pristine. Benroyal must prefer his antiques to anything made of flesh and blood.

I've already tucked my own little secret into the waistband of my cargoes. The stolen flex will be my contribution to Cash's cause. This morning, I cut open a seam to hide it. I've ignored the safe mode switch, but I've already flicked the data sync on. No idea how long it'll take for a sync to complete, but it's worth a try. The chance to hand over all Benroyal's secrets—gift-wrapped with a tiny card—is too much to resist.

I look through the arch. Sitting at his desk, he's waiting for me.

"You may come in, Miss Vanguard."

I step inside. One of his ancient books is open. I stare into the blue-flamed hearth, the wasted fuel perpetually burning.

"I was surprised you asked to see me," he says. "To what do I owe the pleasure?"

"Take care of my family," I say.

"I haven't forgotten our bargain. The Larssens are quite well, I hear."

"It's just that . . . the south side is a dangerous place. Maybe you could—"

"Ah, I see. You'd like me to set them up someplace more suitable, more in line with your new status, is that it? Perhaps a modest townhouse, north of the Mains?"

I nod.

"And why should I do that?"

I let go of all the tension in my body. I am wounded prey. "I'm asking. Please."

"Is that all? Surely you haven't come all this way only to beg trivial favors." He pushes his book aside and smiles indulgently, as if he were my best friend or benefactor. Or father. "I am at your service. Do tell. What is it that you really want, Miss Vanguard?"

I'm no good at pretending to break so easily, and somehow, today it's not what he wants. I switch tactics. "I want to win."

"You have won, Miss Vanguard. I'm very pleased with your triumph at Sand Ridge and I—"

"Put me in the mountain rally."

He blinks, shocked that I've interrupted. "I think not. The exhibition was embarrassing enough. Despite your last performance, I don't like the thought of a real circuit loss. You've proven a bit inconsistent, and I suspect you need more time."

"I can win the series and bring home the Corporate Cup. I need to show the others I can compete on any course. It should be my rig pulling into the winner's circle. Every time."

He pauses. My boasting seems to please him. There's a sliver of real satisfaction in his eyes now. "Ah, and Benroyal Corp at the top of every scoreboard."

I nod.

He stands up, then moves toward the biggest bank of screens. He swipes away today's feedcasts to uncover the images underneath, the ancient pictures that have become so familiar—the statues, the Colosseum. "You never went to school beyond the eight-year core, did you? No languages or ancient history?"

I shake my head.

"No matter. South Siders need not trouble themselves. Better to focus on the present." Another flash of teeth. His false smile turns sympathetic. "It's a shame, nonetheless. I've made it a point to study the past. From it, I've learned how predictable most of us are. . . . Look back through thousands of years and you'll see the same desires, the same weaknesses, the same paralyzing fears. Every great conqueror understood how to leverage those driving impulses. But to be truly exceptional, to build a lasting empire, the trick is not to overreach. Do you know what that means, Miss Vanguard?"

Slowly, I shake my head. I don't know how to play this game.

"It means you must never grasp at things you are not strong enough to hold. It is a lesson every good student of history must learn." He glances back at his books. "From Khed II of Cyan, I learned the limits of expansion. From Alexander the Great, strategy. But it's the Romans I admire the most. The emperors managed public relations so well."

Benroyal knows I'm ignorant and unschooled—at first, I'm sure all his talk is just to remind me. To make me fear him all the more. But when he steps closer . . . I read something else in his face. He craves approval. Allegiance. Admiration.

He slips an arm around my shoulder and I freeze. Terrified, I focus, desperate to control my breathing, the breakneck run of my pulse. When he speaks again, his silken voice rings like an invitation. Listen and learn, it seems to plead . . . welcome to the family.

"Most people require little more than pomp and pageantry—a few holidays, a glittering spectacle, a few vouchers for this or that. It's the illusion that matters."

"The distraction," I whisper.

"Inevitably, there are always the few who see through it. But I know well enough how to deal with that." He pulls up a newsfeed of Toby Abasi. The screen is muted, but I read the captions. Traitor. Terrorist. Call for Execution.

When my breath catches, Benroyal turns on me, tilting my chin to examine me. His touch breaks the spell. Quietly, something new claws its way through my anger and fear. Calm. Self-control. My skin burns and every part of me wants to tear him apart, but for once, I don't let my expression betray me. I can play this game. I can learn from you, Benroyal. My lips curl, and I wear his smile, grinning hard until I'm sure he's looking into his reflection.

His eyes flare and brighten. "Have no fear, Miss Vanguard. I know how to take care of my best assets. I gave your friend a generous leave—and I'm sure I could improve the Larssens' circumstances should you continue to win. You'd be quite satisfied with such an arrangement?"

"I'm happy to be the distraction. As long as it gets me what I want."

His smile widens. "Your attitude is much improved, Miss Vanguard. Perhaps I should let you go after all. I'd very much like this year's Corporate Cup."

In the elevator, Hank raises an eyebrow.

"We're in," I answer.

I don't dare pull out the stolen flex until I'm in the bathroom. Cloaked by steam from the shower, I hold the card and stare at the screen.

DATA SYNC: 91% COMPLETE

Shaking, I swipe through the file names. The sync captured hundreds of documents—maps, formulas, distribution routes, delivery schedules. Benroyal's whole black sap empire is compressed into raw data and images. And best of all, money. I spy the numbers to at least a dozen accounts, and it looks like King Charlie stashes most of his dirty profits anonymously, in banks in Manjor, Bisera's financial center. Makes sense. Every other criminal in the universe hides their credits there, so why shouldn't he?

I can't wait to see the look on James's face. He's going to love this.

After stuffing the flex back into its hiding place, I clean up and go back to my room. Two seconds later, I collapse on the bed. I'm getting another headache and my ears need to pop. I swear, these migraines are getting worse. A fuzzy crackle ebbs in and out, sometimes for a few seconds, other times for a minute or more. With my concussion, Dr.

Menar said I might have these symptoms, but part of me is afraid to mention them to anyone.

What if they pulled me from the next race?

I can't risk a last-minute detour before our escape, so I'll just have to ride this out. Palming my own flex, I text Bear.

PV: MEET ME TONIGHT. THE USUAL SPOT.

I wait for his reply. Half an hour. Nothing.

PV: PLEASE.

Ten more minutes drift by.

BL: *WHY?*

James made me swear not to breathe a word about our plans, so I can't tell Bear the truth, at least not via flex. Yet, if I can't come up with a rusting good reason, I know Bear won't see me. Not that I blame him. I've been nothing but heartbreak for him and his parents. Even so, I have to make him listen and pace me in the mountain rally. For a dozen years, the Larssens sheltered and cared for me. They protected me. And now, for the first time, I must protect them. I have to get them on the right transport next week.

I hate myself for playing on Bear's emotions. But I'd despise myself a million times more if I left him behind. I'll do whatever it takes to keep him safe, whether he likes it or not.

PV: PLEASE, BEAR. I NEED YOU.

BL: TONIGHT.

I wait at the deli at Picker's Grocery and take in everything that's familiar. I know this place, with its battered glass cases and scarred wooden tables. Crates of spices and pickled pale ochre-root are stacked against the walls. The butcher is busy, cleaving his last cuts for the day. The sound of his knife against the ancient block. A hundred times, I've heard its rhythm.

I lean against the counter until the butcher notices I'm ready to order. When Mr. Neeland looks up, it's as if he doesn't know me. Like I haven't stood in this same spot and ordered a number two special at least a hundred times. I look down at my new clothes—my tank, slim cargoes, and racing jacket. Do I really look so different? Has a little polish and gloss erased the girl who lived on Mercer Street?

Yes. To him, I'm a stranger who's wandered too far south of the Mains. I can tell by the wary pinch around his eyes. His crow's-feet are deep, sun-spotted crackles. "Can I help you?" he asks.

"Can I get a number two? Extra ochre-root, easy on the sauce?"

He nods. I reach for my flex, but pause as a shadow falls on the counter. I feel his presence behind me, the warmth looming over my shoulder. I'm afraid to turn around and see him again.

Bear greets Mr. Neeland and hands over his own flex. "Put this on my folks' account," he tells the butcher.

I don't argue. It's a matter of pride for Bear and I don't need to flaunt Benroyal's money around here anyway.

"And for you?" Mr. Neeland replies, wiping his hands on his apron. "What're you having, son?"

Bear shakes his head. "Nothing for me."

After Mr. Neeland swipes the charge against Bear's flex, he stuffs a sandwich and then hands over my order. I forgot to order something to drink, but it's too late. Mr. Neeland has already turned away, scuttling to the back room of the deli. I turn a bit, just enough to catch a sideways glance at Bear. I'm the one who called him here, but now I can't seem to face him at all.

"You want to sit down?" I ask.

He says nothing, but steps away and claims a seat at the table in the farthest corner of the room. It's late. No one else is eating here. I follow.

We sit across from each other. When I finally muster the courage to look up from my uneaten sandwich, he's staring at me.

"What do you want?" he asks.

Back at the Spire, I'd rehearsed my plea a dozen times. Now the words won't come. I look into his sunken blue eyes and forget everything. "I want you and your parents to come to the next race. I want you to be my pacer."

"Why?"

I've never seen him this way. Closed off. Flat. Empty. Bear isn't angry. He is drained and colorless. I used to look at him and see a quiet light, clear skies, and the first blaze of morning on the dunes. That light is gone, and I don't know what to do to bring it back any more than I know how to summon the sun.

"I need you. In the race."

"You have a pacer," he says. "Use Dradha."

I'm not sure why I ever thought I could avoid bringing Cash into this conversation—Bear isn't going to let me off the hook so easily. "I can't do this without you."

"What do you want?" he repeats. "Really?"

"I need you in the race. You have to come with me to Cyan-Bisera."

"I don't want to. Not now."

"Please. Do this one thing, and I'll never ask again. Everything depends on it."

"I don't care about the circuit anymore. You can win without me."

"No. I can't. We leave this Thursday at noon. There's a spot for you and Hal and Mary on the transport. Sand Ridge Launch Yards. Bay number four."

"Are you still with him?"

I'm not sure Bear heard a word I said, and I don't know how to answer. He's here. This corner is our fragile truce, but my promise to James, my oath to keep Cash's secrets, hangs like a noose. I need to tell Bear. It's the only way he'll agree to come along. "Cash can't pace me in the race. I need you, Bear. I can't make it without you. Things are not what you think. You're in danger."

"Is this another threat? Benroyal told me about the DP clinic raid. How you practically begged James to have them shake my parents down, how he didn't really want me on the team in the first place. Even then, I still loved you. I stayed. Like a fool, just to be with you. But you just kept pushing me away, Phee. I don't know who you are anymore."

"No. It wasn't like that. Listen to me. You have to get on that vac. It's not safe for you here anymore."

"And I'm safer on Benroyal's payroll? Watching you and Cash?"

"No, Bear. You have to leave with me. I can't tell you why. Just come with us, and I'll explain everything. I swear to you. We have to get out of here. I hate this life."

"Don't come to me for escape when you're tired of Cash," Bears says. "Come when you want to be with me."

His chair slides back with a grinding scrape. Bear is already on his feet, turning away. I reach for his arm, but he recoils.

"Bear. Please. Listen to me." I try to block his way. "I can't let you get hurt. I'll die if anything happens to you." My voice thickens into a teary croak, but he's not listening anymore. He pushes past me, and there is nothing I can say or do to stop him.

When I leave Picker's Grocery, I see the Onyx parked on the corner. I climb in and hand my sandwich to Hank, who's waiting for me along with Cash. "Going anywhere else tonight?" Hank asks from the driver's seat.

I shake my head. "Take me back."

"I talked to James," Cash says. "Can you believe it? It's on. Benroyal took the bet."

I don't answer. I can't even think about that right now. If I do, I'll fall apart. Everything that ever mattered to me, the anchors that always held fast are all coming undone, and I'm drowning. Silent, I lean against the door. My whole world has changed in such a short time.

Quietly, Cash sits beside me. He doesn't take my hand or push me to talk. He's waiting for me to say something first. I'd reach for him, but I can't. I understand it now, the look in Bear's eyes. I feel that absence of light. I can't live without my best friend, the boy who's stood beside me for so long, I don't know how to run without him.

"I tried," I whisper to Cash. "He won't listen to me."

"It's going to be okay," he says.

"No, it's not. I was just a runt. A scared little girl stuck in a string of windowless rooms on Mercer Street. I was hungry and alone. One day, Bear's parents delivered supplies. He found me, Cash, hiding under a bed. He smiled at me first and gave me his coat." I stop, my voice too halting and ragged. "I can still remember what it smells like. Bear is my family. I can't lose him. James won't let me tell him the truth."

"We won't leave them behind."

In panic, I lurch forward. "Take me to the Larssens'. Right now. Hal and Mary will listen, if I can just tell them everything."

Cash pulls me to him. "Benroyal's watching your every move. Don't flex them or show up at their apartment. Don't give him an excuse to suspect you."

"But I can't let Bear—"

"Leave it to me. He will be there. Hal and Mary too. I swear it."

I wish I could believe him.

CHAPTER THIRTY-TWO

THURSDAY COMES LIKE A DEATH SENTENCE.

We pass three other teams on the way to launch bay four, and I'm pretty sure Max Courant mouthed something nasty as we drove by. I heard he broke two ribs and a wrist when I drove his rig into the wall during the Sand Ridge 400. He's still wearing a special splint.

Figures. My car flips six times and I don't fracture a single bone, but I give that weasely sap-hole one little tap and he shatters. Pity I won't get the chance to do much more damage in the next race. If everything goes according to plan, I won't face him on the course for long.

It's petty to care so much about it, yet I don't relish handing him—or any of these corporate clone drivers—a rally victory. But I have a lot bigger things to worry about. In a matter of days, I won't be part of the circuit anymore.

Soon, I'll be burning, a thick ash cloud rising.

After the team finishes loading my covered rig and our gear on the behemoth transport vac, Cash and I ascend the ramp, following Goose to climb aboard.

James and Benroyal, along with the rest of the Sixer entourage, are taking a smaller, more luxurious vac, of course. Living it up in one that's not so grim and gray, like this monster made of Pallurium bolts. I bet King Charlie's already outside our sweatbox atmosphere, moving across space bridges in high style.

Cash and I linger on the last open loading deck. I squint and search for any sign of another approaching vehicle. Even now, a tiny part of me clings to a fragile hope. Maybe he'll come. Maybe he's changed his mind after all.

There's nothing to see. Not even the wind moves today.

"Quick, quick." Auguste walks back out to me. He clucks his tongue. "Obey the schedule. We are waiting to close the doors, spitfire girl."

So much depends on this race, but a selfish impulse dances through me. You don't have to do this. It's not too late to jump and run back to Mercer Street. "I can't leave. Not without Bear."

"Have a little faith in me." Cash cups my cheek. His thumb catches a falling tear. "I'll never break a promise."

I nod, but I don't follow him into the passenger hold. I'll wait on the deck until the doors shut out the noonday sun. I want to look out on Castra one last time.

Even though I've never traveled to another planet, I know how it works. After we rise above the pitiful protection of the Castran atmosphere, the flight crew docks our uni-vac into its Orbital Charging Shell. Without our craft locked into the OCS, we wouldn't be able to make it far out here, let alone drift through folded space.

The actual trip is supposed to feel like an eye-blink, but the lock and launch phase eats up three hours. We are securely pinned in our seats while the crew is caught up in a series of checks and tests and protocols, a bunch of stuff I don't understand. Now that we're juiced up and armored, we navigate our way to the nearest space bridge.

When we first broke through the atmosphere, I'd expected to see the glimmer of stars right away. Instead, it seemed a curtain of black had fallen. There was nothing visible but endless, starless night. But now that we've reached the giant man-made space bridge, the turning satellite wheel, I see the swirl of golden light all around—nebulae as blue green as sea foam, and billions of jeweled stars, rubies and diamonds, winking bright.

"Ladies and gentlemen," the captain's voice drones into our headsets. "We're fully calibrated, so we'll be charging the bridge in approximately two minutes. For those of you who haven't traveled with us before, welcome." The captain's voice slips into a quick, rehearsed monotone, but I'm not listening anymore. Tightly, I'm clutching Cash's hand and cursing under my breath.

Put me on any road and as long as I'm behind the wheel, I don't break a sweat. But hurtle me through folded space, at the mercy of another driver, and yes, I'm rusting white-knuckle nervous. One of my headaches takes root. Tendrils of dull pain stretch and unfurl inside my skull.

"It's no big deal, really," Cash reassures. "I've done this a hundred times."

Banjo and Auguste are strapped into the seats across from us. "Yes, yes," Auguste says. "Have no fear. Almost there."

I close my eyes. I just want people to stop talking.

Banjo, with his good-natured twang, interrupts my cleansing breaths. "Once you have a good puke, you'll be good as new."

Yeah, I think I'm going to hurl.

Our vac drifts into the open center of the space bridge. I

think something went wrong. I heard a soft ping in my headset, but I don't feel the rumble of engines or the skull-rattling quake of g-forces at work. Nothing's happening. In a blink, all we've managed to do is coast through the calibrated rim.

Wait. No. My gut says otherwise. My nervous system sends out a distress call to every cell of my body, a buzzing relay that says: *You were someplace else a second ago, only that somewhere is now far, far away and we're not sure if all our particles are accounted for, do you copy?*

I repeat, do you copy?

My stomach answers. Affirmative. I reach for my gray airsickness tube and slip the attached rubber mask over my face. I lose everything I ate for breakfast and then some. A push of a button and tiny jets of water and mouthwash rinse out the nasty acid tang. As I spit the last of it, it's all suctioned up and out.

I look around and see that several other members of my team have done the same, including Banjo. I shove the apparatus back into its chamber and take a deep breath. Cash is fine; he doesn't look the least bit green.

"That wasn't so bad, was it?" he asks.

I shake my head. Except I'm lying. That was completely weird.

Cash smiles, like I'm not the most repulsive thing he's

ever seen. Like he actually can't get enough of me, even after watching me vomit in outer space.

"Feel better?" he says.

I nod, and this time it's the truth.

The captain's voice comes through our headsets again. "We'll be preparing to enter Cyan-Bisera's atmosphere shortly. Until then, we hope that you enjoyed the flight, and we ask that you bear with us for a few minutes as we interface with our crew on the ground. Your seats will unlock as soon as it is safe for them to do so. At that time, you may stretch your legs and make your way to the forefront of the hold. You might want to catch a glimpse of the view."

Another soft ping interrupts, and the latches on our safety restraints click open. I stand up and drag Cash out of his seat. I might still be a little woozy, but there's no way I'm going to miss this. "Let's go."

All of us disentangle and make our way to the observation point. A hatch opens, revealing a floor-to-ceiling convex window. The view steals my next breath. I've caught images of Cyan-Bisera on feeds and through Cash's telescope, but up close, it's more beautiful than anything I've ever seen.

There is so much water—teeming seas and oceans of

rich drowning blue. I'm used to the endless brown of Castra, but there's hardly any to be found on Cash's home planet. Pristine clouds swirl over the black deltas of great rivers. Fingers of land reach out from two visible continents, every rise and valley emerald, dappled and veined with gold and orange and red.

I see the Biseran Gap, the deep slash cutting through the center of the largest land mass. From here, the ancient canyon blazes like a firestorm, a thick line of flame dividing one half of the world from the other. Just to the west, I can even make out the Pearl Strand, the demilitarized zone between the two countries, with its endless fields of giant white poppies. From here, the strand is a ribbon of snow, melting into the singed embers of the Gap.

This cannot be real. Something so full of light and life must be an illusion.

Cash rests his palm at the small of my back. We stand silent for the longest time. It's the captain's voice that breaks the spell.

"Preparing for re-entry," he says. "Please return to your assigned seats in the passenger hold. Six minutes until countdown."

We land on the outskirts of Belaram, Bisera's capital. As

we climb down the exit ramp, I gulp my first breath of the atmosphere. My headache disappears, swept away by the scent of balm leaf on the breeze. I'm so conditioned to the scorching heat of Castra, it's a shock to breathe in cool moisture. Every pore of my skin opens and drinks in the nourishment.

We're only halfway down the ramp when the roar begins. At the edge of the launch yard, a crowd swarms. They press against the gates, shouting and chanting in Biseran. But they aren't circuit fans. They are here for Cash, clamoring, pulling at the fences to get a glimpse of him. It occurs to me, I don't know if they are cheering or crying out for blood. Suddenly, I tense up, afraid.

Dradha. Dradha. Ay-khan banat bakar. Eb banat bakar.

I lean into Cash, to be heard above the roar. "They're calling your name. What are they saying?"

"Ay-khan, the evening star," he whispers in my ear, then turns to wave at the crowd. "Eb banat bakar. It means 'he returns.'"

It's then I finally see it. The hope shining in each face. Despite every lie, every bit of gossip on the feeds . . . here, Cash isn't a spoiled aristocrat or a gambling pacer. He is his father's son. They believe in him. They believe in the promise of impossible things. And for the first time, I think I do too.

When he takes my hand again, Cash's eyes are bright, maybe with unshed tears or with relief or joy at coming home. All I know is when the smile lights up his face, his people answer, cheering louder than before.

Eb banat bakar. Over and over and over, a thousand voices strong.

CHAPTER THIRTY-THREE

MY TEAM JUMPS INTO THE BACK OF THREE WAITING ONYXES.
I sit with Cash and Auguste in the lead rig. We disappear
behind dark, tinted windows, and the crowd parts to let us
ride into Belaram. Cash's people line every street, laughing and shouting and throwing red poppy blossoms, as if
they've been waiting for this moment for a hundred years.

As we leave the good road, and move onto a narrower
street, I look out my window. The city's nothing like Capitoline, with its clean lines and endless sun-bleached hori-
zons. These streets are a riot of sound and color. Tangled
vines and moss cover the ancient facades of crumbling
high-rises. The buildings are patchy layer cakes—mis-
matched levels of brown brick are sandwiched between
gray stone walls. From hundreds of balconies, yards of

silk hang to dry. Each faded swath billows and flaps in the breeze, waving as we pass.

When I crack our windows, I smell rainwater and spices and roasting meat. Beyond the crowd, I hear voices calling and the stomp of feet. Ragged laborers hustling to work. Sidewalk vendors guarding their wares from the mob. Quick-fingered children running from shops. It's dirty and jam-packed and noisy as anything.

I love this place.

Auguste glances at the beggars lining the walk. "It would seem Bisera has seen better days."

Cash frowns. "My brother has no concern for his people."

"They seem to love you well enough." Goose snorts, then reaches into his breast pocket for his handkerchief. Nervously, he dabs his forehead.

Cash doesn't answer, and I can only guess what he's thinking. His country's been caught in the crossfire for so long, and the weight of a kingdom seems to press down on him. I can see it in his eyes—despite the warm homecoming, he's anxious about so many things.

When our Onyx turns right, we pass through a set of gates and leave the crowds behind. Our road curves, leading us up to the elevated heart of Belaram. Here, the squalor is cleared away. The whitewashed villas of merchants and noblemen jut above the rest of the city. On these wide streets, there are even a few gleaming skyscrapers. One of them looks like a mini version of the Spire.

I scowl at Benroyal's handiwork. Even here he has to make his mark.

Our driver lowers the screen between us. "Almost there."

"The hotel?" I answer.

He nods. Our convoy of Onyxes turns another corner. I see the marquee, but I can't read the Biseran script. As we pull under the circular portico, Goose sits up. Cash and I both look through the glass to see what's spooked him.

Someone is waiting for us. It's a diplomatic motorcade, half a dozen sleek black rigs. I catch a glimpse of the flag they're flying. A red, five-point star on a field of black.

I've seen the emblem on a million feeds. Cash's ay-khan. The evening star, the symbol of the Royal House of Bisera. For a split second, Auguste's eyes widen in full-on alarm, but he's quick-witted enough to recover. By the time we get ready to step out, he's already put on his most charming smile.

Cash reaches for the door, but Auguste stops him. "Perhaps you should stay."

Cash shakes his head. He and I step out of the rig. While the rest of the crew does the same, Gil and Auguste flank us, moving slightly ahead. "Battle stations, everyone," Gil mumbles under his breath. He laughs, but I don't think he's joking.

Three thick-necked bodyguards slide from the front seat of the third rig in the motorcade. They open the backseat doors. Three men, one more guard and two more-richly dressed passengers, step out and move toward us in a lock-step gait.

Even though they are all Biseran, they are not so different from Castran Sixers. Their suit jackets are cut a bit longer and their ties are fat and old-fashioned, more like knotted scarves, but the finely tailored threads have the same silken sheen as Benroyal's.

The guards and one of the passengers give a slight bow, but the taller man from the backseat stands proudly and smooths the lapel of his jacket, as if he had nothing better to do. I stare at him. His expression is stern and ugly, and his features and imposing height give him away. It's the same face I saw on the gallery portrait. He is a cold, bitter reflection of Cash.

"Hello, little brother." The dark familiarity in his voice chills me to the bone.

Before Cash can answer, Dak's well-heeled lackey bows again. "I welcome you on behalf of His Royal Highness, Prince Dakesh Mohan Benyaran Bahkra-Anan, Prince of Belaram and Lord of the Eastern Isles, Royal Knight Companion of the Most Noble Order of the Evening Star, of the Royal House of Bisera, Steward of the Crown and First Son to Her Majesty, Queen Napoor." He takes a breath and wipes his brow. "I am Her Majesty's foreign minister, Ammad Negendra."

I do not like this diplomat. I sense his closed-mouth smile hides the hungry snap of teeth. He waits for us to bow before His Royal Highness. Most of us nod or awkwardly lean forward, but Auguste obliges best, gliding into an elegant low sweep.

Cash stands tall, his face blank, betraying nothing.

"Thank you, Minister Negendra," Auguste purrs. "We are not worthy of this unexpected visit."

"Unexpected? Surely you would expect His Royal Highness to take great interest in your arrival. After all," he says, bowing a third time. His voice drips with false sincerity. "You have been gone for so long, Prince Cashoman. It is not every day that we have the pleasure of serving the queen's second son. And of course, we hold Mr. Benroyal's interests as close as our own. We want to ensure that your stay is most pleasant."

"Thank you again, Minister," Auguste soothes. "We are at your service, Your Royal Highness."

Nagendra, the rusting jackal, interrupts. "Perhaps we might be of assistance to you? We are prepared to take on passengers and any burdensome cargo. Indeed, you need not stay here. We would be delighted to host your entire crew at the palace."

Dak nods, still saying nothing. His guards approach, as if to escort us all into the waiting vehicles. They stop when Auguste raises his hands in protest. "Minister, I thank you, but again, we would not dare impose on your hospitality and I'm certain Mr. Benroyal would insist we stay here. In fact, if I'm not mistaken, he and Mr. Anderssen have just arrived at the palace to greet Her Majesty, Queen Napoor? I believe they have important matters to discuss. Surely we should not detain you from receiving the Castran diplomatic envoy?"

Dak flicks his hand at Negendra, dismissing him to verify our story. The servant steps back and makes a call. He touches his earpiece and nods several times during the conversation. After he is done, he approaches his master and whispers something in his ear.

"It would seem you are correct. The queen awaits. That is disappointing . . ." Dak stares me down, and for the first time, he smiles. "We were looking forward to spending more time with Cashoman. We've missed him since he ran away."

Cash's fingers flex, then curl. His expression's cool, but the rage is there, just under the skin.

Dak springs, pulling Cash into his embrace, in a mocking show of brotherly concern. He leans into his ear, and I strain to hear the thread of his whisper. "Run along, Cashoman, play your little games, run your foolish races. But watch your back. Step out of line on your own and I will end you."

Cash smiles and grips him tighter. "Could you hear them, my brother, all the way at the palace? Eb banat bakar."

Flinching, Dak breaks away. Without another word, His Royal Highness, sap-hole of the realm, turns on his heels. Nagendra, along with the rest of the servants, scrambles to catch up. A minute later, the motorcade is gone.

After they disappear, Cash pivots toward the hotel, but I'm still so stunned that Auguste has to grab me by the arm to get me moving again. I feel the shake in his grip. A fat drop of sweat trickles down his temple. He wipes it away, swiping the back of his free hand across his eyes.

"Yes, yes," he says. "Perhaps our stay will be much less complicated if we avoid the palace."

CHAPTER THIRTY-FOUR

THE NIGHT BEFORE THE RALLY, I STAY IN CASH'S SUITE WHILE he sits by the window, staring at the lights of Belaram. It's three a.m. by the time I finally stop tossing and turning. Still, I wake up too early.

At the foot of the bed, I spy a tidy stack of clothes. Black pants and a black shirt, creased and starched and folded. The crisp IP uniform doesn't belong here. The second I look at it, I know. Cash won't be slipping into his circuit gear today. He's traded it in for this new disguise. He is leaving.

Groggy, I stumble out of the bedroom, then stand against the loft's railing to look down at the rest of the suite. I'm dumbstruck by the mess, the room service carts that weren't here last night. The scattering of dirty plates and crystal glasses. On the counter, empty wine bottles lined up in drunken rows. It's as if someone dumped an all-nighter across the entire room.

Cash is there, a bottle in each hand. They clink as he empties them into a sink and sets them aside. I wonder if he slept at all.

"Cash . . ." My voice comes out in a sleepy croak. "What happened? Who trashed this place?"

"Hank helped me out. You were sleeping." His eyes sweep the room. "That should be enough, I think." He pauses. "But I have to go soon."

"We both have to go soon. We have pre-race interviews in three hours."

"You have pre-race interviews in three hours. I have a food service truck full of ice-packed bluefin to catch in forty-five minutes."

"You're leaving."

Someone pounds on the doors of the suite. Cash checks to see who's there before opening. It's Hank. He thrusts a helmet and a pair of spit-shined boots at Cash.

"You have big feet." Hank smirks. "Took me a while to snag these. See you in a few?"

Cash nods, taking the gear. "Wait for me. I'll be out in a sec."

After Hank leaves, Cash meets me at the bottom of the stairs. We're face-to-face, and playfully, he drives me back up, one step at a time.

"You have to go and get ready. And I have to blaze." He puts on his best sad-face smile, the one I know he's wearing to melt me.

"You can't leave. The race."

"I won't be in the race."

I snatch the gear from him. I've got a step's advantage, but I still have to tilt to meet his eyes. "Who's going to pace me? How am I going to win and make this work if you're not even there?"

"You'll have a pacer. I haven't forgotten my promise. Bear will know what to do. The Larssens will be there. I swear it."

I stare at Cash, lit up by the thought of my family, safe and waiting. I nearly drop the boots.

Cash takes them, sliding past me. He ducks into the bathroom, and I move into the doorway as he slips into the uniform. He's more handsome than ever, even with the emblem of Benroyal's Interstellar Patrol embroidered over his heart.

Cash stares at the mirror, frowning. But he looks the part. For the moment, he is all ruthless eyes and jutting chin, and I see a dangerous man. With his visor down, he'll be another sleek soldier in polished jackboots, just another IP officer patrolling the capital.

When he turns on me, I balk. "Why do you have to do this?"

"It's better this way. I can't show my face in that rally. I need to go ahead and set some things up."

"If you don't show your face, Cash, everyone will notice. Look at the way the crowds were waiting for you, shouting out your name. If you try to sneak off, they'll know something is wrong."

Tenderly, he runs his fingers through my hair, then traces a path down my shoulders until our hands link. "That's exactly why I have to go. The crowds. The feedcasters. The whole circuit complex will be crawling with security. Once the race starts, I won't be able to slip away. And the longer I stay in Belaram, the more I put us all at risk. The whole city's crawling with royal informants, hungry spies who'd love to feed my brother information for the right price. It's better if I leave now."

I sigh, resigned.

"My friends are waiting, Phee. They need me. Before we rendezvous, I'll have my hands full. Evacuating hundreds of rebels isn't easy work, and by the time you get there, we'll have to be ready to move. To a safer base, closer to Cyan."

I don't answer. He wraps his arms around me, and I rest my cheek against starched cotton. "So all this"—I wave at the bottle-strewn room—"is just for show?"

"To make the Sixers believe what they've heard in the feeds. To show them I am everything they think and nothing more, just a spoiled amateur who stays out too late and gambles and drinks. Hank will confirm that I'm too sick and hungover for the race, and you'll lock the bedroom doors. Standing orders. Do not disturb. By the time they catch on, we'll both be gone."

"And you'll be?"

He touches my cheek. "I'll be waiting. I'll always wait for you."

I start to argue, to stall him again, but he presses his lips to my throat and works his way up to my mouth. When my breath catches, we both know he's won. "We'll only be apart for a little while. I promise."

I kiss him one last time before I mouth the words *I stand with you.*

Bidram arras noc.

After I'm dressed and my last pre-race interview is done, an Onyx arrives to take me to rally headquarters, the circuit complex near the starting line. Our motorcade crawls through the security checkpoints and we finally reach our compound made up of luxe quarters for Benroyal and a separate garage designated for our crew. Enormous metal hangars overshadow red poppy groves and ancient stone lodges. It's a strange sight—Bisera's past so crowded by the Sixers' present.

When I walk into our garage, everyone is waiting for me. Billy and Arad. Banjo and Gil and all the rest. Every member of my team mills around my new slip-covered rig.

"We've got her fixed up and ready," Gil says. "Made a few cosmetic adjustments."

Navin, our detail man, pulls off the slipcover so I can take a look. My new ride is supposed to be identical to the one I wrecked, but this one could not be more different. The sweep of gold paint, the side racing stripes, the crimson blush of the hood—it's all gone. My rig is drenched in black. Everything, from roof to wheelbase, is a glossy midnight mirror.

"What about my number, the Benroyal mark?" I ask, surprised.

"It is there, spitfire girl," Auguste says. "Look closer."

As I walk around the rig, I see it. The phoenix crest and the side detailing are barely visible, painted in a quicksilver, iridescent finish. The wings on the hood seem to move, a ghostly shimmer against the pitch-black.

The paint scheme is killer, unlike anything I've ever seen. I'm speechless.

"Auguste thought we should capitalize on your dramatic finish in the last race," Gil explains. "The smoke and ash. Rising from the wreck and all that."

Yes. The hint of light in the dark.

"You might wanna take a look inside," Gil says.

I lean through the driver's side and check out the interior. Everything is the same, save for one detail. A mechanical throttle. No more touch-screen triggers.

"Yesss," I growl, high-fiving Banjo.

"Took the fabricators three whole days to get it right," he says.

I crack a real smile for the first time today. "Thanks, you guys."

Looking around at my crew, I see the pride and excitement on their faces. I feel the weight of it. They believe I'll take the lead today and win the race.

In a few hours, I'll be nothing more than smoke and skid marks on a hairpin turn and they will be left to answer for it. I can only hope that Auguste and Gil have enough wit and clout to deflect Benroyal's wrath away from my crew.

I'm in such a daze—awestruck and anxious—that I don't notice right away how quiet it's gotten. Everyone on my team is gone. Auguste has silently ushered them all out of the garage. "Another surprise," he says, escorting three more people inside. "One last detail . . ."

The Larssens. Here. In this room.

"Bear," I gasp. Without thinking, I run to him and put my arms around him, but he is frozen. With his hands still at his sides and every muscle tense—he might as well be made of stone. I pull back and look up. He is staring through me, as though I were nothing. Right now, I wish I were.

I focus on the concrete floor. His parents rescue me, surging forward while Bear is unmoved.

Hal squeezes the life out of me, and then Mary does too.

"My Phee," she whispers. When she takes my hands in hers, I feel the warmth and care in her calloused fingertips. This woman's patched me up and taken me in a hundred times. She will always be a mother to me, and I will always be her south side girl.

"I'm so sorry," I answer. "I wanted to tell you."

"We know. Your friend the Dradha boy came by the apartment, the day after—when Bear came home." She's kind enough to leave some things unsaid.

Cash kept his promise, and I can only imagine how hard it was for him, after all the insults and hits he's taken for me. I look in Bear's eyes, desperate to find some trace of the bond we once had. "I'm glad you changed your mind."

"I'm here for them." Even his voice sounds far away, as if he's disconnected his heart and there's nothing left inside but empty space.

Mary's smile tells me not to give up hope. Give him time, her eyes beg.

Auguste offers her his arm. "I'm sorry to interrupt, but we are running out of time. Barrett and Miss Vanguard must prepare for the event. May I escort you and your husband out? I believe James has already arranged transportation for you."

Mary nods, then embraces me again. "Stay safe," she says with a knowing look. "And we'll see you after the rally."

Unless something goes wrong during the race. Unless I don't make the rendezvous. Unless we fail to escape.

Finally, I'm alone with Bear. For the first time in my life, I don't know what to say to him. Turns out that won't be an issue; he can hardly wait to leave.

"I'm going to go change," he says. "I'll be on the headset."

"How are we going to work this out?"

"Got here yesterday. I'm ready."

"You were already here?" I ask, more than a little upset. "No one told me."

"I was busy. Scouted the terrain. Double-checked all the pace notes for your route."

The detachment in his voice, the way he stares past my shoulder; it stings. I try again. "Is there anything we need to talk about? Are you sure we're okay?"

"Cash told me what to do."

"So we just need to go over the route."

"I've been briefed." When he steps toward me, I read his eyes. He can hardly stand to be near me. But he moves in anyway, so no one else can hear. "I have to go. Now, before the race starts, or we won't have time to get ahead of you. I'll be waiting with Hank."

And then he's gone. I sag against the exit doors. An hour until I slip into my rig, and I'm alone. Outside this compound, a million eyes watch the feeds, ready for us to perform, but my thoughts keep wandering back to the family I've lost and the one I've found.

Before the race, there's one more person I need to see.

On my way inside, I run into Goose.

"Are you ready, ma chère?" he asks. "It's almost time."

"Where's Mrs. Benroyal?"

He shrugs. "I suppose she is in the lodge, entertaining Mr. Benroyal's guests."

"Can you take me there? I don't want to be seen. I mean, there's something I need to tell her."

Flustered, he backs away, palms up. "We do not have time for this."

"It'll only take a second. Please. Come with me. I have to see her."

He sighs and offers his arm. "Quickly, then."

We cut through the grove behind Benroyal's lodge. We're halfway up the steps to his private terrace when I hear the hum of chatter and music. A party's in full swing. Through open archways, I catch the flicker of giant flex screens, all fixed on the latest circuit coverage. Seeing it all does nothing to help my pre-race jitters. My stomach's in knots because of the rally, but for Benroyal and his friends, it seems the victory celebration has already begun.

Auguste waves me back. "Wait here. And stay out of sight. By now, you should be preparing for the race, and I am not going to answer for this foolishness." He leaves and I pace the lowest risers, shaded by the balm-leaf trees.

A few minutes later, he returns, but this time he's not alone. Goose escorts a pale, thin woman onto the terrace. A fragile Sixer doll, weighed down by a train of ruby silk.

My mother shuffles down the flagstones.

"You have two minutes," Auguste says. "James is here, and I do not need him asking questions."

"I can handle James," I say.

He guides her to me. I look up. Her silhouette's haloed

by late-afternoon glare. As a little girl, I dreamed of this moment. I imagined how she'd take me into her arms and tell me how much she loved me and how sorry she was that she had to give me up.

But James was right. This isn't a fairy tale.

She stands an arm's length away, in the shadow of the grove, and I see a shrunken, hollow version of myself. A storm front gathers in me. I hate her. I hate her so much that I need to hold her tight, until she drowns in my tears. I need to shake my fists and demand all the reasons why.

But I can't. Now that we're face-to-face, I'm paralyzed.

I was so young when she abandoned me, too small to hold even snatches of her memory—an image on my father's flex is all I've ever had, and it doesn't match up with the weak, vacant-eyed stranger standing here now.

She looks at me, puzzled and lost, a sap-brained mad woman too far from her last fix. "You're a pretty girl," she says.

I open my mouth to ask a million questions, but Auguste stops me. "Tread carefully. Some days are not as good as others. She is easily upset. Be delicate."

"Can you give us a minute?" I say.

Auguste nods. He heads back up the stairs, leaving us. I know I don't have much time. "Do you know who I am?" I ask her.

"Of course I do." The uncertainty in her voice doesn't match her words.

"I'm your daughter, Phoebe Van Zant."

Her fragile smile melts. "Don't say that name. Don't say it. Don't say it. Tommy is gone. He's not coming back and I have to . . ."

I reach for her, to calm her down, but she touches her throat, flinching away. "They give you things to make you forget," she pleads hysterically. "But I remember. She's out there. You have to find her. You have to keep her safe."

All the anger and bitterness rage through me again, yet every time I look at her, pity overcomes it. She wasn't the mother I wanted, but I got the family I needed. I see her haunted eyes, and I realize that I'm the lucky one. I'm Hal and Mary's daughter.

A soft cry rises in my throat, but I quickly smother it. She is broken down and lost, but I am strong. I am strong enough to face her without lashing out. I stare forward, waiting until her gaze locks with mine. "It's okay," I soothe. "I found her. She's safe. I promise."

The words don't taste like forgiveness, but I don't hate her anymore.

She sucks in a breath and stops struggling. When she smiles, it's like a break in the clouds, a brief moment of peace between tempests. She reaches out, takes my chin in her hand. "You're a pretty girl."

Auguste comes back down the stairs. "Ma chère, I'm afraid you must say good-bye."

No. He hasn't given me enough time. There's so much I need to know. I close my fingers over hers. I have seconds left to build a memory, linking the grove's red blossom scent with the fragile softness of this woman's hands. Wildly, my mind reaches for a better ending to the story. Maybe I can take her with me. I can find a place for her. I can save her, even though my father could not.

"Who's down there?" a voice calls from the terrace. "Phee?"

It's James. He hurries down and takes me by the arm. "What are you doing? You shouldn't be here." He stops himself when he sees we're not alone. "Auguste, will you take my sister back inside? I'll see that Phee makes it to the hangar."

Goose nods, but suddenly, I don't want him to leave. It occurs to me that I might not ever see him again. "Will you be at the starting line?"

"Go. Immédiatement. See you on the feeds, spitfire girl. You must be brave. The race is a long one."

If only he knew.

As I watch him walk my mother back, James lets go of

my arm. "You shouldn't have done that," he says quietly. "If Benroyal sees you talking to her and suspects something . . . What did you tell Auguste?"

The urge to snap at him is almost overwhelming, but I resist. "I didn't tell Auguste anything. No one else saw us. I needed to see her. I thought maybe we could take her with us."

James shakes his head. "He'll never let her go. And I can't risk everything."

"But—"

"She built her own prison years ago. She chose Benroyal, Phee. And in his twisted way, he loves her more than anything else."

"Who needs that kind of love? It will kill her."

"He'll keep her safe enough. He has to. If anything happens to Joanna—"

I finish for him. "He gets nothing."

He nods, but I'm no more relieved. My mother . . . I feel our ending slip away, like a thread cut too soon. The race is about to begin, but I am so drained.

James must see it in my face. He braces me, holding me at arm's length. "I know this has been hard on you. I haven't always given you credit, but I want you to know . . ."

"What?"

He doesn't answer right away. I trail as he heads back

for the hangar. "It's going to work out, Phee. No matter what happens today, Cash, Hank, all of us will do whatever it takes to protect you."

For so long, I thought I had James figured out. He was the survivor, the man who stood by and looked out for himself. But I'm staring at him now, and suddenly, I don't think I know him at all.

"If something happens, I'm prepared," he says.

"Stop it. I don't want to talk about that, James."

"Listen. For once, I need you to hear what I'm saying." He leans in, forcing eye contact. "Locus and all that our family's built—it's our legacy to you. There may be dark days ahead, but I want you to know it's all set up, most of it sheltered in accounts Benroyal can never touch."

"It's not like that, James. I don't want your money."

"Phee, this isn't about what you or I want. Someday, you'll understand that. Things weren't always the way they are now, and they can be different again. You and Cash . . . one day, you can make room for the Magna Carta, for everything Benroyal's tried to keep only for himself."

I open my mouth, but it's as if he reads my mind. "I know you're not a Sixer, Phee, and that's what makes you the best heir. You can use your inheritance for good. There are ways to out-game Benroyal and there are tools to repair the damage he's done. Come what may, I'm going to make sure you have them."

I'm not ready to think about what that really means. That kind of money and power—it's the last thing I want. "You're the silver-tongued CEO, James, not me. I wouldn't know the first thing about leading a whole company."

"It's just something I want you to start thinking about. Not right now. I just want you to be prepared when that day comes."

"What aren't you telling me?" I ask. "You talk like this is good-bye. Aren't you coming with us?"

"Please," he teases. "Why should I run? I have money, influence, a hundred places to hide, both here and on Castra. I'll be fine. I just wanted you to know, no matter what, everything's going to be all right."

We reach the hangar doors, but as my crew waves me inside, I'm more worried for him than ever before. I've come to learn James's tells. The glasses never came off.

CHAPTER THIRTY-FIVE

I'M STRAPPED IN, IDLING ON THE BLACKTOP STARTING LINE.
Feed cameras everywhere. Vacs overhead.

My new rig shivers; the engine is growling at me, telling
me to put my foot to the floor. I've got the chance to race
in a real point-to-point rally, not an endless sprint around a
track, but for once, my jittery pulse doesn't slacken into the
usual stone-cold zone. A dull ache blossoms at the base of
my skull; one of my headaches is brewing and I'm a knot
of panicked energy.

No rivals flank me at this starting line. Instead, the trail
of rigs stretches behind me. One by one, seconds apart, we'll
each get our moment to launch forward, hurtling toward
the mountains and a finish line that's hundreds of miles
away. Thanks to my victory at Sand Ridge, I'll have the best

head start, but Courant and the others will be snapping at my heels soon enough.

And this time, I'm running for real. I have thirty-eight minutes to rocket over seventy miles, to take the right fork at the top of the mountain pass and duck into a blind spot, the one place on the course the live feeds can't reach.

I flip down my visor and the VR screens come to life. The clock counts down. My green flag will flash in a matter of seconds. I hear Bear's voice through my headset. "In position, route is all clear," he says. "Go time."

Three . . . Two . . . One. I blast off, tires squealing. It's almost nothing but straightaway for the first forty miles, so I punish the floorboard, jamming the accelerator all the way down for as long as I can. Once I get more altitude, snaking up the treacherous summit, the turns will get fierce and tight. My competition will catch up and I'll have to force the RPMs down just to maneuver without skating off course and over the cliff's edge.

Of course, the whole plan is to run this rig off road, to tumble and fall a thousand feet. But I'd prefer to crash this baby on purpose, not in a moment of shaky recklessness. If only Bear would say something. I've never raced without his steady voice to center me.

I grapple with the silence for as long as I can, but when the road narrows and the emerald foothills disappear, I can't take it anymore. I can't hear their roar in the distance, but my rig's exhaust cam shows me Fallon and Banks are gaining already. I'm climbing too high and the rough terrain is too much. I can't do this alone. I can't even blurt out how scared I am and how badly my head is throbbing, because I don't know who's listening over the line. "Talk to me, Bear."

"Making good time, slow down a bit. You've got the first turn in two miles, maybe twenty seconds," he says. "Take it easy and you'll be fine."

Somehow, I've softened him. I can hear it in his voice. "How many 'til the second marker?"

"Six," he says. "And then . . ."

He doesn't have to finish. I know we're halfway between the second and third points. I run through the getaway script in my head one last time and gulp a ragged breath. I'll stay on track until the last crucial moment. Then I'll take the right fork. We're praying my rivals aren't stupid enough to follow, choosing the race's losing route. But if they do, I'll have to blaze or leave an obstacle, crippling them in my wake.

Gripping the steering wheel, I will my skull-splitting headache to disappear. It's not working.

"My . . . my head," I stammer. If I don't stop bugging out, I'm going to end up smashing my rig against the twisted rock face of the mountain.

"You're hugging the twists too hard," he says. "Ease up, Phee. Please."

"Bear, I need you. Talk me down."

A long silence, then a sigh. "Remember your second race? The time we beat Harkness up in Bellamy Heights?"

I blink. "Yeah. I nearly flipped the Talon on the third corner. Almost smashed into somebody's iron gates."

"But you didn't," Bear says. "And you're not going to crack up now. I won't let that happen."

His words take my panic down a notch. The pain behind my eyes hasn't let up, but with Bear on my side, I know I can deal. We'll negotiate the route together, just as we always have.

In the distance, someone's pulled a trigger to catch up. I look and see a purple rig rip through the space between Fallon and Banks. Rust. Courant's decided he wants a rematch. He's hurtling toward me. In reflex, my finger hovers over my own triggers. It's going to kill me to move aside.

I slide right, but he doesn't speed ahead. Instead, he ducks behind me, letting Banks and Fallon pass us both. "Stupid sap-hole son of a . . . What's he playing at?!"

"He thinks he'll coast in your wake and slingshot later," Bear answers. "Wants you to drag him all the way to the finish line."

A blur of color flashes beside me as three more rigs—

Winfield, Balfour, and Kimbrough—pass us. I'm glad to see Coop get around me, but as for Maxwell . . .

"Courant can kiss my exhaust!"

"Actually, looks like that's his plan."

Whump. I brace against the bump and scrape as Courant's rig nudges my back end. It's nothing more than a love tap, but I'm sure it's just a taste of things to come. He's baiting me, waiting for me to make an insane move.

"Be careful," Bear says. "The turn's ahead."

The fork looms before me. I loosen my grip on the throttle, slowing down a hair. "C'mon, Courant, get off my back," I whisper. "Take the left fork." Surely he wants to win. Ahead, I see Coop and the rest of my rivals break left, taking the broad route to easy victory. Maxwell would be a fool to follow me up the narrow twist.

Speed up. Swerve right. Check my tail. The slash of purple's still there. Blind, vengeful, arrogant Courant. He's forced my hand, and now I have to make him bleed. "How far 'til—"

Fear darkens Bear's voice. "At this rate, you've got maybe two minutes."

I speed up, then slow down. Again and again, I try to throw Courant off, but he won't pass me. I can't have him on my tail in the blind spot. No witness to my escape. I jerk the wheel and skate dangerously close to the outer edge of the road, tossing gravel and catching him off guard. Before he can react, he pulls ahead. I drop behind him, turning the tables at last.

The next hairpin turn is seconds away—I must act now or not at all. I never thought my life was worth that much, but people are depending on me to come through. This is no time to lose my edge.

I have to take Courant out of this race.

I swing right. Just as he mirrors my move, I rocket forward, clipping Maxwell's rear end on the way out. The feeds will say it was haphazard, but the tap was fiercely calculated. While I speed away, Courant fishtails and spins, skidding toward the inside of the mountain. I wince as he slams into the railing, crashing to a brutal stop. Courant will survive to race another day, but not against me. Not ever again.

I gasp, shell-shocked I actually pulled it off. Soon a response crew will descend. The clean-up will close the route to other rigs. I've bought myself a few precious minutes in the blind spot.

After I take a few deep breaths, I wait for Bear to get back on script. If everything's in place at the rendezvous, he'll warn me about an obstacle ahead. That's my signal to spring into action.

A few more seconds tick by. The feeds are consumed

by Maxwell's crash. I swipe the volume up to listen. ". . . already stumbled out of the wreck, but we all thought she was going to get herself killed up there . . . Jack, any word if she's turned up on the other side of the pass?"

"Watch out for debris after the next turn," Bear says. "There was a lot of overgrowth when I scouted this morning. I don't know if they cleared all of it out."

That's my cue. I swallow a deep breath and try not to throw up all over my gear. I make one more ascending turn and grab the throttle stick. Moon and stars, I hope this rig won't fail me. I clench my fist and burn a trigger. My rig surges forward, fueled by a screaming burst. Hold on, baby, hold on . . . I wrestle the steering wheel, squeezing tight to keep this bullet on the right trajectory.

I have to make a stupid move. They have to believe I'm going to skid off the . . .

"What in the . . . Phee . . . what . . . doing?" Gil shouts into my headset. The blind-spot pass has turned his signal into little more than static and crackle. ". . . crazy? Shut that speed down . . . before you . . . up there."

Wish I could tell him that's the whole plan.

I've managed to keep my rig from careening completely out of control. I punish my brakes and the car squeals to a whiplash stop near the outside lip of the road. I'm a few meters from a windswept drop. It's time to play my part.

"Something's wrong," I shout into the headset. "My steering's off and the engine's smoking. I can't get a visual. I can't see through the—"

On cue, I run into a gray cloud. I squint into the woods. I can barely make out Hank and Bear, hiding in the trees. Hank has done his job and tossed three cans of industrial-grade smoke onto the course. The thick, billowing plumes obscure us from any rogue vacs. Even if the feeds could pick up anything, they wouldn't know what's going on.

I have to keep talking my way through this. "I'm caught on something. A tree branch or a deep rut. I can't get her loose!" All the while, as the smoke hides my movement, I'm prying myself out of the six-point restraint, scrambling out of the rig. Hank and Bear dash onto the road.

I hear the clash of broken voices on the line. "Don't move . . . Shut her down . . . Get out . . ." My team yells in the background; they think I'm still gunning the engine, foolishly spinning my wheels. Gil pleads with me to stay put. "DISENGAGE, PHEE. DO NOT TRY TO PUNCH IT."

"No!" I shout. I have no idea how much he's picking up. "I can get out of this. I've got some traction."

The engine's still running, but I left it in neutral. Hank and Bear jump behind my beautiful rig. They push, straining until it rolls closer to the edge of the road. I don't have much meat on my bones, but I lean in to help. Our combined leverage shoves the car another precious two feet.

"NO . . . IT'S . . . I CAN'T . . . I . . ." I rip the headset and helmet free and toss them after the car. We watch Benroyal's circuit rig smash and flip and twist, buffeted by rocks and branches on the way down a thousand-foot plunge. The ugly scream of metal against stone sounds like a dying dream.

The fuel tanks explode; the roar of flame is deafening.

CHAPTER THIRTY-SIX

I'M FROZEN, STANDING AT THE EDGE OF THE CLIFF.

"Move out, let's go." Hank tugs at my shoulder. "Clean-up crew will be on our tails. Let's go."

I killed my rig. I'm dead to my crew. My skull is pounding and I can't get a grip on the shakes rippling through me. When my knees buckle, I nearly drop.

Bear puts an arm around me and drags me back on my feet. He's about to lift me over his shoulder when I finally snap out of it and break into a run, following Hank back into the woods. Once we're sheltered behind the sloping tree line, Hank hands me a new headset, so we can communicate on the go.

"Keep moving." Hank leads the way, hiking down the mountainside at a furious pace. "Watch your step. Don't want to break your legs on the way down. Two more miles."

Bear catches up. He stays close, watching out for me every step of the way. My legs are too short; I can't keep up with their pace and I know I'm just slowing them down. I'm rusting useless anywhere besides behind the wheel.

We run until my lungs scream and wheeze. I trip on a rock and tumble forward, slashing my jaw against the tip of an evergreen branch. Bear catches me before I face-plant. When I reach to wipe the blood away, the red smears my hands like diabolical finger paint.

Hank tosses me a scrap of black fabric. I press it against my jaw until the cut stops oozing.

"Did Hal and Mary get out?" I ask.

"James made sure they got on the transport. They'll be hours ahead of us. Probably halfway there by now."

"What about James?"

Hank shrugs. "His vac was still on standby when I left. Said he wanted to stay and keep Benroyal occupied and off our scent for as long as he could. Don't worry. James is smart. He knows when to stay, and when to cut and run."

Hank takes off again before I can gasp out any more questions. We don't stop moving until we reach a thick knot of trees at the base of a hollow. Hank rushes ahead and starts prying at the tangled limbs.

Wait. The branches aren't haphazard, they're woven together, a clever screen to hide our getaway vehicle. It's a tank. We're climbing inside a rusting anti-vac tank. Inside this giant black beetle, it's dim and hot; there's barely room to breathe or stretch our legs. I lean against one of the low walls and slide to the floor. Hank flips three switches and a bank of screens blinks to life.

"Where did this come from?" I ask him.

"Cyanese Army," he says, swiping icons on a touch panel. "Love their hardware. Corporates make everything complicated, but Cyanese weapons? Totally idiot-proof. Everything's lock and load, point and shoot, start and go."

Idiot-proof or not, I don't know how to drive this monster, but Hank certainly seems to know what he's doing. He climbs into the turret seat and two seconds later, we're off, lurching toward a narrow road at the far end of the hollow.

With arms folded around my knees, I try to relax. We've got miles to go and we're not home free yet, by any means. There's a vac waiting to fly us to the rendezvous, but we can't jump on until we're much farther away from the course.

I glance at Bear. Now that we're eye to eye, sharing the same cramped airspace, it feels like the wall has risen between us again. I suppose it's easier to talk when you don't have to look someone in the eye.

I stare at the blinking panel just over Bear's shoulder. The screen bathes him in red light. "I wish I hadn't ruined your life," I say.

"Me too."

His voice isn't much more than a murmur and I can't tell if he's joking or not. He moves from his spot against the opposite wall of the tank. At first, I think it's just to get farther away from me, but then he wedges himself beside me. We're shoulder to shoulder, pressed in on both sides by equipment and compartments. I open my mouth, but Bear cuts me off before I can get a word out. "Don't," he says.

I read his silence.

Don't speak.

Don't explain.

Don't tell me you're sorry.

Don't hurt me anymore.

I want to lay my head against his shoulder and tell him how much I still care, but I can't. Bear needs time to heal and space to forgive. And I'm going to give it to him.

I lean back and close my eyes.

I'm relieved when we make it all the way down the mountain. At the narrow break in the trees, I'd half expected a squadron of IP to be waiting for us, ready to arrest us all. Instead, we climb on an unassuming vac and head for the rendezvous. We soar, flying high over the mountains heading west.

In the passenger hold, three hours crawl by, and I'm anxious to land. I know the plan. Hank's drilled it into our heads well enough. We'll touch down at an old rebel base. Cash and his allies will be waiting, and we'll all have to pull together to get everyone evacuated. If we move to a stronghold farther west, near Manjor, it will be easier to get more support from the Cyanese. More importantly, we'll be farther from Benroyal's soldiers, who stay close to the Gap. The distance will give us the chance to plan a real coup, a revolution that will put Cash on his father's throne. And I'll have the chance to help my own planet. I won't rest until Benroyal's black sap empire is burned to ash.

Finally, the vac begins to descend.

"How far?" I ask Hank.

"Almost there," he says, tapping the bolt-rimmed window beside his seat. "Take a look."

I lean over him to catch a glimpse of the landscape below, but see nothing but forests and mountains and land-bridged valleys.

We sink, and suddenly, we're dangerously close to one of those land-bridges, a massive, low outcropping. I exhale when we clear it, dipping into its shadow. Near the end of our descent, I finally see what Hank's talking about.

Far below us, underneath the shelter of the rock, there's an enormous man-made wall, gated and half shrouded by flowering vines and lichen and the leaves of hundred-year-old trees.

It's perfect. Shielded by ragged stone and practically undetectable from the air. We fall and I see the bell tower jutting above the gates. This place is ancient. No way did a few rebels build this. "Where did this come from?"

"Used to be a sanctuary," Hank explains. "A secret refuge for Biseran monks, but it hasn't been holy ground for a hundred years. Whole complex belongs to Grace Yamada. Her family bought it years ago. Lucky for us, it's a pretty good hideout."

We land and the vac powers down.

I hear voices and shouts as we climb out. Here, ours isn't the only vehicle that's ready for flight. Two Cyanese fighters flank a trio of transport vacs. There are dozens of people, moving cargo, rushing across the courtyard, prepping to leave.

When Cash said we'd meet a "few friends," I didn't actually think he meant a small army. And James wasn't kidding when he said the Cyanese were aiding the rebels. From the looks of it, these guys are more than well-equipped. It's a motley crew here—mostly Biseran, but there's a handful of Castrans like Hank and me, and even a couple Cyanese. Most of them are dressed in fatigues or some kind of makeshift uniform.

Modern structures, concrete barracks, have been added to the yard, but the ancient bones of this place still stand. A few women and children mill closer to a much older building, a crude stone temple-like structure on the far end of the courtyard.

"Who are they?" I ask Hank.

"Special Intelligence. See that four-year-old?" he mocks, jerking his chin toward one of the younger brats, a wide-eyed boy who stumbles forward when he sees us. "One of our best operatives."

It's a lame joke, but I smile anyway.

"Daddy!" The little guy rushes Hank, who pulls him up into a fierce hug.

How many times have I looked at him, working his post at the Spire, watching all our backs, and never stopped to consider he might have his own worries? I guess everyone here has someone they're fighting to protect. For too long, I was best at saving my own skin. Not today. Not anymore.

From a distance, a woman waves at Hank. "Excuse me," he says to me. "Meet me back at the vac in ten minutes? Moving out soon."

I nod. After he leaves us standing in the yard, I turn and glance in every direction. Which of course is a mistake.

All the movement makes my head hurt worse than ever before. Where are the Larssens?

Where is Cash?

I turn to Bear. "We should find your parents. Make sure they made it all right."

I stop when fuzzy static buzzes in my ears. I'm still wearing my headset. When I hear the snatches of communication, I think it's just evacuation chatter.

Razor, this is Gold Lion. Asset tracked, we are inbound.

Confirmed, this is Razor.

The screech of their voices is too loud. I can't figure out how to turn the volume on my headset down, so I pull it off, letting it curl around the back of my neck.

"Are you all right?" Bear asks.

"It's too noisy. My head's hurting worse."

In the distance, the sound of laughter rises above the bustle in the courtyard. I turn and spy a couple kids running circles around a tall, black-haired soldier.

One look and I'm weightless. It's Cash. He doesn't see me yet, and it's still too far to shout.

Repeat, eyes on, target is designated.

More chatter. The voices are not coming from my headset. "Can you hear that?" I ask Bear.

He shakes his head, looking confused.

My palms slam against my ears, but I still hear the static and coded exchange.

Roger, target acquired, strike package is en route. ETA to fireworks is thirty seconds.

The wind shifts and a warm gust blasts through my hair, cutting through the cool breeze. My brain is going to explode; I can't turn off the crackle and fuzz in my skull.

The distant roll of thunder in the sky.

No. Not thunder. It's the roar of airborne engines.

Gold Lion. Inbound. Strike package. Target.

Nonono . . . this isn't rebel evac chatter, this is military squawk, IP communication before an attack. Why can't anyone else hear it?

"Bear!" I shout. "It's . . . it's . . . Find Hank . . . Hal and Mary . . . anyone . . . tell them it's an ambush!"

Bear blinks for a second, but when I point to the sky, I sense he hears the far-off rumble of incoming aircraft too. "Go!" I beg him. "Please!"

Bear runs for the transport vacs.

I wheel back toward the bell tower. Cash and the kids are still so far away, a hundred yards outside my reach. I bolt, screaming all the way. "CASH! GET THEM OUT. TAKE COVER. IT'S AN ATTACK!"

Cash looks up and sees me. I don't know if he can make

out my words, but he turns and starts moving people toward the transport, urging them to move faster.

As I run, I shout at every passing soldier. "AIRSTRIKE. INCOMING!" They are wired, ready to relay my message. Springing into action, they load weapons, lock into defensive positions, and move their families into the waiting vacs. One of them quickly takes off.

But my warning has come too late. I'm so small and I can't make my body move fast enough. I pass a makeshift gun deck; a rebel gunner locks a magma cannon into place. Behind me, Bear shouts, "Phee! You're going the wrong way! Go back to the vacs!"

I look up and see the swarm. Three of Benroyal's black IP fighters. A giant artillery vac. A squad of jet-packed blitz birds ready to rain down fire. We have all been betrayed. How did they know? How did they find us?

BOOM.

An explosion rocks the ground and I fall to my knees. I look up—the bell tower is completely gone. The handful of women and children still in the courtyard panic, stampeding to the transports. I huddle under the gun deck and claw at my ears to shut out the screaming roar, but it's no use, the ringing's even worse inside my head. Where is Cash?

Bear catches up, ducking under the deck ladder. "Phee, I found my folks. Their vac's taking off. Come on!"

He grips my shoulder, but I shake him off, stumbling onto my feet and squinting into the ragged smoke. Cash scoops up a pair of little ones; he's jogging toward us.

BOOM. BOOM.

More blasts in all directions. On the walls, defending soldiers spray the sky with fire. Two rebel fighters ascend, ready to fend the IP off. A score of our own jet-packed guns sprint off and jump, rocketing into the fray.

Cash reaches the gun deck and closes in on us. "Bear," he says. "Help me. Get these kids on a transport. I've got to go back and get the rest."

Then he looks at me. "Go with him. Get onto one of those vacs."

"I'm staying with you!" I shout over the flaming roar. "I'm not leaving you out here to get killed!"

"We don't have time for this," he says. "Let's go. Now."

He's right. If we stay and argue, we'll get picked off by enemy blitz birds or artillery fire. Cash passes the children off to Bear. They tremble and cry, burying their faces into his broad shoulders. As soon as Bear hustles off with them, Cash takes me by the arm and drags me back toward the transports.

We're halfway there when he hears a woman scream, then the whine of a frightened child. He lets go of me and turns toward their cries. "Phee, get out of here!" he shouts back at me. "I'll meet you at the vac!"

He jogs off, disappearing into the smoke.

Fireworks in the sky. Debris rains as our first fighter is shot down. A rebel drops from the gun deck. The magma cannon is empty, now unmanned. Even as my skull pounds and my weak legs want to give out, I know what I have to do.

The soldiers can't make it back to those vacs without ground support. Cash will die.

I run.

CHAPTER THIRTY-SEVEN

I BOLT FOR THE GUN DECK AND SCRAMBLE UP THE LADDER. Crouching behind the magma cannon, I center my weight behind it. Wait. No. I don't how to work this. Hank said Cyanese weapons were idiot-proof, but there's a whole bank of blinking switches at the base of the cannon, and it's not as if someone left me rusting directions.

I start to panic, but then I spy the triggered handles behind the barrel. As I get a grip and rock the handles, the barrel moves. I squint through the bull's-eye target tracking screen and slip my fingers through the trigger holds. My hands are shaking; I ignore the pain radiating from the base of my neck. I talk myself into a steady zone.

"It's just a steering wheel with built-in triggers. That's all this is."

I strain to roll and turn the heavy trigger holds, looking for a target in the sky. At first, I track an IP fighter, but it moves too fast. I'm no soldier—I can't get a lock on it. Instead, I sight their biggest weapon, the hulking artillery vac.

I close my fists around the triggers. CRACK. The charged ball of fiery sap arcs up. The recoil drops me on my exhaust. The magma explodes and dissipates in the open sky.

Rust. I missed. And now the enemy knows someone's manning the gun deck.

I scramble up and try once more. This time, I squeeze every muscle in my core and widen my stance. When I sight the vac again, I take a breath and hold it.

CRACK. The magma screams along a sure trajectory. BOOM. A fiery blast against the aircraft's hull. It's not enough to bring it down, but maybe a few more hits will do the job.

Shots fire across the deck. I huddle behind the cannon, squinting to look for the enemy. An IP blitz bird hovers at ten o'clock; he's seen me and he's ready to take me out.

"Phee!" Cash screams. I flatten myself against the deck and struggle to block out the roar in my brain. I don't know where his shout is coming from. The static chatter in my head and the voices on the ground—I can no longer tell them apart.

"Phee!" Cash is on the ladder, climbing up to get to me.

More shots. The blitz bird's getting closer. I drop, putting my back against the cannon. "Cash! No! Get down! Get out of here!"

He ignores me, jumping up onto the deck.

The crack of gunfire, closer than ever before.

"Phee." Cash presses into me. As I pull him closer, I see the dark, blooming stain. He's been hit high in the leg.

I jerk and pivot, grabbing the trigger holds, even as I kneel. With teeth gritted and tears in my eyes, I fire blindly, over and over until I hear the blitz bird drop and crash into the courtyard smoke. "Mother-rusting sons of—"

"Phee . . ." Cash's voice is strained. "Climb down."

BOOM. BOOM. BOOM.

"No." I claw at his jacket, pulling it off. I tie it around his leg. "I won't leave you!"

"The vacs won't wait any longer. I can't get down."

"Yes, you can." I crawl toward the edge of the deck, looking down for an escape route. I see one last rebel vac in the distance. It's already hovering two feet above the ground, but one of its bay doors is still open. Soldiers are pulling evacuees inside.

"We can make it," I lie. I scan the courtyard again, scouting for signs of other enemy soldiers. A figure darts toward us. I don't have time to remount the cannon and I don't think the barrel will turn all the way around.

I look back at the figure sprinting straight for us. When he yells, I can't make out the words, but I know the voice. I would recognize it anywhere.

My heart comes to life again, pounding as I watch him dodge and weave. He's an easy target for anyone in the air.

"Bear! Up here!"

A bullet whizzes past him. At first, I think he's been hit, maybe in the back, but then he surges forward, doubling his speed. He's a blur, rushing up the ladder. When he reaches the deck, the roar in my brain turns into a blinding squeal. I can barely see him anymore; he and Cash become fuzzed-out shapes. My eyes roll back for a second, unable to handle the input.

When I open my lids again, I'm seeing little more than dark patches and halos of light. I might as well be blind. I feel Bear's hot breath on my face. I reach out, my fingers graze his chin. "Bear. I can't see." There's a groaning snarl in my voice—I sound like a frightened animal. "I can't see! You have to get Cash."

"I've got you. We'll get you down," Bear says. "I'll carry you, if I have to."

"I've been shot," Cash says. When he reaches for my hand, I feel the blood on his fingertips. "Hurry. Get her to the vac."

Bear locks an arm around my torso.

"No!" I yell. "I'm not leaving without you both!" I feel the hesitation in Bear even as I fight his hold.

"Take her. They can come back for me," Cash argues. "Please. Take her. Keep her alive."

Bear jerks me off my feet and drags me back, pulling me down the ladder. I scream at Cash and fight to hold on to the gun deck, but Bear is too strong. He pries me away and lifts me into his arms, holding me in his fiercest embrace.

"Take me back. Please go back," I sob. "Please."

"I'm sorry." He chokes. He is straining too hard to run and carry me. For him, there is no more room for words, only savage, gasping breaths. My forehead falls against his chest. He smells of ash and burning wood, copper and sweat. I focus on the acrid scent, desperate to sense something beyond the hammering roar in my skull.

The artillery fire on the ground and the sound inside my head—it's all one throbbing bundle of noise, one that matches the rhythm of Bear's pace. In his arms, I am carried forward, rocking up and down, back and forth between flame and smoke.

We stop. I feel more hands, more arms about me. They are shouting and lifting me up into the vac. I lie on a surface that vibrates with movement. I am rising.

"She can't see," Bear says. "Help her."

Someone examines me. Checks my vitals. Cuts open my

zip-front. Rolls a bio-scanner up and down my body. "I'm getting a bad reading. Interference. A frequency coming from somewhere on her. Lieutenant Kinsey, get over here, check her head."

Hank kneels beside me and runs his fingers over my scalp.

"Cash Dradha was shot," Bear shouts, his footsteps retreating toward the bay doors. "I have to go back and get him."

"Negative," Hank snaps. "We are moving out. His orders. We'll relay remaining ground forces. They'll pick up Dradha, if he's still alive."

No. I can't lose Cash.

I hear the groan of the closing doors. A scuffle. The stomp of boots all around me.

"Let me go!" Bear says. "You can't just leave him to die!"

"Wait, back off, soldiers." A voice asks, "Larssen, is that your blood? Did you get hit out there?"

More voices. More movement. People are scrambling around us both.

Bear slumps beside me. I feel his presence even as my brain is singing death, telling me to go to sleep. He reaches for me, our fingers lace, but they are already pulling him away. I'm too weak to keep his blood-soaked hand in mine.

I don't know where Bear is anymore. They have taken him from me.

The vac boosters fire. We are climbing high. The medics shout to be heard.

"Look at this." A female medic touches the scar on my neck, the throbbing knot of agony at the base of my skull. My old wound, stitched the night the DP first picked me up. I scream when her fingers knead the spot. "Hand me that bio-scanner again."

"Something's implanted," one of them gasps. "I'm picking up the frequency. It's a tracker."

"What . . ." I choke. I can't even whisper now.

"Get a surgery kit, stat. Clear that table. We have to get it out." The medic says, hovering over me, "Oh my god, Hank. She led them here."

The needle sinks into my neck. My fists relax, my fingers uncurl. I have so much blood on my hands.

CHAPTER THIRTY-EIGHT

I AM LYING IN A FIELD OF WHITE POPPIES. NIGHT IS COMING. The last peep of sunlight turns the clouds into rosy wisps against a dark sapphire sky. In the afterglow, giant snow-colored blooms droop from the stalks. I am drunk with their scent.

He walks toward me, but I don't have the strength to reach out for him. I open my mouth. I'm so parched, all I can do is whisper his name. "Cash."

He answers, only I realize it's not him. I open my eyes, and it's just a fever dream. I'm lying on a cot. With the beds all around me, I must be in some kind of field hospital. The open flaps of the giant tent whip in the breeze. In the distance, I see the pale blossoms. Green velvety stalks tower like trees.

I blink and adjust to the dim light. Hank is leaning over

me. I try to sit up, but he touches my arm. "Take it easy. We almost lost you."

When my head hits the pillow again, a growling pain awakens, rippling up my spine and all the way to the base of my skull. "How . . ." My throat is on fire. It hurts just to swallow.

Hank sits on the edge of my cot. There's something in his hazel eyes, but I can't read if it's pity or regret. "There was a two-way transmitter, a tracker. We think Benroyal must have had it implanted the night you were arrested."

No. The first time I woke up at the hospital. I remember the stitches on the back of my neck. The pain. Bagged and tagged, I was Benroyal's asset from the start.

"I couldn't see," I croak. "I was blind."

"You're lucky it was temporary. That tracker could have fried you. Hal took a look at it. It had a built-in receiver, but it wasn't actually programmed to pick anything up. It was only programmed to track you. You weren't supposed to hear anything."

"But I did."

"Hal thinks the accident at Sandridge probably damaged it, kicked on the receiver. And when you started picking up chatter on that IP frequency, your brain couldn't handle it. We got it out," he adds. "But your location had already transmitted."

I know what he's thinking. *You led them to us. You betrayed us. You wounded us all.* How many of his men are injured or dead because of me?

I groan and reach for my neck, but Hank stops me again.

"Don't," he scolds. "You'll rip your stitches."

His words trigger a sickening flash of déjà vu. I roll onto my left side and try not to vomit onto the concrete floor. It's then I see who's sleeping in the bed next to me.

"Bear," I cry out. The whisper is hoarse and hollow.

He doesn't answer, and I think he must be unconscious. When his chest rises, I catch the soft wheeze of his breath, but he is much too pale, little more than a ghost.

"He's going to make it," Hank reassures. "For a while, we were worried. The bullet in his back tore him up pretty badly. Mary's got him pumped full of anti-gel and painkillers. He'll come out all right."

"How long have I been out?"

"Couple of days." He pauses, then slips a flex into my hand. "When we tried to upload the files, the card erased itself. This is all we got. The whole thing's corrupted now. He set us up, Phee."

I turn it over, recognizing the stolen flex. I read the frozen screen.

You must never grasp at things you are not strong enough to hold.

Rage burns through my tears. This whole time Benroyal knew I had the card. He might as well have put it in my hands. The flex, the implant, the secrets in his study were all just a game to hunt down his enemies. Maybe he suspected James and Cash. Maybe he was certain all along. I think of each move I made, bolting home, running into Yamada, chasing Cash to the sap house. Benroyal tracked every step. He played us. Me, most of all.

"Where is James?"

Hank shakes his head. "We know Benroyal's men boarded his vac, but James wasn't there. It's been complete flex silence, and no one knows where he is. Locus is a mess and the newsfeeds are going crazy. The rumors are wild, Phee. They say Locus was nearly bankrupt. That James committed suicide."

"Suicide?" The word trembles on my lips. James can't be dead. I know he is. I'm positive he isn't. I don't know which is the lie. "Locus can't be bankrupt. James said he had everything taken care of. Did they kill him?"

"I don't know."

"What about Cash?"

He looks away. "Phee, I . . ."

Wide-eyed, I wait for him to finish.

"I went back myself, to pick up our wounded, but there's been no sign of him."

"No." I sit up. "There has to be something. We have to go back."

Slowly, he shakes his head. "There's nothing to be done. There's nothing left."

"But he can't be—"

"That base is smoke and ash. He's gone."

I shudder, unable to control the ugly, wracking sobs. My sorrow is a silent drowning choke. Hank moves closer, to console me, but I flinch and curl into myself.

"I'm sorry." He stands up. He knows there's nothing left to say.

After the attack, we never made it to Manjor. Instead, we fled Bisera altogether. We took shelter in the snow-white sea of the Pearl Strand, the neutral border zone between Cyan and Bisera. Here, we make camp and pick up the pieces.

It's been a month since the ambush, and I've fallen into a routine. Wake up. Report to Hank. Do whatever needs to be done. The Cyanese keep sending more supplies, so we usually have our hands full unloading incoming vacs. Otherwise, I volunteer for grunt work or patrol duty or infirmary shifts with Bear. I prefer construction detail. It's not that I'm good at putting up tents or laying brick, it's that I crave the sense of building something. Despite everything, that's why we carry on. Stone by stone, we mend a rebellion.

We worked on the armory today. It's nearly done, and already half full of weapons. We're finished for now, and while the rest of the crew heads to the mess hall for dinner, I slump onto the soft grass outside its front doors. On my knees, I lift my flask, then gulp the last of the water. I'm worn out, but still not tired enough. Can't seem to quiet my mind. I need to take a walk after dinner. Go for a climb. Seems that's the only thing that gets my brain off high alert.

I shouldn't be so on edge. They say we're safe in the Strand. That we've put down roots in ground too sacred to be attacked. I look up, spying the proof. To the east, the forests of giant poppies march up and out of our little valley, every inch hallowed ground. To the west, up the slope, is the Hill of Kings. Nine centuries' worth of tombs still stand, a memorial to better days. Hard to believe Cyan and Bisera built it together. For almost a millennium, they lived in peace and buried their leaders side by side. Every day, I'm drawn to those graves, yet I avoid them for the same reason: Dead or alive, this is where Cash is meant to be. Fallen, he'd be laid to rest. Standing, he'd rally us here.

I close my eyes, and I can still see him, smell him, feel the slick of his blood on my fingertips. The memory's too painful, so I pull a flex from my pocket. On it is the antidote. The one thing that takes the edge off my grief. I've watched this bootleg feedcast a dozen times. I keep watching because it gives me hope. I see it and know our gamble wasn't all for nothing.

On the tiny screen, Charles Benroyal sits inside the Castran Assembly House. He is near the dais, watching from the sideline of the visitors' gallery. Up front, he is barely visible, hidden in a tight knot of suits. Around him, Sixers and feedcast crews fill the space, while politicians occupy every seat on the floor. Predictably, the real public's been forced outside, onto the atrium and steps of the House. For this particular press conference, there's only room for the allied elite.

Prime Minister Prejean stands at the grand podium. Above him, Castran flags and corporate banners. Before him, a panel of bulletproof glass. On the periphery, soldiers in black, lined up in neat little rows.

It is the day after. The day after the mountain rally, the day after the ambush, the day after everything. Prejean takes one step forward and begins his formal statement:

"Yesterday, citizens of Castra and Bisera came under attack in a series of calculated and deadly terrorist acts. During yesterday's rally, His Highness Prince Cashoman Dradha was taken by force. We do not know if he is alive or dead, or whether or not he's being held for ransom.

Phoenix Vanguard, who was one of our own, is also missing, and we are devastated by the loss."

Was. Already, I belong only in past tense. When he pauses, I zoom in on Benroyal. King Charlie's expression is grave and tight, but his eyes dance. I'm certain he knows exactly where I am. And where Cash is. Behind the mask, he is smiling at me.

Prejean continues. "As of this afternoon, the facts are few. Midway through yesterday's rally, Miss Vanguard disappeared. Her rig exploded, but no evidence of her remains have been found. And while we are certain Prince Dradha was kidnapped, we have not yet determined whether she was the victim of a tragic accident or a willing accomplice in violent, treasonous acts."

Again, the look. That secret smile in Benroyal's eyes. Prejean's words—I bet every one of them was scripted by Benroyal. Of course, the vague explanations and omissions make sense. King Charlie is waiting. He doesn't yet know how he'd like to twist the facts. Cash and I, we are cards to hold. Later, he can lay our bodies on the table.

"At this time, the Castran Circuit Control Board is currently investigating Locus Informatics and a wager that may be linked to yesterday's attacks. As of now, all shares are frozen. Our administration gratefully acknowledges the contributions of Benroyal Corporation, which has generously offered to fund operations of the courts, until these matters are settled."

Benroyal can barely keep a straight face. He pretends to close his eyes, as if lost in private anguish, but I know he's savoring victory. He doesn't see what's coming.

Prejean begins to wind down the speech. "Yesterday was a terrible day for our nation, but we are proud of the heroic efforts made by officers of the Interstellar Patrol. After discovering a terrorist base, our men and women made a valiant stand to rescue Prince Dradha and capture the enemy. Tragically, five officers were wounded and eight were killed. We salute these fallen soldiers. We grieve with their families."

I scan the faces in the chamber. They've lost no sons or daughters. On the floor, no one is mourning.

The prime minister makes his final plea. "And it is for these fallen brothers and sisters, I beg. For Castra. Because our very way of life is at stake, and we must do whatever it takes to root out our enemies and bring them to justice."

He is nearly breathless now, carried away by his own words. You could almost believe them. At last, he stares into the cameras. His eyes don't scan the floor anymore, because this message isn't meant for the gallery. It's meant for the rest of my world, for South Siders in their living rooms and for those who stand outside.

"Today, I ask you, our citizens, to help. When Domestic Patrol officers knock on your door, share any information you have. If you are able and of age, answer the enlistment call. Stand with me, and contribute to the cause of freedom."

When he finishes, the soldiers take one step forward. Crisply, at attention, they salute the audience, while the Sixers and politicians politely applaud. Quickly, I scan the sea of people and pinpoint the bogus feedcaster, a second before he reaches into his bag. He slips two steps closer to the dais. The pod of raw sap barely fits in his hand. It's a small, gray, thin-skinned ball, the kind designed to rupture easily when used for fuel. But the pod doesn't stay in his grasp for long. In one quick, desperate stroke, he hurls it.

"Give us Abasi!" he shouts as it bursts against the bullet-proof glass. The dull thud is startling, and the murky splatter still makes my stomach twist. It's like watching a corpse hit the ground. The entire chamber sucks in a breath, and for one long second, holds it. Then the IP guards descend on the rogue dissenter. They pounce and drag him from the House.

And it begins.

The chamber doors part, gasping open like an intake valve. As the IP guards pull the man through it, a spark of anger pistons through the crowd in the atrium, igniting a roar so strong, it breaks through the lines of the soldiers. A riot is born, and the feedcast ends with the sound of a thousand shouts as the mob surges into the House. The cut's so abrupt, you'd almost miss the eye-blink of footage. But it's there. I see the look. I freeze the screen and stare at him.

Benroyal isn't smiling anymore.

CHAPTER THIRTY-NINE

AFTER DINNER, I LEAVE BEAR IN THE INFIRMARY. HE DOESN'T like it when I hang around during his physical therapy sessions, while he hobbles back and forth and builds up his strength. Maybe he can't chase Hal and Mary off, but I'll let him be. I can give him that much.

It's the quiet hour. The breeze carries idle chatter—the sounds of soldiers gathered around tables, and children being tucked into their beds with stories and songs and prayers. I cut through the eastern edge of the camp, past the barracks and the armory. Hank is on evening watch. He acknowledges me with a nod and a fist over his heart. We trade greetings. Bidram arras noc.

The night wind gusts and sings, and I turn up my collar, grateful for the warmth of the uniform. My coat, my shirt, my cap. It's all army surplus, the no-nonsense gear the Cyanese hand out to refugees. It's all dark blue, thickly woven, stripped of all its stars and silver thread. Colors, but no country. Like my Earth-born father, I have a new world, but no home.

I keep hiking until the clearing disappears altogether, until I'm deep into the endless field of towering blooms. I find just the right stalk, one thick with thorny buds, and I climb. I struggle, hand over foot, until I've breached the canopy, where the night meets the sweet, heady scent of velvet petals and rain-kissed leaves.

My fingers are sticky with bitter earth and fragrant nectar, but I'm secure enough, perched between two twining stalks. I tilt my head and stare into the sky. This is what I do. Every night, I look for the Evening Star.

Tired and restless, I come here to find him. I tell myself that he isn't dead and that the IP picked him up. I imagine what he must face each day while I'm here, safe and well-fed. Then I spin other futures. We recover Cash. James. Abasi. All of them, safe and alive. We march into the Spire and bring back my mother. Finally, one last task.

I face Benroyal, and he falls.

A rush of air. In the moonlight, a barden soars past my perch. I spy his black feather crown and the pearl-bright sweep of his wings. Slowly, he glides through the tangled swirl of poppies, moving east, then doubling back. He lingers here and there, drinking from a bloom, then winging through the stalks, searching for whatever creeps in the dark.

The barden flies up, circles one last time, then disappears. No prey in sight, I guess, so he must keep going. I wonder how far, and by what road. A thousand miles from here, the Palace in Belaram. Behind the horizon, the Gap. Beyond the stars, Castra is worlds away.

But if I close my eyes, I can still see it. I can still feel the scorch of midday, the sun rising over Capitoline. The memory of it burns like a flame in my heart. It's a fire I tend every day. I can't forget.

Because somewhere, there's a battle waiting. In the Spire, there's an unsettled score. A revolution's coming, and when it does, I'll be ready. I won't run. I won't lay low the way I used to do on the streets. This time, I'll rise, every talon curled and sharp.

I stretch out my hand and look to the skies. I reach for my Evening Star.

ACKNOWLEDGMENTS

"IT'S EITHER EASY OR IMPOSSIBLE."—SALVADOR DALI

I can't believe you're reading this. If you're really reading this, *Tracked* is an actual book. So can I just say? I can't believe we pulled this off.

Because *Tracked* is my impossible thing.

It wasn't easy to write it and bring it into the world, and I'm so grateful for all the people who helped me do it. I will never stop giving thanks.

To Sara Crowe, my agent and friend—you are my champion. Always in my corner, you've never failed to help me answer the bell. Thank you for everything. I could not have done this without you and the rest of the team at Harvey Klinger.

To Heather Alexander, my editor and advocate—you are my lamppost in the dark wood. I have learned so much from you, and your patience and tenacity are a gift. My words will be forever influenced because of yours.

To Stacey Friedberg, my editor and sounding board—thank you for pacing me through the last leg of the race. And to the rest of the crew, at Dial and beyond—Jill Bailey, Lauri Hornik, Regina Castillo, Irene Vandervoort, Dana Chidiac, Mina Chung, Lori Thorn, Elizabeth Rupp, and Jennifer Dee—thank you for your generosity, patience, and hard work.

To my husband, Chris, who always, always encouraged my writing dreams and defended them against the relentless monster of self-doubt. Thank you for your strong arms and loyal heart. Everything that's best in Cash and Bear? I borrowed from you.

To my son, Conor, who never fails to dream the grandest dreams. Thank you for teaching me to believe in them too.

To my truest friend, Caron Ervin, who has the kindest, fiercest, most admirable spirit. Thank you for the honor of your friendship. I owe you so much for carrying me, through thick and thin.

To my parents, who didn't laugh when I said I wanted to be a writer. To my mother, Marilee, who is endlessly encouraging, and my father, Charles, who's been with me the whole way, vicariously chasing the dream, getting just as choked up as his sentimental daughter. And to the rest of my family—to all my J's and C's. (And N's and K's!) I love you very much.

To Rosemary Clement-Moore, Kate Cornell, Candace Havens, Sally Hamilton, A. Lee Martinez, Tex Thompson, and all my friends at DFW Writers' Workshop who were never too busy to encourage or spur me on. Thank you for always listening.

To Julie Murphy (my darling JAM), who is strong where I am weak.

To Amber Swindle, for reading draft after draft.

To Jen Bigheart, for all the laughter and happy songs.

To Donna Lufkin, for inspiring so many of us.

To Mary Kole, for teaching me so much when I was just an embryo writer.

To Neil Gaiman, for your life's work, and also, for the hug.

To Dave Grohl, for your life's work, and also, for the distortion.

To my bookish friends, online and off, who have been comrades in arms—Erin Bowman, Mindy McGinnis, Victoria Scott, Lindsay Cummings, Kari Olsen, Kristin Treviño, Natalie Parker, Christa Desir, Jeramey Kraatz, Stacy Vandever Wells, and Britney Cossey, I'm looking at you. Also, the Fourteenery and the Freshman 15s and my Dallas Darlings and Austin Girls and the Houston Horde and the Lufkin 6 and the Literary Lonestars and so many more. You know who you are. I love you guys.

To the infamous, mercurial Mr. Happenstance, who taught me that a good deal of luck—finding the right person at the right time— can make all the difference.

Lastly, to you. I sincerely and humbly thank you for reading *Tracked*. It's not mine anymore. It's yours. May you always believe in impossible things.